A RARE MURDER IN PRINCETON

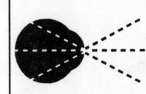

A Rare Murder in Princeton

Ann Waldron

WHEELER PUBLISHING
An imprint of Thomson Gale, a part of The Thomson Corporation

THOMSON

GALE

Detroit • New York • San Francisco • New Haven, Conn. • Waterville, Maine • London • Munich

THOMSON
━━━━━━━━ ✳ ━━━━ ™
GALE

LIBRARY OF CONGRESS CATALOGING-IN-PUBLICATION DATA

Waldron, Ann.
    A rare murder in Princeton / by Ann Waldron.
      p. cm. — (Wheeler large print cozy mystery)
    ISBN 1-59722-308-5 (lg. print : pbk. : alk. paper)
    1. Princeton University — Fiction. 2. College teachers — New Jersey — Princeton — Fiction. 3. Women detectives — New Jersey — Princeton — Fiction. 4. Large type books. 5. Princeton (N.J.) — Fiction. I. Title. II. Series.
PS3573.A4226R37 2006
813'.54—dc22   2006015014

Published in 2006 by arrangement with The Berkley Publishing Group, a division of Penguin Group (USA) Inc.

Printed in the United States of America on permanent paper
10 9 8 7 6 5 4 3 2 1

ACKNOWLEDGMENTS

I should like to thank the people who work in the real-life Department of Rare Books and Special Collections at Princeton University. They are much nicer and more interesting than the characters I made up for my wholly fictional, geographically inaccurate Department of Rare Books and Special Collections. Most helpful were Alfred Bush, Steve Ferguson, Charles Greene, Gretchen Oberfranc, Linda Olivera, Ben Primer, Meg Sherry, and Jane Snedeker.

Kim Otis, Ted Cashel, and Mary Cason answered questions about other matters.

Heartfelt thanks for manuscript reading to Lolly O'Brien and Amanda Matetsky.

ONE

"So good of you to have me for dinner, but, dear boy, you didn't tell me you had bought the murder house . . ."

Coming down the stairs, McLeod Dulaney heard the old-fashioned phrasing of the man talking to George Bridges at the front door. The voice obviously belonged to the dinner guest George had told her to expect, Nathaniel Ledbetter. She stopped and looked down at the pair of them.

George was her old friend from an earlier stay in Princeton — tall, about her own age, with a head of thick curly black hair turning gray. Ledbetter was a portly man who looked rather like a glossy gray tomcat with his thick mane of gray hair and bristling gray eyebrows. He took off his galoshes and his gray overcoat, and pulled down the gray cardigan he wore as a vest beneath the jacket of his gray tweed suit.

Ledbetter followed George through the

door at the bottom of the stairs, and McLeod continued down the stairs and joined them in the small front parlor of George's house.

"The murder house?" she asked Nathaniel Ledbetter, who was just sitting down on George's new sofa.

He stood up when McLeod came in. "Oh, yes, this is the murder house," he said with an air of authority.

"What do you mean, 'murder house,' Natty?" George asked.

"Surely you remember when Jill Murray was murdered?" said Ledbetter.

"Vaguely," said George.

"I don't," said McLeod, who could not abide not knowing what people were talking about. "Who was Jill Murray and where was she murdered?"

"She was murdered right here in this house," said Ledbetter, staring, puzzled, at McLeod. He held out his hand. "I'm Nathaniel Ledbetter," he said.

"I'm sorry," said George. "You shocked me, Natty, and I forgot my manners —"

"I have often said you didn't have any, dear boy," interrupted Natty.

George went on as though Ledbetter had not spoken. "McLeod, this is a former professor of mine, Nathaniel Ledbetter. He always was a terrible know-it-all. Nat, this is my good friend, McLeod Dulaney, who's going to stay here while she's teaching a writing seminar at Princeton this semester. She's my first houseguest."

"I'm glad to know you, Ms. Dulaney. I've heard about you. You're from Florida, aren't you? What do you think about our winter weather?"

"It's cold," said McLeod. "The camellias were in bloom when I left Tallahassee three days ago." It had been beautiful, in fact, the pink and red and white camellias amid glossy green leaves all over town under live oaks festooned with Spanish moss, and McLeod felt a moment's pang for the camellias and azaleas she would miss, but only a moment's. She concentrated on Natty Ledbetter. "Tell me about the murder," she said.

"You two sit down and I'll get drinks," said George. "You'll have a martini, I assume, Nat, and what about you, McLeod?"

"I'll have a martini, too," said McLeod.

"Good girl," said George and left for the kitchen.

McLeod sat down on the sofa in front of the tiny fireplace and looked at the fire while Ledbetter sat down in a small wing chair. She turned to him. "Now, this murder," she said. "Who was Jill Murray?"

"She was a lovely woman. A widow, who lived here alone. It was in the autumn — beautiful weather, I remember — and Jill disappeared. Nobody knew what happened to her; she just vanished. Finally, her son came over and searched the house thoroughly and found her body down in the basement. She had been beaten severely. And the police never found out who did it."

"Good heavens!" said McLeod. "How long ago did this happen?"

"Oh, let's see. Ten, fifteen, maybe twenty years ago, I would say."

"And it was never solved?"

"No, I think the police finally decided that she had been working in her garden — her hands were still crusted with dirt — and a tramp, somebody from Trenton, had come up here and tried to rob her and then killed her."

"And the house? Has it been vacant since then?"

"It was for a long time. Her son kept it for years because nobody wanted to buy it, and then came this man from Texas who bought it, but he didn't stay long. I guess George bought it from him."

"And people still call it the murder house?"

"Always will," said Ledbetter. "Things don't change all that much in Princeton."

George arrived with a tray that held three martinis and a plate of baguette slices with smoked salmon. He handed out the drinks, and Ledbetter, brown eyes gleaming, proposed a toast: "To your new house, dear boy."

The murder house, thought McLeod uneasily.

George added another stick of wood to the fire.

"Ms. Dulaney, I'm delighted to make your acquaintance," Ledbetter said. "As I said, I've heard so much about you. And I understand you've written a most interesting book about Elijah P. Lovejoy."

"Elijah P. Lovejoy is my hero," said McLeod.

"Admirable man," said Ledbetter. "He was lynched, was he not, out West somewhere?"

"In Alton, Illinois, near Saint Louis," said McLeod. "He was a Presbyterian minister and the editor of an abolitionist newspaper. A pro-slavery mob came to destroy his press, and he was killed."

"I see," said Ledbetter. "And what are you working on now?"

"I'm not working on another book," said

McLeod. "I do have a newspaper job, you know — on the *Star of Florida* in Tallahassee — and they're good about giving me a leave of absence. This is the third time I've come to Princeton to teach for a semester. I'm lucky."

"I would imagine it makes for a full life," said Ledbetter.

"McLeod has the energy of three dynamos," said George.

"Hardly," said McLeod. "Mr. Ledbetter, you're not teaching anymore? You're at the library, George said."

"Natty, McLeod will interrogate you," said George, "while I go to the kitchen for a few minutes."

"What do you do at the library?" asked McLeod, thinking that George knew her pretty well. Curiosity about people — and everything else — ruled her life. And she had found that her white hair — it had been white since she was in her thirties — permitted her to ask even more questions.

"I'm director of Rare Books and Special Collections," said Ledbetter. "Do you know what that is?"

"Manuscripts? Rare books?"

"You're right. The term 'special collections' includes not just manuscripts, but graphic arts — a wonderful collection of prints — and the theater collection and Western Americana, a coin collection, and a few other odds and ends. It's a big tent."

"What's your special treasure?"

"We have many. We have cuneiform inscriptions on clay cylinders from Nebuchadnezzar's time. We have papyrus manuscripts, illuminated manuscripts, incunabula — that is to say, books printed before 1501 — one of them, incidentally, is *The Hypnerotomachia Poliphili* from 1499, and we have . . ."

McLeod had met her match, someone who knew more than even her curiosity demanded. Natty described photographs taken by Lewis Carroll, mentioned an autograph (meaning handwritten) manuscript of a poem by Emily Dickinson, talked about a book of Oscar Wilde's poems inscribed by Wilde to Lord Alfred Douglas. "And of course, we have all of F. Scott Fitzgerald's papers," he said, "but that's enough."

"How did Princeton get all these things?"

"Gifts. Generous alumni over the years have given us their libraries and book collections. And benefactors give us money to make our own purchases. A loyal group called Friends of the Princeton University Library gives money for purchases and lectures and exhibitions."

George came in to say that dinner was ready.

"I am afraid I've bored your guest," Nat said to George as they went to the dining room. "I do go on. I get carried away."

"Not at all," McLeod said. "It's fascinating."

"It's hard to bore McLeod," said George. "Her curiosity is insatiable." He smiled at her sympathetically and patted her shoulder. But then he opened the gate for more. "Nat, McLeod is a real Trollope fan," he said. "You did tell her about your Trollope holdings, didn't you?"

"No, but I shall," said Natty. "We have the manuscripts of ten Trollope novels — *The Eustace Diamonds* and *Orley Farm* are the best known of the ten. We also have *The American Senator*, *The Claverings*, *Lady Anna*, *The Landleaguers*, *Lord Palmerston*, *Marion Fay*, *Mr. Scarborough's Family*, and *An Old Man's Love*."

"I never even heard of some of those titles," McLeod said.

"Natty, I'm impressed that you can remember all ten titles and recite them at the dinner table," said George.

"Alzheimer's has not set in for me yet," said Natty. "Dear lady, come over to Rare

Books and I'll show you our Trollopes."

McLeod, who really was extremely fond of Trollope, happily agreed to pay him a visit, thinking that being called "dear lady" was not as bad as "dear girl."

Dinner was outstanding — a creamy cauliflower tomato soup and duck à l'orange, with fruit tarts for dessert.

"George, you're an even better cook than you were before," said McLeod.

"Very fine, my boy," said Nat.

"I spent two years in Brussels — I learned a lot about food," said George. "But I bought the tarts at Chez Alice."

It was while they were having coffee in the living room — George had rebuilt the fire — that Natty spoke to McLeod again. "I'd like to interest you in a man whose papers we have. You might want to write about him — Henry van Dyke."

"Is that the man who wrote 'The Other Wise Man'?" she asked.

"Yes, but he wrote many other things, too," Nat Ledbetter was saying when George interrupted him to ask what "The Other Wise Man" was.

McLeod and Natty spoke at once and then told him together.

"It's a Christmas short story," said McLeod. "My mother loved it."

"I heard it read out loud at church when I was a boy," Nat said. "It was quite popular. But van Dyke did many other things. He was a famous Presbyterian minister and he was later for twenty years a distinguished English professor here at Princeton. He wrote many books. He is the only member of the English Department faculty whose collected works have been published — in twelve volumes, no less. He was a great fly-fisherman and was ambassador to the Netherlands. He was a most fabulous man. And I do wish somebody would write about him. Do come over to see the Trollopes, and while you're there, take a look at the van Dyke papers — there are boxes and boxes of them, including letters from, I believe, six presidents of the United States."

McLeod promised she would indeed be over to see him and his treasures as soon as she could. And soon after that, she yawned, apologized, and said she really had to go to bed.

"I've been driving all day for three days, and I'm exhausted," she said.

Natty Ledbetter said he had to go, too, and George helped him on with his coat, hat, scarf, and gloves.

"I'm sorry I had a guest your first night

here," George said after Natty had gone. "But I wasn't sure which day you'd get here, you know."

"This time I only stopped twice on the way up — Thursday night with my mother in Atlanta and last night with Rosie in Charlotte. I should have telephoned. But I wasn't sure I could make it from Charlotte in one day. Don't worry. I enjoyed Natty." She yawned hugely. "George, I'm going to bed. Sorry I'm not helping with the cleanup."

"It's all right," said George. "You're excused. Go to bed."

It took McLeod's last ounce of energy to get up the stairs, into her room, and snuggle under the down comforter on the bed prewarmed with an electric blanket. She was asleep before she could dwell on all that Nat Ledbetter had talked about: cuneiform and incunabula and Henry van Dyke — and the murder house.

Two

The next morning, McLeod had a chance to get a better look at the murder house. She and George had a leisurely breakfast and tried to catch up on all that had happened to them both in the past three years.

She did like George Bridges, McLeod thought after breakfast as she buckled down to unpacking and settling in. He had called her in Tallahassee as soon as he learned she was going to teach a writing class during the spring semester. He had for years worked as assistant to Princeton University presidents, three presidents in all, then he had gone off to Brussels for two years to work for one of these former bosses at some European Union education apparatus. He was back in Princeton now, back at the university with a huge promotion — vice president for public affairs.

"I've bought a house," he had told McLeod when he called to congratulate her on her appointment to teach nonfiction writing at Princeton. "It's on Edgehill Street — you know, the little one-block-long street between Stockton and Mercer. You can stay with me while you're here. You can have your own room and private bath."

"That sounds palatial," McLeod had said.

"The whole house is tiny, but it seems palatial to me — I've lived in apartments for years. It's wonderful, but it's bewildering, too. I look at the yard, and I ask myself, 'Now what is all that space for?'"

"Mowing?" suggested McLeod.

"Not just mowing," George said. "It all needs lots of work. I could see that when I bought it. But it obviously used to be a nice yard."

"You'll deal with that eventually," said McLeod cheerfully.

"I know," said George. "Oh, well. Do stay here. I'll be very glad to see you."

"And I'll be glad to see you," said McLeod. "Thanks so much for calling."

And she *was* glad to see him, she thought now as she hung up clothes in the guest room closet. She and George had had a little fling two years ago, the second time she taught at Princeton, but she had not seen him since. Still they had kept in touch. It would be nice to resume the friendship, even on the platonic basis he seemed to have in mind, she thought.

George had urged her to try to arrive on a Saturday or Sunday so he could be home when she got there, and when she had turned into his driveway on Saturday, he came out on his little porch, grinning at her, his black curly hair rumpled, and looking as full of vitality and brio as ever. She cut off the engine, popped the trunk open, and got out of the car, as George came down the steps and gathered her, thick coat, tote bag, and purse into a huge bear hug.

"McLeod, I am so glad to see you," he said, holding her tight and rubbing his cheek on hers.

"I'm glad to see you, too," she said. "And I love your house. Aren't you cold? You don't have on a jacket even — just that sweater. And it's cold up here."

"Your blood is thin from living in Florida," he said. "But it *is* cold." He pulled two of her suitcases out of the trunk and started up the steps to the porch. "Come on in. You'll love it."

"I love it already," McLeod said as she went in the door, with its stained glass panels, and saw the square hallway with a staircase winding upward.

The house was indeed tiny, she thought,

but darling. On the left was a small parlor and on the right a large dining room with bookshelves and a bay window at one end. Through the panes of the bay window McLeod could see the backyard, which didn't look too bad, she thought. A door led from the dining room to a kitchen that was small but surely big enough to allow George to cook more of his wonderful food.

"It looks like you've really settled in," said McLeod.

"The downstairs is in pretty good shape," said George, "but upstairs is still a mess."

Upstairs were three bedrooms — one for George, a guest room, and a third that George was setting up as his study with more bookshelves and a desk and computer, copier, and fax.

"Impressive," said McLeod, although the room was in some confusion, with cartons, as yet unpacked, stacked on the floor and no curtains or shades at the windows, no pictures on the walls.

"Lots of work to do in here," said George, "but you can use any of this equipment anytime."

"I brought my own laptop and a little printer," she said.

"And here's your room." George made a wide gesture, ushering her into the guest room, which was at the front of the house, facing Edgehill.

"It's charming," she said. "I love the wall-paper."

"Don't the flowers look like camellias?"

"A little bit, I mean they have petals," said McLeod, "but camellias don't grow on trel-lises."

"Picky," said George.

"I love the wallpaper," McLeod said again. "What more can I say? Actually, I can say I like all of it. I love the pictures — where did you get the watercolors of the campus?"

"Oh, I bought them at a charity auction," George said. "I knew you liked watercolors and these were done by a local artist."

"They're great," said McLeod. "Nassau Hall and Stanhope and Murray-Dodge . . . It's the perfect guest room, George, the desk by the window and a wing chair" — she was walking around — "the big closet and the nice bathroom and the ancient oriental rug. . . ."

"Don't you like all the old rugs? I bought them in New Hope last weekend at a sec-ondhand store — I wouldn't dignify it by calling it an antique store."

"You've had fun furnishing this house, haven't you?"

"I'm not near through," said George. "I

moved at breakneck speed after you said you'd stay here, and got the guest room finished, but everything else is still in a mess. Come see my room."

George's bedroom, which overlooked the backyard, was as bare as the study, with a bed, chest of drawers, and another full complement of unpacked cartons.

"It's a perfect house," said McLeod, ignoring the disarray.

The next week passed in a whirl of getting settled. George left for work every morning before McLeod was up, and usually worked late. She seldom saw him, but she had plenty to do — finish unpacking at home, settle into her office at the university, and get reacquainted with the Princeton campus.

In the office of the Humanities Council in Joseph Henry House, Frieda, the administrator, welcomed her for her third visit to teach the class on writing about people.

"It's good to be back," said McLeod. "I love it that I get to return now and then."

" 'Return, return, O Shulamite; return, return that we may look upon thee,' " said Frieda. "That's from the Song of Solomon."

McLeod had forgotten Frieda's skill at

producing a quotation for nearly every occasion.

"And now, I'll take you upstairs," said Frieda. The "offices" for visiting writer/teachers on the third floor of Joseph Henry House were not really offices, but cubicles with a work surface, shelves, a few drawers, and a file cabinet.

"We've given you the choice cubicle this time," said Frieda.

It was indeed the choice cubicle, located by the window overlooking what one architect had called the "kaleidoscopic octagonals" of Chancellor Green Hall, once the Princeton University library, a remarkable building designed by a nineteen-year-old architect.

During the next few days, she got familiar with the university computer system and obtained a decal for her car from the parking office so she could park in the garage down near the hockey rink.

As she walked all over the campus, she admired the old buildings she knew from past visits and stood stock-still, amazed, before the new sculpture in front of the Art Museum. The sculpture consisted of twenty very tall — at least nine feet — headless, armless men standing on a low concrete platform. Walking up to her office from the garage, she had come upon the sculpture, Picasso's *Head of a Woman,* which used to be in front of the museum. Now it stood below the I. M. Pei–designed Spelman dormitory.

Well, she thought, we had *Head of a Woman* and now we have twenty headless men. Why not?

One cold afternoon, she walked down to the brand-new Ellipse dormitory to see the Sol LeWitt painting on the arched ceiling of a tall passageway — and admired it wholeheartedly.

The cold weather made her think of knitting again, and she went out to the shopping center to buy yarn. She decided to knit George a sweater — she had made enough sweaters for her children, Rosie and Harry — and she picked out a beautiful gray wool and then selected a dark blue for doing some figures across the front. She would go all out, she decided. Surely, he would like a hand-knit sweater? The saleswoman assured her she could return the yarn if George didn't like it. When George saw it, he did like it and was obviously pleased that she would knit him a sweater.

She asked George about the sculpture in front of the Art Museum. "Do people like it?" she asked.

"Older alumni hate it," he said. "Young people like it. A Polish woman named Magdalena Abakanowicz is the sculptor. It doesn't belong to the university — it's on long-term loan from the parents of three alumni."

"And the Sol LeWitt?" she asked. "Did he come out and do it personally?"

"It seems he doesn't do any of the finished work anymore. He designs it and he has workers who actually produce the finished product."

"It's a very beautiful ceiling," she said.

"Everybody likes that one," George said.

She met her first class on Thursday and marveled again at how astonishingly bright Princeton students were — and at how they seemed impervious to the cold. While she bundled up in a shearling coat, a knitted cap that came down over her ears, a heavy muffler, and warm mittens, most of them drifted about in jackets and jeans as though it were Indian summer. If it got above freezing, a few wore shorts and one lad appeared one day in flip-flops.

She ran into people on campus she knew from her previous teaching stints and made dates for lunch and accepted invitations to dinner.

When she came home at night to the little

house on Edgehill — nearly always empty — she thought of Jill Murray and her murder. She put off doing her laundry — the washing machine and dryer were in the basement where Jill's body had lain for — how long? Days? Eventually she had to have clean clothes, so she went down the steps to the basement. She saw no stains on the concrete floor, and thought, Well, that's one hurdle passed, and put her first load in the machine.

THREE

She did not forget Nat Ledbetter. The first time she was in Firestone Library with time to spare, she went to the Rare Books and Special Collections rooms on the first floor. To get to the collections, you pass through an exhibition gallery, and McLeod paused at a permanent exhibit, behind a store-front kind of window, which looked like a stage set. It was a replica of the office of Jonathan Belcher, CAPTAIN-GENERAL AND GOVERNOR-IN-CHIEF OF THE PROVINCE OF NEW JERSEY FROM 1747 TO 1757, when it was a colony of Great Britain, according to a nearby plaque. The governor had given his entire personal library of 474 books to the little new College of New Jersey, along with two terrestrial globes and his portrait. Now the books that had survived the ravages of fire and time were lined up behind an eighteenth-century desk; his portrait (red faced and wearing a magnificently curled gray wig) hung on the wall beside the desk and one of the globes stood some distance from it. McLeod stared at this permanent exhibit, wondering what Governor Belcher would think if he knew that the tiny College of New Jersey had metamorphosed into the august institution known as Princeton University. Then she went past the gallery's current exhibition, material drawn from George F. Kennan's papers. Kennan, a Princeton alumnus, had designed the containment policy for the Soviet Union.

Finally, she found the Department of Rare Books and Special Collections and was eventually ushered into Nat Ledbetter's office, where the splendor astounded her. The room was vast, lined with bookshelves full of books — they must be very "rare," she thought — set in dark oak paneling, with heavy brocade curtains at the windows.

Nat stood up behind his big desk and greeted her warmly. "I'm so glad to see you. Sit down. I'd offer you some coffee, but drinks are not allowed in Rare Books."

He still looked gray today, except that he had on a red tie, and beside that he just looked rosier. When Nat asked her if she had come to see a Trollope manuscript, she said yes, indeed she had.

"Let me see if Philip Sheridan is here," he

said. "I know he'd love to meet you. The Trollopes are part of the Sheridan collection . . ." He disappeared through a small door in the inner wall of his office and came back a moment later, beckoning to her.

"Philip is here and wants to meet you," Nat said. McLeod followed him through another paneled room lined with bookshelves, into still a third book-lined room with two desks. A white-haired, beaked-nosed man in a pin-striped suit rose from behind the big desk and smiled at McLeod. He had the rosy cheeks of old age, but he was tall and straight. McLeod thought he must have been blond before his hair turned gray because aside from the rosy cheeks, his skin was pale and his eyes were blue.

"McLeod, this is Philip Sheridan," said Nat. "He's a great collector. And this is McLeod Dulaney — I told you about her. She's a real Trollope fan."

"I'm glad to hear that," said Sheridan. "I'm a Trollopian, too." He came around from behind the desk to shake hands. "This is Chester" — he waved at the young man at the smaller desk — "my assistant and the curator of the collection." Chester stood up and smiled shyly. "Do sit down, Mrs. Dulaney," Sheridan said. He ushered her to a large wing chair, and pointed to a smaller chair for Nat. "Which is your favorite Trollope?"

"I used to think it was the Parliamentary novels — all of them," said McLeod. "But I'm reading *The Vicar of Bullhampton* now and it's wonderful. I believe it's my all-time favorite. I really do."

"Oh, yes, that's the one where the vicar tries to rescue the 'fallen woman,'" said Sheridan.

"That's right. And there are all these plots and subplots — the love affair between the squire and Mary, the murder of the farmer — it's wonderful."

"What edition are you reading?"

"What edition? Oh, you're a book collector, so you *care* about the edition. It's just a paperback I bought secondhand at Micawber."

"I see. Then you're not interested in books except for their content?"

"Some books are quite beautiful — I appreciate that. But I guess I do care mostly about the content. I wish I knew more about books as books. Are you interested only in first editions?"

"I wouldn't say that. Some first editions are unobtainable. Shakespeare's quartos, for instance, are no longer in private hands. But a first edition makes you feel closer to the author."

"And a manuscript still closer?" said McLeod.

"Exactly. And you want to see a manuscript." He spoke to the young man at the smaller desk. "Chester, would you fetch the manuscript of *The Eustace Diamonds,* please."

"Oh, good, that's one of the Parliamentary novels," said McLeod. "I love them, because I covered the legislature in Florida and that gave me a taste of the parliamentary process."

Chester disappeared through still another door and returned to lay a gray carton gently on the big desk. Sheridan moved the carton to a small table that he pulled up in front of McLeod's chair. He opened the carton and looked tenderly at its contents. McLeod stood up as Sheridan lifted another box, this one dark leather, out of the carton; he opened the leather box, slid out the manuscript, and laid it in front of her. It was an enormous pile of paper, at least three inches thick. She lifted the first page — good, heavy, slightly textured ivory-colored paper, on which Trollope had written the novel's title, *The Eustace Diamonds,* and below it, "Chapter 1."

The rest of the page — both sides — was

covered with Trollope's handwriting in brown ink. McLeod sighed in admiration. She knew that Trollope had written ten pages a day, relentlessly, two hundred and fifty words to the page, none of it ever rewritten and all of it fully legible a hundred and thirty years later, with only an occasional word crossed out, an ink blot here and there, a smudge now and then.

She admired the manuscript silently and then looked up, smiled at Philip Sheridan, and said, "I find it strangely moving. Thank you so much. It's an amazing experience — to look at what Anthony Trollope actually wrote."

"We'll make a collector out of you yet," said Sheridan.

"I'm very grateful," McLeod said. "To both of you."

"Thanks, Philip," Nat said and steered McLeod back to his office.

"That was so interesting, Nat. Tell me about the Sheridan collection. Who is he? Do the books and manuscripts belong to Princeton or to Philip Sheridan?"

"Philip Sheridan is from a tremendously wealthy old Princeton family. He went to Princeton and he's always been a loyal alumnus. His father was something of a collector of Americana — he's the one who bought the *Bay Psalm Book.* That's the jewel of the Sheridan Collection."

"What's that?" asked McLeod.

"It's the first book printed in America and it is extremely rare," said Natty. "Philip is interested in Americana but he's more of an Anglophile and he put together this incredible accumulation of British books and manuscripts from the eighteenth and nineteenth centuries. It was my predecessor who got him to promise his books and manuscripts to Princeton. The books still technically belong to Sheridan, but in his will he leaves the collection to Princeton, along with a trust fund to pay for a curator and cataloger. In return, we house his collection for him now — it's quite safe here, safer than it was in his home. And he paid for building those two rooms — they're replicas of his own library. Everything in it is included in our catalog, and researchers have access to the collection. Researchers don't work in his rooms, of course, but in the Dulles Reading Room, and staff members bring them the books they call for, just as they do for other books and manuscripts. The Sheridan Collection is heavily used by researchers, as a matter of fact." He paused for breath. "Now for van Dyke. You can look in the Finding Guide for the van Dyke papers — it's a kind of index." He handed it to her.

McLeod, realizing she had to pay the price of holding a Trollope manuscript in her hands, dutifully looked at the Finding Guide, a large loose-leaf notebook that listed the contents of the collection box by box. Hmmm, she thought when she saw that the collection contained 179 boxes of the papers of three generations of the van Dyke family. Subject headings included things like CLERGY — UNITED STATES — 19TH CENTURY — CORRESPONDENCE. It looked dismal.

Nat Ledbetter did not sense, or just ignored, her lack of enthusiasm. "Now for the papers," he said cheerfully. McLeod could do nothing but acquiesce.

Nat led her back out to the receptionist. "Molly will get you signed in and show you how to get started." It seemed that Nat was washing his hands of her. Molly asked McLeod to sign the daily register and gave her a form to fill out for permanent registration. Then she showed McLeod how to stow her purse and everything else she had brought with her in one of the lockers — not ugly metal lockers, but lockers with wooden doors that measured up to the generally lofty tone of everything in Rare

Books and Special Collections.

"You can only take loose pieces of paper and a pencil with you," said Molly. "And the key to your locker." Then she led McLeod back to the John Foster Dulles Reading Room, an octagonal space with tall windows and long tables for researchers. McLeod filled out a call slip for the first box in the van Dyke collection and gave it to the keeper of the Reading Room, who in turn gave it to a page, who quickly disappeared.

FOUR

McLeod was so overwhelmed by the masses of boring papers in the first van Dyke box — sermons written by Henry's father — that she soon gave up and left the Reading Room and Rare Books and Special Collections. However, she was sufficiently curious that she went to the library stacks and found a copy of "The Other Wise Man" and a book that van Dyke's son, Tertius, had written about his father, and checked them both out.

Outside, she buttoned up her coat, pulled her hat down over her ears, and trudged home to Edgehill Street. Checking telephone messages, she found one from George saying that he would be home that evening and asking if she would like to go out to dinner.

She called him back. "It will be nice to see you for a change," she said.

"Likewise," George said. "I had no idea

that I'd have so little time when you were here —"

"Never mind," said McLeod. "And we don't have to go out. I'll be glad to cook supper."

"Excellent," said George. "Believe me, I'd love not to go out. You're sure?"

"I'm sure. What time will you be home?"

"About seven, with any luck," said George.

McLeod hung up and thought about what to cook, decided on a pork chop and sweet potato casserole, made a shopping list, put her heavy coat and hat and gloves back on, and set out for the grocery store.

She was peeling the sweet potatoes — the most tedious job involved in assembling the very easy pork chop casserole — when the doorbell rang.

A very old, dark-skinned man stood at the door, holding his hat in his hands in spite of the cold. He smiled a dazzling smile at McLeod while she looked at him inquiringly.

"You're the new owner?" he asked.

"No," she said. "I'm a houseguest."

"I used to work for Mrs. Murray," he said. He shivered and put his knitted cap back on. "I just wondered if the new people needed any help."

"What kind of work do you do?"

"Yard work — I'm good with plants — and I'm a handyman, too. I was always fixing things for Mrs. Murray, building shelves and things like that."

He sounded like a home owner's dream to McLeod. Although it did occur to her that he might be Jill Murray's murderer, it was cold and he was old. She took pity on him and said, "Come in."

She got his name — Dante Immordino — and his phone number and told him that George Bridges was the new owner. "It's so sad that Mrs. Murray was murdered."

"It was sad, *molto triste*," he said. "She was a very nice lady. Good to work for."

"You remember her well after all those years," McLeod said.

"I'll never forget Mrs. Murray. She was a great lady."

By the time George got home at seven twenty-five she had made cheese straws and a salad. The casserole was in the oven and a bottle of wine was open.

"Good Lord, the house smells great!" George said when he found McLeod fussing with a newly laid fire in the parlor. "Here, let me do that." He took the tongs from her.

"Why is it that no man on earth can stand

39

to let a woman handle a wood fire?" asked McLeod.

"Some gender roles are immutable," said George firmly.

While they sipped drinks and munched on cheese straws ("I haven't had homemade cheese straws since my mother died," George said), McLeod told him about Dante Immordino. "He used to work for Jill Murray and he sounds like just what you need to help with the yard — if it ever gets warm enough to work in the yard."

"I'll keep him in mind. Do you know how to get in touch with him?"

"He lives with his daughter. He left his telephone number. He said that he loves this house. The people that bought it after Jill Murray died didn't use him and they let the yard go to rack and ruin. He said he missed working here."

"He sounds great," George said.

They ate dinner on small tables beside the fire, and George loved the pork chop casserole.

"It couldn't be easier," said McLeod.

"You always say that," said George.

"But everything I cook nowadays is easy," said McLeod. She told him about her visit to Rare Books. "There sure are a lot of van

Dyke papers," she said.

In turn, George told her a little about a crisis on campus involving the Alumni Office. Then they cleaned up the kitchen and climbed the stairs somewhat wearily and went to their bedrooms. It was still early, and after McLeod was in bed, she opened the biography of Henry van Dyke. It was hagiography — Tertius van Dyke had adored his father — and slow going, but she persevered. Then she got interested in what she was reading and began skipping the worshipful parts to get a quick picture of Henry's life. By the time she slammed the book shut at one o'clock in the morning, she was hooked.

When she got up late the next morning, she was sorry — but not surprised — to find that George had already left for work. She would have liked to tell him what she had found out about Henry van Dyke. Since she had no class and no student conferences scheduled that day, she decided to stay home and finish reading the book.

Then it began to snow.

After she had finished breakfast and *The New York Times,* she went upstairs and settled down with her book, glancing from the page often to look out the window at the falling snow.

George called that afternoon to say that the university was closing early because of the heavy snow and that he would go to the grocery store on his way home from work. What would she like for supper?

"I eat anything," said McLeod. "You know that."

"All right, I'll use my own judgment."

George arrived with bags of groceries. "I decided to stock up," he said. "It's getting messy out there. Watch me as I put the stuff away — then you'll know what all we've got in the larder."

"We've got a lot," she said sometime later, after George had put chicken in the refrigerator and steak and a roast in the freezer, and left quahogs on the counter to make clam chowder for supper.

"And I thought we'd have hamburgers with the chowder," said George.

"Chowder sounds divine, but no hamburger for me. Chowder will be plenty — I haven't been out of the house all day. I don't want to gain any more weight. And all this food — if you're not home more than you have been, it'll never get eaten."

"As you like," said George loftily. "I'll build a decent fire before I make the chowder. Thank God I bought lots of wood last fall."

"I have to say I've gotten interested in old van Dyke," she said as they ate bowls of chowder before the fire in the living room.

"Really?"

"Yes. You know he was a Presbyterian preacher — he was at Brick Church in New York and had all sorts of famous parishioners, including General Ulysses Grant. His sermons were so popular that the New York newspapers reported on them and hordes of people came to hear him — they couldn't all get in the church and lined up outside on the sidewalk. He tried to visit all his parishioners twice a year. He wrote books, too."

"What kind of books?" asked George.

"Every kind. He wrote about religion and he wrote about art. He wrote books about fly-fishing — he was named one of the ten outstanding outdoorsmen of the United States one year, along with Theodore Roosevelt. He wrote a book about Tennyson — he had fallen in love with Tennyson's poetry when he was thirteen years old — and Tennyson himself liked his book so much that he invited van Dyke to visit him in England. While van Dyke was there, the Tennysons had him say grace at meals and conduct the family morning prayers."

"It was a different age, wasn't it?" said

43

George. "Well, I guess he was an interesting old guy. Maybe Nat was on to something good. He sometimes is. More chowder?"

"Yes, please. It's very good. How do you make it?"

George got up and headed back to the kitchen with their bowls. When he got back, he said, "How do I make it? I'm not one of those purists — they won't use anything but potatoes and clams and salt pork. I use onions and thyme and bay leaf and parsley."

"And cream," said McLeod.

"And cream," agreed George. "The purists use milk and a little butter. People in New England can get quite upset when they talk about how to make chowder."

"Cream's good," said McLeod, gobbling up her second bowl.

"Cream's good," agreed George.

"I didn't finish telling you about van Dyke," she said, when she had finished her second bowl of chowder and refused a third.

"Go ahead," said George, who was now concentrating on a large juicy hamburger.

"Some friends of his were so impressed with his knowledge of literature that they raised the money to endow a chair for him at Princeton and he taught English there for twenty years — students stood in line to register for his classes. Members of his church put up the money for him to buy a big house at the corner of Bayard Lane and what I think is Paul Robeson Place. He named the house Avalon."

"The street was called Avalon when I came here," said George. "They changed it to Paul Robeson Place not too long ago."

"Oh, I see," said McLeod. "Later Woodrow Wilson named van Dyke ambassador to the Netherlands, and van Dyke was so upset by the United States' neutrality during World War I that he resigned and went home to urge America's entry into the war."

"Do you think you might do a book about him?"

"No, I don't think so. Who cares about him today? I've had my stroke of luck — a publisher was interested enough in a book about Elijah P. Lovejoy to give me an advance. I'm afraid nobody cares about van Dyke. But I'll go back and look at the van Dyke papers and see what's there — now that I know more about the man, I feel interested after all. And I reread 'The Other Wise Man.' "

"How was it?"

"Oh, it's dreadfully overwritten, but it's still a great Christmas story. It's about a fourth wise man who was supposed to start out with the other three to worship the

Christ child, but he keeps getting delayed because people ask him for help. He never fails to lend a hand and spends all his money on other people and only gets to Jerusalem as Jesus is being crucified. But it illustrates van Dyke's big point: Helping other people is more important than worship."

"Can't fault that," said George. "For dessert, I bought some more fruit tarts. Coffee?"

"I'd love decaf," said McLeod.

While the coffee was brewing, George went out on the little front porch to look at the snow. "I think I'll call your new friend — what's his name — Dante?— tomorrow to see if I can get him to help me shovel the snow," he said when he came in. "It's really coming down."

After dinner they settled down companionably to watch television. McLeod knitted, and George worked on a crossword puzzle, occasionally taking time off to compliment her on the progress she was making on his sweater. It was the most leisurely evening they had had.

FIVE

The next morning the snow had stopped. George was up early and shoveled the sidewalk in front of the house. "The Borough is strict about the sidewalks being shoveled," he said when McLeod came down and complimented him on his promptness. "So I did the sidewalk, but I didn't do the walk to the house or clean the cars off or shovel the driveway so we could get them out. I'm going to walk to work as soon as I can get ready and I'll call Dante from the office. Can you walk to the university all right?"

"Sure, if everybody is as good as you are about shoveling the sidewalk."

"Otherwise, walk in the street. They're all plowed. Everybody does it. It's too bad the garage is so full of junk we can't get the cars inside."

"Don't worry about it. I'll get there," said McLeod.

George left and sometime later McLeod, in boots and shearling coat and muffled in scarves and a warm hat and shearling mittens, was ready to leave, too. The doorbell rang, and it was Dante Immordino.

He smiled his dazzling smile again and this time McLeod invited him inside immediately. "Mr. Bridges called," he said. "He wanted me to shovel the snow."

"If it's not too much for you," said McLeod.

Dante looked offended. "It's not too much for me," he said.

"Of course," said McLeod. "I'm sorry. He left his new shovel here on the porch."

Dante scorned George's new shovel. "Mrs. Murray had a real nice shovel. I'll look in the garage."

It had been twenty years since Jill Murray's murder, McLeod thought. And somebody else — the man from Texas — had owned the house briefly before George bought it. How could Jill's snow shovel still be around? Nevertheless, since she already had on her boots, she followed Dante down the steps and stepped in his tracks to get to the garage door. Dante poked around amid the cartons and garden tools in the garage and came up with an old but very substantial-looking snow shovel.

"Here it is," he said. "It's good." He looked around. "And some of her other stuff is still here." He pointed to boxes on a makeshift shelf of boards on the rafters of the garage. "I put that stuff up there on those rafters for her," he said. "Little Big — that's her son — never took it away, I guess. Little Big, he's an odd duck. He cleaned out the house, but I guess he left these things here and then the other owner just never bothered with those boxes."

"What about all the other stuff — the lawn mower and all that?"

"Some of that is hers, and some of it is not. Some of it must be the other owner's — or maybe Mr. Bridges'." He shrugged, took the old shovel outside, and started his work.

McLeod followed, looked around, and grimaced at the snow on both cars. "I don't even have one of those things you use to scrape the snow off the windshield," she said. Dante said not to worry, that he'd clean the cars off. So she set off for the university, feeling like Ernest Shackleton in all that snow.

That night George was impressed with the job Dante had done. McLeod asked him about all the things in the garage.

"I didn't put that junk there," said George. "The seller was supposed to clean it out but he didn't do it. I'll tell you what: I'm going to clean out that garage. Then we can put both our cars in there."

"And then they won't get covered with snow!"

"That's right," said George.

"What a concept," said McLeod. "Look, I'll be glad to help clean out the garage."

"Thanks. I'll get Dante over to help us, too. Many hands make light work," said George, who liked old maxims. "I'll see if he can come Saturday."

"By the way," she said, "Jill Murray's son was named Little Big. Is that right?"

"Little Big? Oh, I remember. Jill's husband was Bigelow Murray and everybody called him Big. So the son was Bigelow Murray Jr. And everybody called him Little Big."

From time to time she went back to Rare Books, always stopping in the exhibition gallery to look at Jonathan Belcher's office in the showcase. She liked saluting old Belcher's artifacts, then crossing the gallery to Rare Books, signing the day's register, stowing all her belongings in a locker, and proceeding to the Reading Room with nothing but loose sheets of paper and a pencil, then filling out a call slip for the next box of papers, and giving it to Diane, the watchful clerk who sat at a desk. It was like preparing for surgery, she thought. While she waited for the page to bring her order up from the vault, she looked around the octagonal room, with its tall windows on four walls. She enjoyed watching the other researchers, if there were any, and wondering what they were looking for. Some were using rare books, which had been laid reverently before them on V-shaped pillows, and some were going through folders and boxes of papers.

McLeod couldn't get to Rare Books every day — after all, she had a class to teach. The class met for only three hours once a week, but the students seemed to require a lot of conferences with the teacher. They also sent her frequent e-mails, which McLeod answered scrupulously. Then there were the classes themselves to plan, and the visiting speakers to arrange, meet, host, and see on their way. Busy as she was, she went to Rare Books when she could and plowed slowly through the van Dyke papers. When she saw George, she told him about some of the things she found — essays and orations van Dyke had written in college, and the promised letters from six presidents of the United States.

"The plum I've found so far," she told George one night, "is this fight song he wrote for Princeton. It was to be sung to the tune of 'Marching Through Georgia.' I wrote down some of the lyrics:

" 'Nassau! Nassau! Thy jolly sons are we
Cares shall be forgotten, all our sorrows
    fly away
While we are marching through Nassau.'

"Isn't that gorgeous?" she asked.
"Well," said George, "not exactly."

But was there a book in all this stuff? McLeod didn't think so, but she kept on with the research. Sometimes she thought it must be her innate curiosity that drove her, and sometimes she thought it was just deeply satisfying to sit in the octagonal Reading Room and read old letters and clippings. And maybe she persisted because she was interested in all the people who worked in Rare Books and Special Collections. She talked to Diane, the clerk who sat all day at the table in the Reading Room, and found out that she was a single mother whose child had a learning disability. Diane was trying to get him into a special school. Molly, the receptionist, took ballet lessons at night and dreamed of dancing. Jeff, one of the pages, was writing a novel.

She sometimes chatted with other researchers who came to the Reading Room. One was Barry Porter, an English professor on leave from Harvard, who was doing research on Eugene O'Neill.

"What's O'Neill's connection to Princeton? Why are his papers here?" McLeod asked him when they were having a quick cup of coffee in the little café in the basement of Chancellor Green.

"There's an extraordinary collection, despite his brief stay at Princeton. O'Neill matriculated in the fall of 1906, but he dropped out after his freshman year," said Porter.

"Why?"

"Disciplinary and academic problems," said Porter. "He worked in a mail-order house and then went to sea before he started writing plays and went on to win the Nobel Prize. But he had some sort of feeling for Princeton — he gave them a collection of his earliest manuscripts."

Another researcher, or "reader," as the staff called them, was a delightful woman named Swallow. Her hair was white, though not prematurely white like McLeod's. Miss

Swallow might be old, but she was writing a book on botanical painters — Princeton had wonderful books with beautiful paintings of plants and flowers, Miss Swallow told McLeod, as well as loose prints.

"They're all so gorgeous," Miss Swallow said. "I'm writing about the lithographs and researching the lives of the painters. I'm concentrating on the women. Rachel Ruysch in Düsseldorf was one of the first women to earn a living painting, and she did flowers. Her thistle is superb. And Princeton has Elizabeth Blackwell's *A Curious Herbal.* She painted the specimens in the Chelsea Physic Garden in London in the eighteenth century. Did I tell you more than you wanted to know?"

"It's fascinating. How did you get interested in this?" McLeod asked her.

"I'm a gardener, and an amateur painter, and I like to write. I used to write children's books."

"Did you illustrate them yourself?"

"Sometimes I did," said Miss Swallow. She paused and then said, "This is the best project I've ever worked on."

McLeod liked Miss Swallow, liked her looks, her energy, and the way she dressed, in trim pantsuits, always with a nice piece of old jewelry — a silver pin, a cameo, or a coral necklace.

She was a paragon, McLeod thought, and she deserved a super project. If flower painters was her master work, then good luck to her.

Six

If McLeod didn't see Nat Ledbetter as she came into Rare Books, he nearly always stopped by the Reading Room to speak to her when she was there. One day when she was signing in, Ledbetter was on his way out with another man. He stopped to introduce her to his companion, who was the curator of Rare Books, Randall Keaton.

"But everybody calls him 'Buster,' " Nat said.

"I'm glad to know you," said McLeod, shaking hands with Buster, who was dark-haired, dark-skinned, and angry-looking. Almost bellicose, she thought, creating a device to remember his name.

"Have you had lunch?" Nat asked her. "Won't you come with us to the Annex?"

"I shouldn't," said McLeod, "but I will." And she put her coat and hat and scarf and gloves back on and happily went out with Buster and Nat. Later, she was glad she went — Buster turned out not to be bellicose at all, but more of a bluffer, with a tendency to make sweeping statements. Buster the Blusterer, she came to think of him.

"How are you coming with the van Dyke papers?" he asked her.

"Slowly," she said.

"The dullest man who ever lived," said Keaton.

"Hardly," said McLeod. "There's Calvin Coolidge."

"But nobody's writing anything about Coolidge either," said Keaton.

And so it went. Tomato soup (which McLeod had just ordered) was the blandest soup in the world, according to Buster. The news in the paper that morning about global warming, or whatever was the top story of the day, was the worst thing that had ever happened. His cup of coffee was the vilest he had ever had. The director of libraries at Princeton was the biggest fool he had ever seen. That winter's weather was absolutely the foulest yet.

What Buster really liked was books. He was obsessed by books. "It's the most exciting thing I've ever seen," he said when he was talking about a *Book of the Dead* from Egypt. "It's a manuscript on linen, and it dates from the Ptolemaic Period."

McLeod wondered when the Ptolemaic Period was, but before she could find out, Buster had moved on to talk about a copy of Richard Lovelace's *Lucasta,* published in London in 1648, which was up for sale.

McLeod had never heard of Lovelace or *Lucasta* but didn't get a chance to find out more because Buster had already moved on. "But even more important," he was saying, "is the copy of *The Tenth Muse Lately Sprung Up in America.* You know, by Anne Bradstreet, the first book of verse published in America. We must have it to go with Sheridan's *Bay Psalm Book.* I want it more than anything."

"You always want the next thing 'more than anything,' " said Natty. "Maybe we can get it. Let me look at our funds."

She met Fanny Mobley, the curator of manuscripts, on her own. Fanny stopped her as she was leaving late one afternoon and said, "You're McLeod Dulaney, aren't you?"

"I am."

Fanny introduced herself and said, "I just wanted to tell you how glad we are that you're working on Henry van Dyke. We've had those papers a long time and I've always wished someone would do something with them."

"I think he's a very interesting man," said McLeod.

Fanny was a tall woman with longish red hair that was turning gray. That day she wore a fringed, woolly, homespun skirt that fell well below her knees and a gray cardigan over a maroon silk blouse. "I hope you're finding everything you need."

"Oh, I'm finding more than I know what to do with," said McLeod.

"Everyone is being helpful?" asked Fanny.

"Everybody is wonderful. This is a marvelous place to do research."

"I hope so," said Fanny. "Let me know if there's anything at all I can do to help you."

"I certainly will," said McLeod. "Thank you so much."

The next morning, McLeod stopped in Fanny's office door to say hello. Fanny merely scowled at her. "I'm sorry," said McLeod, "are you busy?"

"Very," said Fanny. Still scowling, she got up to close her office door.

Odd, thought McLeod. Miss Congeniality had turned into pure Gorgon.

And she was interested in Dorothy Westcott, who wasn't on the paid staff, but was always around. Everyone called her Dodo. Dodo had beautifully coiffed pinkish blond hair and wore designer suits. She was president of the Friends of the Princeton University Library, the group of mostly rich townspeople who generously supported Rare Books and Special Collections, sponsored lectures and symposia, and financed publication of the *Princeton University Library Chronicle,* a scholarly journal that published articles about material in the collections.

Dodo invited McLeod to lunch one day and asked a few questions about her background and education. She was also interested in McLeod's hair. "You never — well, touch it up?" she asked.

"Good heavens, no," said McLeod. "I don't have the patience. Besides I like to swim and the chlorine turns dyed hair green, doesn't it? I find my white hair is kind of an asset when I'm interviewing people for the newspaper. They tend to tell me everything and I've always thought that was because I look so harmless."

"I see," said Dodo doubtfully.

"Yours looks lovely," McLeod said, eyeing Dodo's well-cared-for pink coiffure with awe. She moved into her interrogatory mode and learned that Dodo "just loved

60

Princeton." Her great regret was that she was not an undergraduate alumna.

"Alas, Princeton was not coed in my day, so I went off to Northampton and Smith, but I came here lots of weekends for dances and football games." She did have a graduate degree from Princeton, "but that's not the same," she said.

"I think it's wonderful myself," said McLeod.

Dodo also regretted that her husband, Bob Westcott, was not an alumnus ("He went to Rutgers, poor soul"), but she had married him, it was clear, when she had learned for certain that he had made lots of money on Wall Street, was going to make even more, and was willing to commute to New York every day from Princeton. "So we live here — the children did very nicely at Princeton Day School until they went to Lawrenceville — and I try to help the university library all I can. Running the Friends is practically a full-time job, but Bob likes me to do it — although he wouldn't stand for a regular job, say teaching, which I am fully qualified to do."

"I'm sure you are," said McLeod.

"And I guess this has a little more prestige than some things," said Dodo. "You work with such lovely people . . ." And she recited a list of names that McLeod vaguely gathered belonged to the richest people in town.

The conversation languished, and McLeod could think of nothing to say except to compliment Dodo on the suit she wore. "Thanks," said Dodo. "I do like good clothes. You have your own style, don't you? I've noticed. At least, your clothes don't come from Talbot's."

"I guess it is my own style, whatever it is," said McLeod, who didn't know whether not buying clothes at Talbot's was a compliment or an insult and hoped it didn't mean she looked like frumpy Fanny Mobley, who certainly had her own individual style. Then something occurred to her. "Did you know Jill Murray?" she asked Dodo.

"Everybody knew Jill Murray. She was quite the grande dame of Princeton," said Dodo. "Of course she was ages older than I was, but she was involved with everything — the Present Day Club, Trinity Church, the Garden Club."

"Who do you think murdered her?" asked McLeod.

Dodo looked around the restaurant, leaned closer to McLeod, and lowered her voice. "I've always thought it was Mary."

"Mary?" McLeod asked.

"Her daughter-in-law," said Dodo.

"Her daughter-in-law?" McLeod had known women who professed to hate their mothers-in-law, but never any woman that she thought would actually be driven to murder. "What was her name?"

"Mary Murray. Do you know her?"

"No, I don't," said McLeod.

"She's married to that ridiculous Little Big Murray, and I think she was jealous of Jill. Of course, some people say it was Little Big that did it, but I never could see that. He's too stupid, really. Jill had a brother, Arthur Lawrence, who was a foul-tempered old man, and some people thought he might have done it, just out of spite. She had another brother, Vincent, but he died before she was murdered. The police never found out who did it. The yard man was under suspicion a little while, but I'm sure it was Mary Murray. She's so quiet and so good, and that's the kind who always breaks out and does something awful like murder."

McLeod shook her head in disbelief. It sounded like utter nonsense to her, and Dodo Westcott was probably projecting her own feelings onto Mary Murray, but she merely said, "Interesting."

SEVEN

One day, Chester, Philip Sheridan's assistant, came in the Reading Room and asked McLeod if she would stop by to see Mr. Sheridan before she left that day.

"Of course," she said. "I'll come right now."

"He didn't want to disturb your work," said Chester.

"I'd love to stop work," said McLeod, and followed Chester to Sheridan's hideaway.

"Ahhh, McLeod. May I call you McLeod?" Sheridan stood up and smiled at her.

"Certainly."

"McLeod, thank you for stopping to see me. I have a little present for you, if you'll accept it." He handed her a book. It was a fat hardcover book, heavy when McLeod took it into her hands. She looked at it and saw that it was *The Vicar of Bullhampton*. Puzzled, she opened it, and looked at the title page. "It says '1870,' " she said. "Is it a first edition?"

"It is," said Sheridan. "Chester and I both spotted it in a London antiquarian bookseller's catalog soon after you came in here, and we ordered it for you."

"But shouldn't it be in the Sheridan collection?"

"We already have two firsts of the *Vicar*," said Sheridan.

"I'm overcome," said McLeod. She sat down in the wing chair, and looked at her new book. "This was very sweet of you. Thank you so much."

"I told you we'd make a collector out of you."

"I'll have to become a collector — out of gratitude."

"For the joy of it," corrected Sheridan.

"How do people become book collectors?" asked McLeod. "How did you get started?"

"I started early. I've been around fine books all my life, and I loved the children's books my father bought for me. My favorite was *The Wind in the Willows*, I read it over and over. I loved Rat and Badger and dear old Toad. It was a quite ordinary copy bought in the thirties but it had illustrations by E. H. Shepard. When my father saw how

I loved the book, he bought me the first edition from 1908 — and I never looked back. I loved those two different editions of the same book. Over the years I bought other editions of *The Wind in the Willows* illustrated by other people — Arthur Rackham, Tasha Tudor, and Michael Hague."

Sheridan said he had turned briefly to collecting Ernest Hemingway. "If you collect Hemingway, you get interested in books about Spain and bullfighting and in the other expatriate writers in Europe between the wars. Just like people who collect Shakespeare have to have Sir Thomas North's translation of Plutarch's *Lives* because that's where Shakespeare got his Roman plots, and Raphael Holinshed's *Chronicles* because that was the source of details for his history plays. I could talk forever."

"Go ahead. How did you get from Hemingway back to the English?"

"Hemingway was the aberration. My heart wasn't really in Americana. My father loved it, and I had a dear friend who was interested in American writers and we used to talk about them a lot. I'm an Anglophile at heart; I really like Dickens and Trollope and Thackeray and even Sir Walter Scott. And Galsworthy and then Evelyn Waugh — well, just all of them. It's been very rewarding."

McLeod took her expensive, heavy copy of *The Vicar of Bullhampton* and put it in her locker, thinking that she would never become a serious collector — it was so much easier to read a paperback than a heavy hardcover. Still, it was nice to own a Trollope first.

When she saw Miss Swallow in the Reading Room, she went over to her and whispered an invitation to lunch. Miss Swallow accepted, and at noon they went to their lockers to get their coats and purses. McLeod brought along her copy of *The Vicar of Bullhampton.*

"I have something to celebrate. Lunch is my treat. Let's go to Prospect."

"That's lovely," Miss Swallow said. "I haven't been there in years." Prospect was an Italianate house, once the home for Princeton presidents, and now the faculty club.

"This is nice," Miss Swallow commented when they were seated at a table by the window overlooking the formal garden that Woodrow Wilson's wife had designed when her husband was president of Princeton.

They both ordered chicken salad. McLeod admired Miss Swallow's pin, a silver angel.

"Thanks. And what are we celebrating?"

asked Miss Swallow.

"This," said McLeod, handing her *The Vicar.* "Philip Sheridan gave it to me. It's a first edition. He found out how much I like Trollope."

"That's just like Philip," said Miss Swallow.

"You know him?"

"Oh, yes, he's lived in Princeton for years."

"Have you always lived in Princeton?"

"For sixty years," said Miss Swallow. "I'm almost a native."

"Then you know about the murder house?" asked McLeod. "That's where I'm staying."

"I wish people wouldn't call it that." Miss Swallow paused. "I knew Jill Murray. She was older — believe it or not — than I, but I knew her. And her murder was so shocking. Nobody could believe it had happened. It was all anybody could talk about for weeks — no, months. And it's equally shocking that it's never been solved."

"Who do you think did it?"

"As I recall, the police interviewed everybody remotely connected with her. Her husband was dead. She had one son and one brother but they were apparently cleared of suspicion. I really don't have an idea."

"Did she have any enemies?"

"Not that I know of," said Miss Swallow.

They ate their chicken salad, spurned dessert, and went back to work.

EIGHT

On the next Saturday morning, McLeod found herself cleaning out the garage with Dante Immordino.

On Friday, George had come home at a fairly decent hour and suggested they go out to dinner. After much discussion about where to eat — Friday night was a dreadful night to eat out in Princeton — they finally went to Lahiere's. It was pretty full, but the maître d' had offered to put them at a table in the bar.

"This is really awfully nice of you to take me out," said McLeod.

"I'm trying to butter you up. I am going to ask the most godawful favor of you. Can you possibly oversee Dante when he comes tomorrow to clean out the garage? The president has asked me to be at an emergency meeting tomorrow. There's no way I can refuse."

"What on earth is going on?"

"A big donor is about to file a suit against the university because of the way his gift has been used," said George. "And Tom wants me to meet with the lawyers and Les to decide on a strategy to deal with it. I'm flattered to be asked to be at the meeting."

"I guess so," said McLeod. Tom was Thomas Blackman, the president of Princeton, and Les was Lester Billings, the vice president for development. "Sure, Dante and I will clean out the garage. Just throw all that stuff away?"

"Just get rid of it, so we can get the cars in there."

"We'll do it," said McLeod. "Never fear. Be of good cheer."

"McLeod, you're a dear," said George, picking up the rhyme. "From gratitude I shed a tear."

"It's a trifle, mere."

"I'm glad you're near."

In an excess of emotion, George had ordered a bottle of champagne, and they had continued rhyming until they were exhausted from laughing at their uses of fear, clear, beer, kir, seer, tear, spear, steer, queer, weir (a tough one that George managed to use), smear, sheer, hear, peer, and leer.

■ ■ ■ ■

Thus, on Saturday morning, McLeod was in the empty house dressed in jeans and a sweatshirt waiting for Dante, who arrived right on time, looking cheerful and kind — could he possibly be a murderer? No, of course not, she thought. They set to work.

Is there a more tedious job than cleaning out a garage? Probably not, McLeod thought. Some decisions were easy. The piles of old newspapers could go — McLeod wondered who could have put them there in the garage in the first place? Dante took them all out to his pickup, promising to haul everything they threw out to the dump or to the recycling center. They decided to discard some inferior garden tools but to keep the best ones. Dante said he would replace the old broken brackets on the wall to hang these out of the way.

Dante carried away the half-empty cans of dried paint and three huge glass jars filled with rusty nails and screws. They sniffed a large round tin and decided the mysterious moldy contents was old dog food, and Dante emptied it into a garbage bag. He then poured the potting soil out of many open bags into the tin. He and McLeod

72

looked at the folded yard chairs and opened them up, discarded some, and kept a few more, which McLeod pronounced perfectly good.

"You can hang them up on brackets, too," Dante said.

"The place is going to be so tidy George won't recognize it," McLeod said.

They kept at it until there was nothing left to be sorted out but the cartons on the boards across the rafters. "And they belonged to Mrs. Murray? And they're still here after twenty years?" McLeod asked.

"They were hers. She had me put them up there," Dante said. He climbed up the stepladder and handed the boxes down to her one by one. Two contained old shoes, and McLeod told Dante to throw them away. One labeled MOTHER'S RECIPES looked more promising, but when McLeod opened it, the recipes were all clipped from moldy, yellow newspaper clippings. McLeod consigned them to the dump, too.

One large carton held old dresses. They looked quite grand — brocade and velvet.

"Marvelous!" said McLeod. "One of my students is doing the costumes for a student play production and he was talking about how he needed dresses like this. I'll give them to him. Little Big couldn't possibly want them at this point."

"Nahh," said Dante. "I'll take that carton in the house for you. What about this?"

Only one much smaller box remained. McLeod opened it and saw it contained old letters from Lieutenant Vincent Lawrence at an APO address to Mrs. John Lawrence on Edgehill Street, with postmarks in the forties. They were World War II letters.

"I'll take these inside, too," said McLeod. Curiosity, her cross and her inspiration, made her want to look at them, but common sense made her want to look at them where it was warmer. She could eventually turn them over to Little Big Murray — if he wanted them.

Dante carried the box of clothes inside and up the stairs to her room. He finished loading his truck, accepted payment, declined her offer of lunch, and drove off.

When he got home, George was extremely pleased that she and Dante had cleaned out the garage. "Congratulations!" he said when he had viewed the results of their labor. "I really can't tell you how grateful I am. But you didn't put your car inside."

"No, I didn't even think about it," she said.

"Give me your car keys and I'll do it and

then put mine in, too," he said.

It was the next Tuesday before McLeod remembered to e-mail Clark Powell, the student who was involved with the play, to ask him if he wanted the dresses, and he responded immediately that he certainly did. She replied that she'd bring the carton to campus and he could pick it up.

The next day George left before she got up, and she brought the carton of clothes downstairs, put it in the trunk of her car, and drove to the university garage. What could she do with the box of clothes? she wondered. She couldn't carry that carton up the hill to Joseph Henry House. Would it be all right to bring Clark Powell down here to pick it up? Then he would be the one who had to carry the carton up the hill. Then she realized she could manage the box if she rode the shuttle bus up to the library stop, which wasn't far from Joseph Henry House. Okay, but I hope Clark appreciates these old dresses, she thought as she boarded the shuttle.

NINE

McLeod left the carton on her desk and went to the library. She planned to start her day that Wednesday at Rare Books, where she could finish up a box of papers that dealt with van Dyke's writing of "The Other Wise Man," and then spend the rest of the day on teaching duties. She arrived at Rare Books and, as she always did, stopped to pay her respects to Jonathan Belcher, "Captain-General and Governor-in-Chief of the Province of New Jersey from 1747 to 1757," or at least the replica of his office that was behind glass. This morning, though, there was somebody in the "office," somebody lying on the faded Persian carpet beside Governor Belcher's desk.

It took McLeod a minute or two to recognize Philip Sheridan. What was he doing, lying in the display of Governor Belcher's office?

What he was doing was being dead, she

realized a second later. She had seen it before.

McLeod ran into Rare Books and screamed wordlessly at Molly Freeman, the receptionist.

Molly screamed back. Nathaniel Ledbetter appeared and stared at the screaming women. McLeod ran to him and clutched his gray tweed jacket. "Philip Sheridan is lying beside Belcher's desk." She ran back through the gallery and Ledbetter followed her, took a look through the glass window, and turned and ran back to Rare Books. McLeod followed him, and to her surprise, Nat hurried past the phone on Molly's desk, past his own office — where there was another phone — and with Molly trailing behind them, through the door into Sheridan's office, where a startled Chester stood up as they ran through. Nat opened a door that McLeod had not noticed before, a door that led into the glass-fronted space that held Governor Belcher's effects.

Chester followed them into the small space and knelt beside Philip Sheridan, who stared at the ceiling without moving. Chester tried to find a pulse, first in Philip Sheridan's wrist, then in the artery in his neck. He put his ear to Sheridan's chest. Fanny Mobley and Buster Keaton and even Dodo

Westcott came in and stood, watching Chester. Diane and a couple of pages came in. The little room was crowded.

McLeod took a good look at Chester, who was somebody to whom she had paid very little attention. He was worth watching, she decided, as he shook his head, and then said, "It's hopeless. He's gone."

He got up and went to his own office; McLeod could see him pick up the phone. The others stood paralyzed around Philip Sheridan. Chester came back. "I called the campus police and I called old Dr. Winchester, Mr. Sheridan's doctor," he said. "Someone will be here in a minute, I guess." He began to weep.

"All right, the rest of you must leave," said Natty. Everyone trailed out except Chester, Natty, and McLeod. Natty said, "McLeod," hesitated, and said, "Oh, all right. You're the writer, aren't you, and you found the body."

Chester seemed to regain self-control, and wiped his eyes.

McLeod went over and patted his arm. "I'm so sorry," she said. "He was such a nice man. Do you suppose it's a heart attack?"

"I don't know. I don't know," said Chester. "He had just had a checkup and he was fine."

By this time, Molly was leading in Sean O'Malley, the university's director of public safety, red-haired and freckle-faced, who greeted Natty, smiled in a perplexed way at McLeod and Chester, and knelt by Philip Sheridan. He was still on the floor when Dr. Winchester arrived and replaced him. O'Malley pulled out his cell phone and spoke quietly into it while Winchester knelt.

"Did you notice what I noticed?" Dr. Winchester asked O'Malley when he stood up.

"You mean the slash in his clothes? Is it a stab wound?"

"Yes, it is. Is there something he could have fallen on in here?" Winchester looked around the small replica of the colonial office.

"I understand that accidental stab wounds are extremely rare," said O'Malley, who McLeod remembered was inordinately proud of the fact that he had audited courses at the Federal Bureau of Investigation. He claimed he knew far more about criminology than he would ever need to know in his present job at the university.

"I guess so," said Winchester. "Looks like a matter for the police."

"I'm way ahead of you," said O'Malley. "I've already called the Borough Police. They'll be here very soon."

Chester, Natty, and McLeod looked at each other helplessly.

"I won't even try to start an investigation," said O'Malley. "Let's leave it to the police."

"Sean, I'm McLeod Dulaney," said McLeod. She told herself that she was after all a trained reporter and positively needed to ask questions while she could. "I met you a few years ago."

"Oh, yes, I remember you," said O'Malley.

"And I just wondered, if Mr. Sheridan was killed by a stab wound, wouldn't there be more blood?"

"Not necessarily. It depends on many factors — the path the blade took, for one thing. A stab wound usually does not bleed the way an incision does."

"So the murderer wasn't necessarily covered with blood when he left here?" asked McLeod.

"Not necessarily. I'd say not, in fact. There would be more blood on the body. It's not easy to see the wound. The sharp instrument went through his clothes, his vest, shirt, undershirt, and then apparently hit a vital organ. The autopsy will show."

The police arrived just then, led, McLeod

was delighted to see, by her old friend Lieutenant Nick Perry, chief of detectives of the Borough of Princeton. Molly turned him over to Natty, whose hand he shook. He caught sight of McLeod and smiled briefly, but he was plainly focused on the business of death. He talked briefly to Winchester and O'Malley, examined the body himself, and stood back up.

"Okay, all of you people" — his gesture took in McLeod, Natty, and Chester — "wait outside. Make sure nobody leaves this department. Sean, what can you tell us?"

"Just what you see, Nick. Stab wound. I did not know the deceased and saw him for the first time just now."

"Dr. Winchester, tell me everything you know about this. We'll have the medical examiner come take a look, but we don't want to waste your expertise, do we?"

Thoughtful old Nick Perry, McLeod thought as she trailed after Chester and Natty, moving aside to let what must have been the entire police force of Princeton Borough enter.

Chester stayed in his office, and she followed Natty into the reception area, where he closed the big double doors into Rare Books. "Nobody is to leave without police permission," he told Molly. "No one." As if to underscore this order, a uniformed policeman came out and stood by the door.

"This is very distressing, very troubling," said Natty after McLeod followed him to his office. "Philip Sheridan — he was apparently murdered."

McLeod sat down, and Natty sat behind his desk. "How could a murderer get in?" he asked. "I don't understand it." He pulled the neatly folded handkerchief from his jacket pocket and wiped his face with it. "I don't understand how a murderer could get into this area."

McLeod nodded in sympathy, but did not point out that perhaps the murderer was already in "this area."

She thought of Chester and decided she should go and see about him. She murmured her sympathy to Natty, and got up. Natty automatically rose as she did. "Let me know if there's anything I can do," she said.

She found Chester sitting at Philip Sheridan's desk, staring into space.

"Are you all right, Chester?"

"How can I be 'all right'?" he asked.

"I know," said McLeod. "I know. But is there anything I can do? Tea? Coffee? Anything at all?"

"Nothing. Nothing. This is worse than the

worst nightmares I ever had, worse than anything I ever imagined could happen."

"I guess it is," said McLeod. "Nobody ever imagines something like this."

"Somebody did," said Chester grimly.

"I guess you're right." She pulled up a chair and sat down beside Chester.

"Had you worked for Philip Sheridan for a long time?"

"I had," said Chester. "It's the only job I ever had. I came to work for Mr. Sheridan right out of library school. He was my employer and my friend, my best friend. And now this —" His voice broke.

"Who could have done it, Chester?"

"I don't know. I don't know." Chester's voice grew louder. "I don't know."

"McLeod, Lieutenant Perry wants to see you." Molly's voice interrupted Chester, who sounded more and more distraught.

McLeod looked around and saw a carafe of water and glasses on a tray on Philip Sheridan's desk, poured a glass for Chester, and coaxed his hand around it.

"Chester, drink this slowly. It will help you," she said. She hated leaving him alone, but she followed Molly out to the main work area.

"The lieutenant asked Mr. Ledbetter where he could interview people, and Mr.

Ledbetter told him he could use the conference room," Molly said. "Those other policemen are doing the crime-scene work. Just like on television."

Natty was standing with Perry and a very young, blond man in the door to the conference room, which was oddly located with windows in the interior walls so that people in the work area could watch what was happening inside it. Lieutenant Perry was frowning at the windows, but Natty pointed out that people outside couldn't hear what was going on. "We'll find another place if this one doesn't work," he said.

"This is fine," said Perry. "We'll get started in here. I'd like to talk to you, Ms. Dulaney first, and then to you" — he pointed at Molly — "and you" — pointing at Natty, "and then to everybody else who was at work here yesterday afternoon or this morning. Come along, Ms. Dulaney."

McLeod followed him into the conference room. Perry looked good, she thought, balder than ever and just as blue-eyed and cheerful.

"MacLeod, this is Sergeant Popper," he said, nodding to the blond young man. "Sergeant, this is McLeod Dulaney, whom I've known for some time. She teaches writing here — I presume you're here for another one-semester gig, McLeod."

"That's right," she said.

"We'll tape this interview, as usual, but I will also take notes. Sergeant, you can take notes, too. It's good practice."

"Yes, sir," said the sergeant.

"All right. Now, McLeod, just for the record, give us your full name." He waited for her answer. "Your home address. Your local address. Phone number. Now, McLeod, what were you doing here? And how did you find the body?"

McLeod told him about Henry van Dyke and his papers and her custom of stopping to look at Jonathan Belcher's office desk and globe and books whenever she came to Rare Books.

"What time did you get here this morning?" Perry asked her.

"It must have been a few minutes after nine," she said.

"And the rest of the staff was all here?"

"I assume so. Rare Books opens to the public at nine and everybody who works here gets in between eight-thirty and nine. They were all here, I think, when we went into Belcher's office."

"And nobody noticed a body lying there in that exhibit, or whatever it is?" Perry asked. "Nobody else?"

"I don't know why I always stopped and looked at it," said McLeod. "I don't think anybody else does. I mean anybody connected with the university. The stray tourist who wanders into the gallery might look at it. But nobody on the staff ever does."

"Does anybody ever go inside that space?"

"I don't know — oh, yes, once I asked if anybody ever went in there, and it seems that once in a great while a researcher will actually want to see one of the books that belonged to Belcher. Nick, it really is amazing the research that goes on around here. A page or a curator would go in to get the book the researcher needed. That's the only time anybody ever went in, so I guess it was a good place to hide a body, a place that nobody ever looks."

Nick harrumped. "I never heard of hiding a body in a glass case in a gallery," he said. "Oh, well. And the deceased is Philip Sheridan. Did you know him?"

"Yes, I did. Very slightly."

"How slightly?"

"I talked to him twice. Exactly twice, I think. Once was when he showed me a Trollope manuscript and the other was when he gave me a Trollope first edition."

"Gave you a Trollope first edition?"

McLeod obligingly described the occasion, and added, "You know he was a very nice man."

"Tell me everything you know about him," said Nick.

"The others can tell you a great deal more about him. All I know is what Natty Ledbetter, the director, told me. Philip Sheridan was a very rich book collector. He went to Princeton University and lived in the town of Princeton. He paid to have his collection installed here and paid for a curator. Natty told me he had left his collection to Princeton in his will. That's all I know about him."

"Okay. Do you know of anybody who might have wanted to kill him?"

"I can't imagine," McLeod said.

"When was the last time you saw him?"

"Last week, I guess, when he gave me the first edition."

"You did not see him yesterday?"

"I wasn't in Rare Books on Monday or Tuesday."

"Well, you can go now. Sergeant, go ask Molly Freeman to come in."

Sergeant Popper got up and McLeod lingered as he left. "It's good to see you again, Lieutenant," she said.

"It's good to see you. I'll talk to you again, I'm sure. And McLeod" — he smiled like a man making a familiar old joke — "don't leave town."

As she left the conference room, the sergeant and Natty were arriving.

TEN

When McLeod came out of the conference room, she found everyone but Buster, Fanny, and Chester gathered in the reception area. Even Dodo Westcott, resplendent in a cherry-colored suit, was sitting in a chair by Molly's desk. The double doors to the outside — the gallery — were still firmly shut.

"Rare Books is closed?" asked McLeod. "I knew nobody was supposed to leave, but nobody can come in either?"

"Oh, we had to close," said Molly. "Obviously, we can't have researchers in here at a time like this." She spoke as though any fool ought to know this. "Of course, we let the police in — and there must have been a thousand of them. And President Blackman came over — he and that cute George Bridges, the vice president for public affairs."

Molly seemed to have such a firm grip on

herself now that it was hard to remember how she had screamed this morning. But then I screamed, too, McLeod thought. "Is George here now?" she asked Molly.

"Oh, yes, they're in Mr. Ledbetter's office."

"Mr. Ledbetter just went in to talk to the police," said McLeod, who thought it would be wonderful to see George, even cry on his shoulder, then realized that that kind of behavior would be entirely inappropriate when George was in his official mode. She sighed and hesitated, unable to leave, but knowing she should get to her office.

Just then George came in, accompanied by an extremely tall gangly man who had to be President Thomas Blackman.

George stopped, startled. "McLeod!" he said. "What are you doing here? But I should have known you'd be involved somehow. Tom, this is McLeod Dulaney. McLeod, Tom Blackman."

"How do you do?" said Blackman. His hand flapped loosely as he reached for one of McLeod's, but his greeting was warm. "You're George's front room boarder, aren't you?" Blackman said. "I'm glad to meet you, even in this troubling situation. I do hope you have a good semester here."

"I'm sure I will. I'm sorry about Philip

Sheridan. He was a very, very nice man."

"He was indeed, and a very generous donor to Princeton. His death is a great loss and the manner of his death is shocking. Well, I'm glad I met you, McLeod, but we must be going. The press are sure to hear about this quickly, I'm afraid."

Then he and George were gone.

"I want to talk to you McLeod," said Dodo Westcott. "But I have to wait to talk to the police."

"Let me go and speak to Chester again. He was so distressed earlier. I'll see you when I come out, and if you're in with the police, I'll wait here for you. How's that?"

Dodo agreed to this plan and continued to sit in the chair by Molly's desk. McLeod found Chester still in his office, but calmer. The glass of water was empty. "Is there someone who could go home with you, Chester," she asked. "Do you live nearby?"

"I lived with Mr. Sheridan," he said dully.

"With Mr. Sheridan?" McLeod could not keep the surprise out of her voice.

"Yes. So you see he really was my best friend."

"I see," said McLeod. Again, she pulled up a chair and sat down.

"He used to live in a big old house in the Pretty Brook area but then he tore out the library and installed it here and smoothed the space over and sold the house. He moved into a much smaller house on Hibben Road. His companion for years and years had lived with him in the big house but he died just before Mr. Sheridan brought his collection here. Mr. Sheridan was already living alone in this smaller house when I came to work for him. I couldn't afford a place in Princeton, and we got along so well that he invited me to live with him. And I did. I lived with him for ten years. I loved him."

All this had come pouring out in a rush. Chester's big brown eyes looked as huge as saucers and shone with incipient tears. McLeod tried to think if there was room in George's house for poor Chester to stay for a while. There was a couch of sorts in the midst of all those unpacked cartons in George's study. Could he sleep there? Would George be upset? No, he was a kind, generous man. She plunged: "Chester, would you like to come stay with us? I'm staying with George Bridges and you could bed down in his study. At least you wouldn't be alone?"

"Thank you, Ms. Dulaney. But I think I'd rather stay in Mr. Sheridan's house. George Bridges was just here — he came in with President Blackman."

"If you change your mind, let me know. Incidentally, George's house in on Edgehill, just up from Hibben Road. Which house do you live in?"

Chester told her the number and described the house.

"Oh, that's very close to Edgehill. It's a lovely house. Even if you don't want to spend the night, then come to dinner," said McLeod. She reflected that the houses on Hibben Road were not what she would call "small." The "big house" in Pretty Brook must have been monstrous.

"I really think I'd better stay in the house," said Chester. "I've always been there and I feel like I ought to be there now."

"In that case, I'll bring you your supper," said McLeod.

"That's very nice of you. I appreciate it, but I could manage, you know. I'm a fair cook."

Natty came in as McLeod was leaving, and told Chester that everybody could leave as soon as they had talked to the police. "We won't try to do any work today," he said. "McLeod, we're not going to provide services to researchers today. We just can't."

"Sure. I understand. You're closed, and I'm leaving, Natty. Could you please tell Dodo Westcott I couldn't wait?"

When she left Rare Books, it was after noon. Murder sure takes up time, she thought as she headed toward her office in Joseph Henry House. Chester's grief had left her feeling unable to tolerate Dodo Westcott's self-centered conversation, though she regretted breaking her word.

She pondered Chester's situation. How could he cope alone, after having that close relationship at work and at home? For ten years, the young man and the older man had apparently thrived on it. She pitied him.

McLeod stopped by the café in Chancellor Green to pick up lunch and finally made it to her office. She was overwhelmed by the number of e-mails, and sat down to answer them while she drank her Coke and ate her chicken wrap. One message was from Clark Powell, the costume designer, reminding her that he was dying for the dresses. Naturally she had forgotten all about them. She replied that he could pick them up at her office when he came for his scheduled conference that afternoon. Good, she thought, that would work out. Except that she never had really looked at the dresses — just glanced at the contents of the carton and caught glimpses of sequins and ruffles — and hated to let them go without seeing them.

She finished up her e-mails, dealt with her phone messages, and then opened the carton and began to take gowns out. They were wonderful — one was black velvet with a high neck and long sleeves, another was pale blue lace with a low waist and satin sash. What looked like a black and gold dressing gown was bundled up. When she lifted it out of the box, it felt heavy. It was heavy, she found, because it was wrapped around something. She shook the object free from the bathrobe and laid it on her desk. It was a very old book with jewels encrusted in its heavy leather cover. It was, she discovered when she opened it, not a printed book but a manuscript written in gold ink, illustrated richly. What *was* it? Something religious — that was obvious from the prayerful postures of the people in the pictures and the halos on their heads. With the colors of the pictures and the gold writing, it was stunning, obviously old and obviously valuable. What on earth was it doing in a box of old clothes?

She went back to the carton. She took out another garment — a sequined black cocktail dress — very carefully. It was wrapped around a gold and silver crucifix. Another dress swaddled a box with carved ivory reliefs on the sides, a very beautiful object from another age. She shook out the last dress in the box and was almost relieved to find that it concealed no further treasure.

She looked at the three objects lined up on her desk for a long time, puzzled, not knowing what to do with them. What were these objects doing in a box of dresses that had been stored in a garage for twenty years? It was unfathomable. She could not just leave them in her office, which wasn't a room, but an open cubicle. The file cabinet, however, did have locks on the drawers. She put the book, the crucifix, and the box in the bottom drawer of the file cabinet, covered them with an old copy of *The New York Times,* closed the drawer and locked it, and put the key on her key ring. She had found a body in the library that morning, and that was enough mystery for one day. She needed time to think what to do.

Then she set about getting organized for her next day's class, and reading the students' first essays. Their assignment had been to interview a person who was an expert in a specific subject — and it was easy to find such experts at Princeton. In fact, she looked forward to reading all her students' stories on these people, and the ordinary task of evaluating their work helped to calm her.

When Clark arrived, he looked at the dresses and thanked her profusely. "I never could have found such a treasure trove," he said, with no idea how aptly he spoke.

"What's the play?" she asked him. He was a nice kid from Chicago who dressed a little more neatly than most of the other students.

"It's a Molière," he said. *"Les Femmes Savantes."*

"The Learned Ladies — lovely," she said.

"We're doing it in modern dress," he said. "Well, fairly modern. These dresses will make all the difference."

"That should be fun," she said.

The phone rang three times while Clark was there, but she did not answer it, knowing that her voice mail would take messages. After he left, she checked and found that George, Nat Ledbetter, and Dodo Westcott had called.

George first. He wanted to make sure she was all right. "I couldn't talk to you when I saw you in the library. And I didn't know you found the body," he said.

"I saw it through the glass darkly, that's all."

"And raised the alarm," said George. "I must say you looked quite shaken when I saw you this morning. Are you sure you're all right?"

"I'm all right. Honestly."

"I'll be home at a decent hour," said George. "I'll cook."

"Fine. Shall I go to the store? I tried to get Chester to come to dinner tonight, but he'd rather I brought his supper to him. He lives close by — on Hibben Road. But I think I'll call him and urge him again to come."

"Chester? Oh, Chester Holmes, Philip Sheridan's assistant. Sure, McLeod. Whatever you think best. I guess he is all alone now."

McLeod called Nat Ledbetter, who told her that Rare Books would be closed to researchers for the rest of the week at the request of the police, who wanted it as undisturbed as possible. "They're looking for the murder weapon," said Nat. "It's an all-out search, Lieutenant Perry said."

"I see," said McLeod. "I understand about closing Rare Books. Are there any out-of-town researchers who will be seriously inconvenienced?"

"One gentleman from California is working on Allen Tate material, but he says he can go to other libraries tomorrow and Friday and come back here Monday. I hope we'll be able to reopen on Monday. And

Barry Porter can easily wait until next week."

"I hope so, too," said McLeod. "Do the police know who did it yet?"

"No, they don't. No obvious solution."

"Thanks so much for calling me, Natty. I really appreciate it."

Dodo Westcott was at home. "The police finally got around to talking to me," she told McLeod. "It was a good thing you didn't wait for me — they took forever. I couldn't help them much. They wanted to know when I saw Philip last, and I said about four o'clock Tuesday. I went in to talk to him about the annual dinner for the Friends of the Library. I had decided to see if he wanted to spring for champagne. Wouldn't that be lovely? Champagne at a Friends dinner? We've never been able to afford it before."

"Did he want to?" asked McLeod, interested in spite of herself.

"Actually, he did not," said Dodo. "Rich as he is, or was, you'd think he would, wouldn't you?"

"I don't know. Rich people seem to be the most careful with their money. That's why they have a lot of it; that's what my father used to say."

"I suppose so," said Dodo. "Anyway, you

must plan to come to the Friends' annual dinner. It's quite an occasion. But that's not what I called about. Today the police kept asking me about when I left the library, or left Rare Books. I told them I was late getting away. Late for me, I mean. Of course, Philip was still alive when I left — I'm sure of that. But they want to talk to me again. McLeod, I'd like to talk to you before I see them again. Can we have lunch tomorrow?"

"I can't, Dodo. My seminar starts at one."

"Would it be all right if I came over to see you right now?"

McLeod looked at her watch; it was four-thirty. She wanted more than anything to get home and have a drink with George and see about Chester, but Dodo sounded odd. "Sure, come on over," she said.

Dodo said she'd be there in minutes. McLeod tidied up her desk — she thought she had better do this since she couldn't close a door to hide the clutter — and decided she'd lock all the student papers in the file cabinet with the mysterious objects from the carton of dresses. The world seemed to have gone mad.

ELEVEN

Dodo Westcott arrived, looking somewhat worn, her cherry-colored suit rumpled and her face tired and lined.

McLeod met her downstairs and suggested they sit in the glassed-in sunporch since her office was so spartan and so open. It was close to five o'clock and the staff was leaving Joseph Henry House as McLeod and Dodo settled on a sofa. Frieda, the dark-haired, dark-eyed secretary, poked her head in the sun parlor door to explain that the doors were on automatic locks. "Just make sure the door you use is closed tight when you leave, McLeod." She paused and declaimed dramatically: " 'O, it's broken the lock and splintered the door . . . Their boots are heavy on the floor.' " In a more normal voice, she said, "That's from Auden. Of course, we hope no one will break the locks, but at least we can lock the doors, can't we?"

McLeod promised to close the door tightly, and turned her full attention to Dodo.

"This *is* nice of you to stay and talk to me. I'm terribly upset by what happened today . . ."

McLeod agreed that murder was unsettling.

"You see, I thought the world of Philip Sheridan," said Dodo. "He was such a *gentleman.* There's no other word for it. And he was so generous to the Friends . . ."

McLeod noted that just a little while ago Dodo had not thought Philip Sheridan was so terribly generous, when he turned down her request for champagne for the Friends' dinner, but she had apparently decided not to speak ill of the dead again.

Dodo continued, "I don't know what we'll do without him. I can't imagine who would want to kill him, can you?"

"No, I can't, but then I don't know anything about him, really. I presume he did get along with everybody at the library."

"Of course he did. He was a towering figure. Everybody adored him. That's what I tried to tell all those policemen. We all looked up to him." Dodo paused and looked at her scarlet fingernails a long time. McLeod looked at them, too, and wished she could manage to find time to get regular manicures and keep her nails long and red. How did other women do it? She had never been able to accomplish this simple feat. "Well, nearly everybody adored him, that is. There was one exception, of course."

McLeod wondered where all this was going. "Who was the exception?" she asked.

"Chester."

"Really?"

"Chester and Philip had some terrible quarrels."

"That's amazing," said McLeod. "I'd say that if anybody adored Philip Sheridan, it was Chester Holmes."

"Of course, in a way, he adored him. But don't they always say it's the spouse who does the murder. Well, Chester wasn't his *spouse,* but you know what I mean. People like that — those relationships — are always charged with such tension. Those people are always so sort of unbalanced —"

"Philip Sheridan, unbalanced?" said McLeod. "Dodo, be sensible. Think about it. Were they emotionally involved? I got the impression that Chester was a faithful apprentice figure."

"He must have been more than that," said Dodo.

"He was good at the work he did at the

library, wasn't he?" said McLeod. "And it must have been a great help to Philip Sheridan at his age to have a young person living at the house. They weren't inseparable."

"I know, but don't you think Chester maybe *wanted* them to be inseparable? If Philip had found somebody else, wouldn't Chester have gone berserk?"

"Did Philip find somebody else?"

"He must have. What else would make Chester kill him?"

McLeod shook her head in an effort to clear it. Dodo was going in circles. "But surely you don't know that Chester killed him? Do you?" McLeod asked.

"No, but as I said, it just seems logical to me," said Dodo. "That kind of relationship breeds violence. You are the kind of person who sees people in the best possible light. I guess I'm more cynical, and I just believe that Chester killed Philip. It's as simple as that."

"It's an interesting point of view," said McLeod, keeping her voice neutral.

"Do you think I should tell the police?" asked Dodo.

"Tell the police what?"

"Tell them that Chester murdered Philip," said Dodo.

"Dodo, do you have any evidence at all

that Chester Holmes killed Philip Sheridan? Motive, means, opportunity — those are the things that count in a murder investigation. Do you have tangible, provable evidence about any of those things?"

"I see what you mean. I just have this strong gut feeling, and my husband says my intuition is incredible. I just seem to be able to psych things out."

"That's a remarkable gift," said McLeod, wishing she was at home having a drink with George. Was she becoming an alcoholic, she wondered nervously. Wasn't wishing for a drink a sign of addiction?

"I knew you'd understand," said Dodo.

McLeod, who was far from understanding Dodo, shrugged. She stood up.

Dodo stood up, too, but more reluctantly. "I was hoping we could have a nice long chat about it. A real heart-to-heart. You're so smart, McLeod. You have a mind like a meat cleaver. You cut right to the main issue."

"Good heavens, Dodo. I don't have a mind like a meat cleaver. It's more like a can of hair spray. It just seizes on a cliché and hardens it into a fact."

"Oh, no. I wanted to talk to you immediately. I think you have good sense."

"Thanks, Dodo, but I'm not a good adviser. I get emotionally involved — I guess everybody does — and don't always see an issue clearly."

"Well, thanks for talking to me," said Dodo. "I really appreciate it. I'll wait and think it over before I tell the police about Chester. Where are you parked?"

"Down in the garage," said McLeod.

"Oh, I'm right on Nassau Street. I found a metered place just like that." She snapped her fingers.

"Good for you, Dodo," said McLeod. "I have to go upstairs to get my things, but you can go out this door. I'll make sure it's closed tight. I'm scared of Frieda. You know, she's a regular martinet."

"I bet you're not scared of anybody," said Dodo as she left. "Thanks so much. See you soon."

"Hope so," said McLeod. When she left, unburdened by the box of dresses she had brought that morning, she resolutely avoided the shuttle bus and walked down the hill to the garage, wondering about Dodo as she went. Why in the world had Dodo sought her out to try to blame Chester Holmes for the murder of Philip Sheridan?

At home she found George in the kitchen.

"I'm sorry I'm late," she said. "Dodo Westcott wanted to talk to me. Have you been to the store?"

"I have. I actually got away early. We have this new guy in public relations — Chuck Hammersmith — and he's terrific. He handled the murder with the press quite well. Tom and I both left early — Tom said there would be so much to do tomorrow we'd better get away while we could."

"That's great. Who is the new guy? I always liked Jim Massey. Where is he?"

"He was fine," said George, "but Chuck is better, I think. Jim got a good job at Stanford — he's vice president. Anyway, I went by Wild Oats and got these felicitous filet mignons. I know you aren't crazy about steak, but these really are superb."

"I know. They look good. I'm delighted."

"And I got some stuffed potatoes from Nassau Street Seafood. I'm just doing a salad. We'll have a feast."

"Lovely. What can I do?"

"Nothing. It's all under control. Go sit down and I'll come make us martinis in a jiffy."

"Splendid. What a nice life I lead. But what about Chester?"

"I didn't forget him. I bought three of everything. Call him. The phone would be listed under P. Sheridan."

McLeod went upstairs to dump her stuff, and while she was up there, she changed into a woolly caftan she loved. Back downstairs, she looked up Sheridan's number and dialed it.

Chester answered and said he believed he would come to dinner after all. He had found out how hard it was to be alone in the house on Hibben Road and he was very grateful. McLeod gave him the address on Edgehill, and relayed the news to George, who sighed.

"It's an act of charity. And it's our duty, but duty's hard," he said. "Let's have a drink and I'll finish up after he gets here. I guess I'd better build a fire."

"I'll go get my knitting," said McLeod.

"Yes, indeed, I think you should work on it with greater dedication. I've never had a hand-knit sweater before."

"I just hope I don't screw up your sweater," said McLeod when she came back downstairs. She got out the sweater, which she had barely started. "This part is pretty straightforward, but when I get up to where the pattern is, I'll have to be very careful."

"Be *very* careful, then," said George. They sat down before the fire with their martinis and a bowl of pretzels, and George said,

"Now tell me how you happened to find the body."

So McLeod told him about her habit of stopping to look in on Belcher's office and how this morning she had seen Philip Sheridan stretched out. "Was it just this morning? It seems like a century ago."

"And your old friend Nick Perry is back on the job. Do you have any ideas about who did it? You've been spending a lot of time in Rare Books."

"I don't have any idea who did it. Philip Sheridan was such a nice man. But accusations are already flying." She told him about Dodo and her talk of Chester.

"Do you think Mrs. Westcott is a reliable accuser?"

"I don't know," said McLeod, then added, "No, I don't think so."

"What did you think of Tom?" asked George, changing the subject.

"He seemed quite nice — in the two minutes I talked to him."

"I like him," said George.

"Who took your place as assistant to the president?"

"A woman. She's good at the job — but not as good as I was."

"Lots of changes," said McLeod.

"Yes," said George.

She was on the verge of telling George about the book and the crucifix when the doorbell rang and they both went to let Chester Holmes in.

TWELVE

Chester could barely wait until McLeod had performed the introductions to express his gratitude for the invitation.

"Chester, this is George Bridges. George, do you know Chester Holmes?" she was finally able to say. While George was hanging up Chester's down jacket, Chester began chattering as he brushed his floppy brown hair out of his eyes. "I am so glad you called, McLeod. I can call you McLeod, can't I? It seems friendlier than Ms. Dulaney. Anyway, I thought I should stay there at the house and answer the phone and deal with all the people who called. Then Mrs. Hamilton arrived, and she has never approved of me. Never. She tries her dead level best to be nice to me, but she just can't. And so when you called, it was like a lifeline to a drowning sailor. I said to myself, 'I can get out of here and she can be in charge and do what she likes.' So I said,

'Yes,' and here I am."

"Who is Mrs. Hamilton?" asked McLeod. They were still standing around in the hall.

"She's Mr. Sheridan's sister," said Chester. "She's his closest relative. I called her this morning. She lives in New York and she came right down. She does like to manage things and I guess it's good she's here, because I want Mr. Sheridan to have a proper funeral and she'll see to *that* —"

George interrupted. "Let's go sit down, Chester. What would you like to drink?"

"Oh, water's fine," said Chester. "I'm not much of a drinker." He followed them into the parlor with its small blazing fire.

"Come on," said George. "Have a drink. McLeod and I are having martinis. Wouldn't you like one? It'll do you good."

"All right, I will. Maybe it will make me feel better."

"It will," George assured him and headed to the kitchen.

"I just hope Mrs. Hamilton is not going to be here for long," Chester said. "It's bad enough that Mr. Sheridan is dead. That breaks my heart. I can't take it in — I'm sort of numb and I guess that's good. But I'm not so numb that Mrs. Hamilton won't get under my skin — even if she is good at managing things."

"What does she do that's so annoying?"

"It's hard to describe. She makes me feel like I don't belong there, even though I *live* there and she doesn't. It's a horrible feeling."

"Maybe you should stay here. George, can't we put Chester up here?" she asked as George came back with Chester's drink.

"I don't quite see how," said George. "McLeod is in my very nice guest room at the moment," he added for Chester's benefit.

"Oh, no, I wouldn't intrude. I'll stay in Mr. Sheridan's house. It *is* my home, after all. The only thing is I can't go to work for a while, because the police are taking over Rare Books."

"I know," said McLeod. "Natty called me. I can't quite see why they need the whole area."

"They're looking for the murder weapon," said Chester, taking a gulp of his martini. "I told them what I thought it was and they're looking for it." He took another gulp.

"What do you think it was?"

"I'm sure it was Mr. Sheridan's own paper knife," said Chester. "It was a splendid ivory-handled knife, very old, designed originally to cut the pages in books — you know, when they used to come with 'uncut pages.' And he used it for a letter opener, too. It was very, very sharp. Some of the old paper knives were dull, but this one was sharp. Mr. Sheridan kept it that way. He had arthritis in his hands and it was hard for him to use a knife. So he kept it sharp. Anyway, it's not on his desk, where he always kept it. So I'm sure that's what the murderer used." With a third gulp, he finished off his martini and set the glass down on a table beside the sofa.

"Would you like another?" asked George, standing up to take the glass. "McLeod?"

"No, thanks," she said.

Chester just smiled. George left carrying his glass.

"Did you tell the police about the paper knife?" asked McLeod.

"Yes," said Chester. "Finally. Most of the day they were asking us all about times — times we last saw Mr. Sheridan and all that."

"When *did* you see him the last time?" asked McLeod as George came back in with Chester's fresh drink.

"I'm going to finish up supper," said George, interrupting.

"Can I help?" asked McLeod.

"No, no. You talk to Chester. This will be easy."

"Chester, when did you see Mr. Sheridan

the last time?" McLeod repeated.

"That's what's so hard. I last saw him when I left about six o'clock Tuesday. How did I know I'd never see him again?" He drank half his second martini.

"You didn't go home together?"

"I left before he did most days. He liked to be alone with his books occasionally, and I would go out and see some of my friends — my other friends. That's what I did Tuesday night. I left him at the library and went home and changed clothes — Mr. Sheridan was a stickler for a coat and tie at work — and went out to the Alchemist and Barrister with some friends. Then we went to a movie after dinner. I didn't get home until almost midnight. I didn't know Mr. Sheridan wasn't home when I went to bed."

"What about the next morning?"

"I still didn't worry. Once in a while, Mr. Sheridan would sleep in, and not go to the library until noon. After all, he wasn't on anybody's payroll. I was. Mr. Sheridan paid my salary, but he did it through the university. Since I'm on the university payroll, I keep regular hours." He polished off his second martini and set the glass down, just as George came in to call them to dinner.

The filets were magnificently tender, the potatoes excellent, and George's salad was marvelously filling since it contained Parmesan cheese, artichoke hearts, bacon, and beet slices as well as lettuce.

George and McLeod drank sparingly of the Bordeaux, but Chester had several glasses as he ate. And he talked. He answered McLeod's questions readily and fully.

"So when I saw Mr. Sheridan in the Belcher room this morning — you had not seen him since late Tuesday afternoon?"

"That's right, and that's what the police kept asking me about. They asked me a zillion times if I could get in Rare Books when it was closed. And I told them I could if somebody was still here — they could let me in. I couldn't get back in if everybody was gone and the alarm was set. They never quite understood about this and they just kept on and on. They asked me over and over, if I came back after I left Tuesday. And they asked me why I didn't see Mr. Sheridan on the floor of the Belcher room this morning, and I said I never looked in there. Nobody ever looked in there but you, McLeod. They want to talk to me some more tomorrow, they said."

"They'll probably talk to you tomorrow and tomorrow and tomorrow," said McLeod.

"I guess so," said Chester.

"A murder investigation is dreadful," said George. "I was a suspect one time, and it was foul."

"Surely I'm not a suspect," said Chester.

"I think everybody is a suspect at this point," said McLeod. "Everybody who had a chance to be at the library alone with Mr. Sheridan on Tuesday."

"That's scary," said Chester. "I thought I was just helping the investigation. It never occurred to me they could suspect me."

"Everybody is suspect until they're eliminated, I think," said McLeod.

"I can't believe anybody would suspect me of killing Mr. Sheridan. He was my best friend. And since my parents died, he's been like my only relative."

McLeod relented. "I'm sure you're not really under suspicion."

"I should think not," said Chester. He brushed his hair out of his eyes and switched topics. "This is good wine," he said, picking up the bottle. "A Bordeaux — Mr. Sheridan always called it claret. He was a real oenophile as well as a bibliophile and an Anglophile." He filled his glass and set the bottle down.

"You said you told the police about the paper knife, didn't you?" said McLeod.

"I did. As soon as I noticed it was missing."

"You said he kept it on his desk."

"That's right," said Chester. "He kept it in a sheath — it was really sharp — and he stuck it in a little antique pitcher that sat on his desk. You know, it was in the sheath, but pointing down in this little pitcher. That was so it wouldn't get lost among the papers on his desk."

"Did he use it much?"

"He used it all the time — to open all his letters — but what he liked best was when we got a book with uncut pages, and he would cut the pages with the knife. He loved that. He loved old things, and an old book that nobody had ever read before — that really pleased him."

"When was the last time you saw the paper knife?" asked McLeod.

"I'm sure it was on his desk Tuesday. Mr. Sheridan opened a lot of mail that day. If he hadn't used the paper knife, I would have noticed." Chester brushed his hair back and poured himself another glass of claret.

"So the police are looking for the paper knife," said McLeod. "Where had they looked when you left?"

"Well, they weren't devoting all their time to looking for the knife," said Chester. "As I said, they spent more time asking the same questions of everybody there. When did you last see Philip Sheridan alive? And what time did you leave Rare Books? Who was there when you left? There were a lot of people to ask questions of, too — Mr. Ledbetter, Mr. Keaton, Mrs. Mobley, Mrs. Westcott, Molly, all the clerks and secretaries and conservators and curators."

"I wonder who was the last person to leave," said McLeod. "And did that person see Philip Sheridan alive? That's key, isn't it? I know how Nick Perry works, and I'm sure he's keeping careful notes and making charts of times and people. How can they prove when somebody leaves? John could say, I left at five and Mary and Joe were still there and Sheridan was still alive. And Mary could say, oh, no, John was still here when I left at five-fifteen. It's too bad everybody didn't have to punch a time clock."

"That's all the university needs to improve employee relations — time clocks," said George, speaking for the first time in a long time. "How about some ice cream and coffee?"

"No, thanks," said Chester. "I'll just have another glass of wine."

"I'll pass, too," said McLeod. "Are you going to have ice cream, George?"

"I guess not, but I'll make a pot of decaf if you'll have some."

"I'll always have decaf coffee," said McLeod. "I'll clear the table."

They all helped to clear the table and load the dishwasher while the coffee dripped. When they were sitting in the parlor, McLeod asked Chester, "But you say the police weren't conducting an all-out search for the weapon?"

"No, one man was looking all over our office," said Chester. "He was tearing things apart. I guess he'll move into the other areas tomorrow or the next day when he finishes in ours."

"The thing is," said McLeod, "there are millions of places to hide a knife in that place. Think about all the file drawers and books on shelves upstairs and more books downstairs, and all those boxes of papers in the vault. What a job!"

"Yes," said Chester thoughtfully. "I guess I hadn't realized how big a job it would be." He had brought the bottle of wine with him and he filled his glass again.

McLeod sipped coffee and looked at George. He must be tired of Chester, who seemed settled in for a long night. She could always ask Chester more questions, but that would just make him stay longer. Nevertheless, she plunged ahead. "Chester, you were there a long time today. While all this questioning was going on, did you gather any idea about who was the last to see Philip Sheridan alive?"

McLeod saw George glaring at her, and felt a pang of guilt, but brushed it away.

"Well, as you might expect, Molly and the other support staff left first, pretty much right at five. I remembered that much. I think when I left at six that Mr. Ledbetter and Mr. Keaton and Mrs. Mobley and Mrs. Westcott were still there. And one of the conservators was working away at something he didn't want to stop and leave. And oh, yes, Mary Woodward — she's a curator, a jack-of-all-trades curator, and she was still there — and then . . ." He named another curator, whom McLeod had not met.

"Do so many people stay after five, when Rare Books is closed to researchers?"

"Oh, yes, they all say that's when they can get some work done," said Chester.

George pushed his chair back and stood up. "Listen, you two, I've got to go upstairs and do some work. You'll excuse me, I know, Chester. I'm glad you could come tonight. Let me know if there's anything at all I can do. This is a terrible business." He shook hands with Chester, who had stood up, too.

"I certainly will, Mr. Bridges, and I'm so grateful to you and McLeod. Thank you so much. It was a delicious meal."

"See you soon," said George. "Good night, McLeod."

"I guess I'd better be going home," said Chester. He brushed his hair out of his eyes.

McLeod opened the coat closet and handed him his jacket. "I'm so glad you came. You must let us know if there's anything at all we can do. Good luck with Mrs. Hamilton. I'm sure you'll charm her into submission."

"Thanks," said Chester, "I certainly hope somebody charms her into something." And he left.

THIRTEEN

McLeod closed and locked the front door, turned out the lights, and climbed the stairs. George came out of his office to apologize for deserting her. "I feel sorry for Chester Holmes, but I was getting tired of him, and he was drinking so much I was afraid he would pass out and stay forever."

"What did you think of him?" asked McLeod.

"I guess he's a nice chap. He seems to have been devoted to Sheridan. I hope Sheridan left him something in his will."

"I didn't even think about that," said McLeod. "I like him. He's always so *nice.* I forgot to ask him something —"

"You asked him every question it is possible to ask," interrupted George.

"No, I forgot to ask him about Dodo Westcott."

"What about Dodo Westcott?"

"You know — how she thinks he's the

most likely suspect. I just wonder what he thinks of her."

"Another day, another question," said George.

"That's right. Well, I'm going to bed. I'm tired. See you in the morning — maybe."

"I'm going to turn in, too. I'm going to the office very early," said George. "I have a breakfast meeting with Chuck Hammer-smith. You know this is going to be very hard on the university, public relations-wise. A big donor killed, and if Chester's right, the murderer will probably turn out to be a member of the staff. It could be a disaster. So I called him just now and set up the breakfast meeting."

"If anybody can handle it, you can," said McLeod cheerily. "Okay, see you sometime. I have class tomorrow afternoon."

"Right. Good night, McLeod. Inviting you to stay here was the smartest thing I ever did. It's one way to be always in the thick of things."

"Now you're being sarcastic — or is it ironic? I can't keep them straight."

"I'm being perfectly sincere. I'm glad you're here."

"Thanks, George. I'm glad I'm here, too. Good night."

■ ■ ■ ■

McLeod tossed and turned for a long time before she went to sleep. She was trying to decide how to find out what time people had left Rare Books on Tuesday and thus find out who had been the last to see Philip Sheridan. Would Nick Perry tell her what he knew? She was sure he would not. Then could she possibly go around and ask the same people the same questions that the police had asked them? Not likely, she thought. Oh, well, a way would open up — she was always able to find out things the police couldn't or didn't find interesting.

Then she remembered that she had never told George about the things that had been in that box of dresses. It had been a long day. She finally slept.

She woke up late on Thursday and looked at the newspapers while she ate her breakfast at the kitchen table. *The New York Times* had more news about the murder than the Trenton *Times* did, and she read Philip Sheridan's long obituary with interest. He had certainly lived a life of privilege — son and grandson of extremely rich railroad tycoons, schooling at Exeter, Princeton, and Oxford. He had never married and was

125

survived by a sister, Lucia Hamilton of New York City, and several cousins.

As for the murder itself, there was very little in either paper. Police were investigating; a stab wound had apparently been the means of murder; no suspects had been named by the police. And that was about it — nothing new.

McLeod folded the papers and went upstairs to get dressed. She wrapped up warmly and walked to her office and settled down to get ready for her class that afternoon. This work required her full attention for several hours; she was planning to discuss the students' essays on faculty members, turned in last week. She was rather disappointed in them; it seemed to her that too many students had made what they thought were "safe" choices among the faculty, interviewing distinguished but not controversial professors. Two students had showed originality — one young woman had written about how hard it was to get an appointment with the world-famous writers who taught creative writing, and a young man had written a sympathetic interview with a professor who had been suspended for a year for misuse of a departmental fund. She e-mailed each of the students to make sure it was all right to photocopy these papers and distribute them in class for discussion. Frieda's assistant did the copying for her, thank heavens.

She was interrupted by one phone call — from Dodo, who wanted to know if she and George could come to dinner next Wednesday.

"Good heavens," said McLeod. "That's lovely of you. But I can't speak for George. He's working terribly hard at his new job and he almost never gets home before dinner. I'm sure I can come, but you'd better call George yourself."

Dodo promised to do so and get back to McLeod. "And don't forget the Friends' dinner next Saturday," she said.

At twelve, McLeod went next door to the café in Chancellor Green and had a bowl of soup and some crackers.

At one-thirty, class members began trailing into the big seminar room on the first floor of Joseph Henry House and took seats around the wide table. The class was lively as she led the discussion on their choice of subjects. They talked about the murder — most of them had never heard of Philip Sheridan and did not understand the position he had occupied in Rare Books and Special Collections.

"It's weird. A rich alumnus gets bumped

off in the library," said Clark Powell. "It's not as though it was a faculty member or a student or something."

"It would make a wonderful mystery story, wouldn't it? I wish Princeton offered a course in mystery writing," said Olivia, one of the two who had written good papers.

"Maybe they will," said McLeod. "But right now we have to talk about your papers on professors. I have to say I was disappointed in them," and she went on to talk about how boring a profile could be if it was just a puff piece.

One of the students who had written a "soft" paper on an exemplary faculty member spoke up and said, "I see what you're trying to do. You want us to go beyond the mouthpiece position and get more controversial and offbeat subjects, don't you?"

"I couldn't have put it better myself," said McLeod.

She was well pleased as she walked home to Edgehill. As she climbed the three steps to the little front porch, she noticed that one of the stained glass panes in the front door was missing. The door was not locked, she discovered, and opening it, she saw the colored pane lying in shards on the hall floor. She closed the front door behind her and felt cold air still coming in from the hole where the pane had been.

It dawned on her that someone had broken in. Was the burglar still here? Did she hear steps upstairs? Fear weakened her knees and made her feel faint. I'm such a coward, she thought, stepping quickly back out the front door. She walked down to the sidewalk by the street and called 911 on her cell phone. A police car was there in seconds. At least the whole Borough force isn't tied up with the murder, she thought.

The police car pulled into the driveway and the policemen got out. McLeod explained what had happened. They told her to stay outside while they searched the house.

She stood on the walk and stomped her feet to keep warm until the police came out and told her she could come in. "Looks like somebody did break in," one of them said. "One of the bedrooms upstairs is a real mess."

"I'm afraid I am messy," McLeod said.

"No, you didn't do this, I don't think. This guy was looking for something. Come see."

Upstairs, her room had been ransacked. There was no doubt about it. Drawers had been pulled out and emptied, clothes ripped off the hangers in the closet, her suitcases pulled out from under her bed and opened. "It's awful," she said.

"It's kind of scary when somebody breaks in your house," agreed one of the officers. "Can you tell us what's missing?"

"I can't see anything that's missing right now," said McLeod. She looked in the little wooden box that held her tiny collection of jewelry, a gold bracelet her mother had given her, a string of pearls that Holland Dulaney had given her before he died, a couple of pairs of good earrings — it was all there, and the rest was costume jewelry. "The only remotely valuable thing I had was my laptop computer and it's still here. I can't think of a thing that's missing."

"What about the rest of the house?"

"You know, it's not my house," said McLeod. "I'm just sort of a tenant, staying here for the semester. This is the only room where I own anything. I don't suppose I'd know if anything was missing anywhere else."

"Who's the owner?"

"George Bridges. He's at the university. When he comes home, he can tell if anything is missing."

"No television set?"

"There's a small one in the dining room," said McLeod. "It's kind of a family room.

We can see if it's still there."

The three of them looked in George's bedroom, which seemed to be in order, and in his study, which also looked undisturbed — the computer, printer, and fax were all still there — and went downstairs. The television and DVD player were still in the dining room, and the microwave was in the kitchen.

McLeod could see nothing missing from the basement, which looked relatively undisturbed.

"Can George call you when he gets home?" asked McLeod. "And tell you if other things are missing?"

"Tell him to call this number," said one of the officers, handing her a card as they walked toward the front door. "And see if you can't get this pane replaced. The cold air is getting in."

"I feel it," said McLeod. She thanked them for their prompt appearance and thorough examination of the premises. With many assurances of goodwill, the police departed.

When George got home, he was angry and bewildered that someone had broken into his newly bought home.

McLeod understood. "I've always read how people said they felt 'violated' after their house had been burglarized," she said. "Now I see what they meant. But is anything missing? The police want to know."

"I can't think of anything," said George. "Oh, wait a minute, I do have the ancestral flat silver." He checked the drawer in the dining room and decided every fork and knife and spoon was there.

"This is weird," McLeod said. "What were they after?"

"Something of yours," said George. "Yours is the only room that they tore apart."

"I know," said McLeod. "And I don't have a thing worth stealing." She thought fleetingly of the objects she had found in the box of old dresses. But who on earth would have known they were there? And then George distracted her.

"McLeod, do you know what I'm going to do?" he was asking. "I'm going to get an alarm system. I've always hated them, but one burglary is one too many."

"I think you're right," said McLeod. "I'm all for an alarm system — in theory. I've heard all these stories about how the people that live in the houses with alarms can't open their own doors without setting them off and all that kind of thing. But surely you could learn to cope with it."

"I think I could manage," said George.

"I'll call about it tomorrow."

"Do you think Dante could replace that pane?" asked McLeod.

"That's a good idea," said George. "I wonder where you get red glass. I guess he'll know. I'll call him and then maybe I can cut a piece of cardboard and tape it over the hole — keep out some of that cold air that's pouring in here." He went to the telephone in the kitchen and fumbled around among the pieces of paper in a small basket on the countertop, and finally found what he was looking for.

"Dante said he'd come over first thing in the morning," he said when he hung up the phone. "Do you have any cardboard?"

"Not that I can think of. You send your shirts to the laundry, don't you? Don't they still stuff cardboard in them?"

"Sure they do. Good thinking." He hurried up the stairs, two steps at a time, and returned with two pieces of cardboard. McLeod watched him measure the hole in the door, then measure the cardboard, and then try to cut it with scissors.

"Don't you have a box cutter?" she asked.

"I don't know," he said. Finally, they got the cardboard cut to size. Then they needed masking tape and had none. McLeod finally took adhesive tape from the first aid shelf in the bathroom medicine cabinet and used that to hold the glass in place.

"I'm exhausted," said McLeod.

"I should think so. I think we'd better go out to eat."

"Oh, no," said McLeod. "I don't want to have to come back to the dark and empty house."

"I see what you mean," said George. "And I have to call the police and tell them nothing is missing. We'll just eat here. We have lots in the freezer."

For what was almost the first time that day, McLeod thought about the murder, and asked George if he had heard anything.

"Nothing new," he said, "but the administration is concerned." He grinned. "We issued a statement to that effect."

FOURTEEN

McLeod spent most of Friday trying to bring order out of the chaos of her room. She went downstairs when Dante arrived to repair the glass in the front door. George had gone off to work — of course, she thought. I'm like a wife, somebody to do the stay-at-home chores, but I'm not a wife. Then she had to admit that the arrangement was fine with her right now. She didn't want to be married again and she liked being able to live in Tallahassee for long periods of time and Princeton (or some other place) for short periods. She honestly wouldn't want to be married to George and have to be the wife of a university administrator.

When he came, Dante clucked over the broken glass. "It's a puzzle," he said. "Who would do such a thing?" He shook his head for a long time, but finally he said he knew where to go in Trenton to get red glass. He measured the hole for the pane and prepared to leave. But he was concerned about the burglary. "Mrs. Murray never had any problem with burglars," he said.

McLeod wondered if she was supposed to be ashamed that Jill Murray had managed to avoid burglars while she had not.

"You need a dead bolt on this door," said Dante.

"What good would that do?" asked McLeod. "They could still break a pane and reach in and undo the dead bolt, couldn't they?"

"It's the principle," said Dante. "A dead bolt is better."

That was logic for you, McLeod thought. It was unanswerable.

"Mrs. McLeod, you still have that box of old clothes?"

Evidently Dante thought her last name was McLeod. That was all right, lots of people got confused. "No, Dante, I took it to my office."

"You better get that dead bolt," Dante said again as he was leaving.

"George is going to get a burglar alarm system," McLeod said. As she went back upstairs to work on organizing her room, she wondered what a dead bolt had to do with that box of old clothes? Had Dante known about the things wrapped in the dresses? Did anyone else know? She must tell George about that box.

Cleaning up after a burglary is worse than moving, she thought as she hung skirts and dresses on hangers in the closet. It was worse than moving because of the personal threat involved in the ransacking of her possessions. Some of her clothes were too rumpled to put back in the closet, so she set them aside to take to the cleaners.

Who had done such a thing? It was vile, she thought. She gathered up the sweaters and underwear that were lying around on the floor and took them down to the basement to wash them — she could not bear the thought of wearing them after some hideous unknown person had manhandled them.

What on earth had they been looking for among her paltry possessions? Why hadn't the rest of the house been ransacked? The burglar must have been interrupted. George was just lucky he didn't have a mess to clean up like she did.

She made her way up the stairs to her room to get on with trying to restore order. She went back downstairs when Dante came back from Trenton. He quickly inserted the new glass and puttied it in.

"All finished," he said.

McLeod inquired about payment, and Dante said Mr. Bridges had made an arrangement.

"Fine," said McLeod. "Thank you so much."

"Non c'e problema," said Dante. "Be careful. Be careful."

McLeod promised she would. It was lunchtime, and she decided to walk over to the campus and get some lunch and perhaps find out if there was anything new about the murder. It had been two days since it happened. Surely there was something to be learned. Just as she was leaving, George drove up.

"You left the office?" she asked, incredulous.

"Yes, I came home to meet the man from the burglar alarm company," he said.

"I'm off," she said and started on her way. George was indeed very upset about the burglary, she reflected as she walked.

The little café in the basement of Chancellor Green offered a limited menu, but she bought a roasted vegetable wrap and a bottle of apple juice, turned to survey the room, and saw Fanny Mobley at a table by herself.

"May I join you?" she asked.

Fanny silently moved her purse so McLeod could put her food down on the table but did not speak or smile. She wore a heavy rust-colored wool cardigan over a mauve dress with a long skirt, and to McLeod looked dowdy beyond belief. I wish she would cut her hair and comb it, she thought. Regretting the impulse that had made her approach Fanny, McLeod sat down, smiled in what she felt was an idiotic way, and began babbling.

"I'm glad to see you. How is everything in Rare Books? Have you recovered from the murder? Are you able to get any work done? Such a terrible thing to happen. How are you surviving?"

Fanny, pausing in her steady pursuit of spooning up soup, said briefly, "Yes, everyone is wildly inquisitive about it."

Oh, dear, thought McLeod, it was one of Fanny's bad days. "I didn't mean to intrude, or pry," she said. "It's just that I have come to like everybody in the department and I liked Philip Sheridan. . . ."

"Oh, everybody is just crazy about Philip Sheridan now that he's gone to what might be or might not be his reward," said Fanny.

What did that mean? wondered McLeod. "Didn't you like him?" she asked.

"He added to the manuscript collection

in major ways," said Fanny. Having finished her soup, she unwrapped a sandwich she had brought from home, put it down, unscrewed the cup-top off her thermos bottle, and poured a beverage into the plastic cup. She took two gulps, sighed with relief, and took a bite of her sandwich.

"Pâté," she said. "I love it."

"It looks divine," said McLeod, encouraged by a not-ill-humored remark. "Did you make it?"

"Oh, no. I bought it at Bon Appétit. It's the only sandwich I like. I can stand the soup here but that's about all." She took another gulp from the thermos cup.

"I think the food is okay here — it's university food services, isn't it? And it's so close to my office in Joseph Henry House."

"It's close to the library, too."

Fanny seemed to be relaxing. Maybe she was basically shy and had to get used to each person all over again for every encounter. "Have you been at the library long?" McLeod asked her.

"Twenty years," said Fanny.

"I seem to hear a faint English accent when you talk." McLeod persisted, always eager for more information about people. "Do I?"

"Yes, I suppose you do," said Fanny. "My

mother was English and I spent a lot of time with my grandparents in England."

"Is that where you got interested in rare books and manuscripts?"

"As a matter of fact it was. My grandfather worked at the British Museum. He was a curator in the manuscripts department." She took another drink out of her thermos cup. "I was fascinated with what he did from the time I was a little girl. Once in a great while he would take me to work with him and show me something. One time it was a will in Old English from the later Anglo-Saxon Period, about 980 A.D., as I recall. The woman who died was very wealthy and she freed a slave priest in the will, and issued orders for three slave women to chant the Psalms in her memory. I'll never forget that."

McLeod was fascinated and listened intently as Fanny told about other wonders her grandfather had shown her. "I knew when I was eight years old that I wanted to work with manuscripts," she said.

"That's fabulous," said McLeod. "I love stories about people who know what they want to do when they're children. I always knew I wanted to be a newspaper reporter but lots of people don't have a clue when they're young."

"Lots of people don't have a clue about what they want to do even after they're grown," said Fanny. "Buster Keaton never has had a clue."

"Really? You mean he just happened to become interested in rare books?"

"Staggered into the field," said Fanny. "I don't think he has a clear idea of what it's all about to this day."

"Heavens," said McLeod. "But he's pretty good at his job, isn't he? He must be."

"It depends on what you call 'pretty good.' I know Philip Sheridan thought he was terrible."

"Really?" said McLeod. "Did Buster know Philip thought he was no good at his job?"

"He must have known. Philip made it plain to everybody that he thought Buster was hopelessly uninvolved," said Fanny. "Buster, of course, put up a great show of respect for Philip, deferring to the greater knowledge of rare books that Philip plainly had. But I don't think that cut any ice with Philip. Subservience did not mean a great deal to Philip Sheridan. And I did sense that Buster was beginning to tire of his role as lifelong learner from Philip. It has occurred to me that he revolted — revolted dramatically."

"Have you mentioned this to the police?"

asked McLeod.

"Of course not," said Fanny. "I do my job and they do theirs, I hope. They seemed to be interested only in what time I left the library Tuesday and who was there after I left. All I could tell them was that I left right after we closed and everybody else was still there."

"Let me ask you: Did Philip Sheridan get along well with everyone in the department? Everybody except Buster, I mean."

"Everybody had to get along with him," said Fanny. "He was the mighty money man."

"What about Chester?"

"Chester?" said Fanny. "Of course Chester and Sheridan got along. Chester adored him, worshipped him."

"That's what I gathered," said McLeod.

"Come to think about it, maybe there was some tension there," said Fanny. She drained the last of the beverage from her thermos, and actually smiled warmly at McLeod. "It was so nice to see you," she said. "I have to be moving along. I hope everything is going well with Henry van Dyke, and let me know if there's anything I can do to help you."

McLeod decided Fanny was one of the oddest women she had ever known. It was as if she were manic-depressive — cross as a bear one minute and sweet as sorghum sugar the next. She sat there reflecting on what Fanny had told her. So sweet Philip Sheridan wasn't always sweet. According to Dodo, he had terrible quarrels with Chester, and according to Fanny, he made no secret of his low opinion of Buster Keaton.

She bused her tray and prepared to go to her office. Students never came for conferences on Fridays, but she would check e-mails and phone messages and leave everything shipshape for Monday. Once there, she found a phone message from Dodo Westcott, but when she tried to call Dodo, she was not at home. McLeod left a message.

As she trudged home, she thought that she really must remember to tell George about the box of dresses.

By Saturday morning McLeod had forgotten the box of dresses and was diverted to another course of action. She suggested to George that they ask Natty Ledbetter to dinner that night.

"Great idea. I have to go to the office so why don't you call him? He's probably tied up — he leads a busy social life. Call him."

McLeod called and Natty, who was indeed free that night, professed to be delighted to come back to the murder house. "Murder's all over the place, isn't it?" he said, and then apologized for making a tasteless joke.

"I always say a tasteless joke is better than no joke," said McLeod.

"Perhaps," said Natty.

She got busy with a grocery list.

That night, when she was coming down the stairs, she had a sense of déjà vu as she heard Natty saying to George in the hall below, "Dear fellow, so good of you to have me to dinner again in the murder house . . ."

She followed the two men into the living room and sat down with them before the fire for a while, and then went into the kitchen to see about dinner. She was cooking this time, and it seemed to make George nervous — he kept coming into the kitchen to check on things.

"It's okay, George. It's fine," she reassured him. The minute he left the kitchen, her own qualms began. Was it really going to be fine? She did have failures in the kitchen now and then, and it would be just her luck to mess things up when she was cooking dinner in George's house for George's old mentor. She wished George were cooking; she would much rather be talking to Natty; she had a million questions for him. But she persevered in the kitchen. Please God, she prayed, let it be all right. It was a heavy meal, but it was the dead of winter in frozen New Jersey, she told herself. A heavy meal was what was called for.

And it was fine. The scallop soup was better than chowder, the men said. The Irish stew was superb, and the dressing for the endive salad was perfect. McLeod sighed with relief, and George insisted on serving the dessert, McLeod's own chocolate mousse, and making coffee.

"Natty, did you know we had a burglary?" George said while they were drinking coffee.

"No, I didn't know. When was it?"

"Thursday," said George. "Two days ago. The burglar must have thought McLeod was an heiress. He really only seemed to be after something in her room."

"Dear girl, he didn't find the Dulaney family jewels, did he?" asked Natty.

"He found them and wasn't interested in my bracelet," said McLeod.

"That's good," said Natty. "But now it's the burgled house as well as the murder house. How did he get in?"

George gave Natty the details, and Natty said that burglaries were disturbing. "I have an alarm system. Do you have one, dear boy? No, I thought not. You should if you have anything remotely valuable —"

"I don't," interjected George, "but I'm getting one. The man was here yesterday."

"I've had one for years. I have some very nice pictures, you know, some choice books of my own, and some prints that I treasure."

"I'd love to see them," said McLeod.

"Natty doesn't show off his treasures," George said.

"No, I hug them to myself, dear lady," said Natty.

McLeod ate her mousse and drank her coffee and then turned to Natty. "Is it true that Philip Sheridan was not as nice as he seemed?" she asked.

"What do you mean?" he asked. "How nice did he seem?"

"He seemed very nice to me," she said. "You know that. But in talking to other people since then, I gather he had feet of clay."

"What do you mean?" Natty repeated. "Nobody's perfect."

"Well, to be frank, Dodo Westcott told me that she thought Chester and Philip Sheridan had problems, and Fanny Mobley told me how Sheridan felt — and talked — about Buster Keaton."

"You know, everybody in Rare Books is

temperamental to some extent," Natty said. "That's why the university brought me in from the English Department to take charge. Everybody used to have his own little fiefdom. Nobody could stand anybody else and they were always feuding. Fanny Mobley was fine one minute and a beast the next. Buster Keaton lost his temper continually and every day he yelled at somebody until she — and sometimes, he — was in tears. It was impossible to set up an exhibition anymore because no two people could agree about the contents."

Natty stopped talking long enough to finish off his glass of wine. George got up and brought out a bottle of brandy, offering it to Natty, who accepted gratefully. McLeod declined; she wanted to listen with a clear head.

"McLeod, you realize all this is confidential," said George.

"George, I wasn't about to put it in the paper," she protested. Turning to Natty, she asked, "But you straightened out the situation, didn't you, when you came in?"

"Oh, yes, certainly. Sure I did. I fixed it so that now everybody has his own little fiefdom. Nobody can stand anybody else and they are always feuding. Fanny Mobley is fine one minute and a beast the next. Buster

Keaton loses his temper once a day and yells at somebody every day until she — and sometimes, he — is in tears." He took a huge swallow of brandy, and grinned at his own wit.

"But they do put up exhibitions," said McLeod.

"Only because I listen to everybody's arguments and then I simply issue a fiat: We will do this and include that, and so on."

"I suppose that's all fixed, then," said McLeod, smiling.

Everybody was quiet for a minute or two, until George suggested they go back to the living room and he would poke up the fire. Carrying the brandy bottle, he led the way.

The men settled down, and McLeod went upstairs to get her knitting. "Natty, did Philip Sheridan take part in all these battles and feuds? I would have thought he'd stay aloof," she asked when she came back.

"He tried," said Natty. "He really wanted just to work with his own collection and keep everything shipshape. His collection was to be his immortality and he wanted it to be as perfect as he could get it. He and Chester were as happy as clowns puttering around in there in their lair. I don't believe that Philip was involved in serious altercations with anybody on the staff. For one thing, as I said, he didn't pay that much attention to anything but his own collection, and all of us were understandably respectful of him. He was already our benefactor, but besides that, everybody saw him as a source of potential power and a source — of course — of funding for future pet projects. And they were always swarming over him — I guess we were all always swarming over him."

"But did he really get mad at Chester?"

"Chester was deferential to a fault," said Natty. "Sometimes Philip may have been impatient with him, but I think at heart he was very fond of Chester. He should have been. Trust Dodo to bad-mouth Chester."

"And did Philip Sheridan really dislike Buster Keaton? Fanny said he did."

Natty reached for the brandy bottle and refilled his glass. "I don't know how Philip really felt about Buster," he said. "He brought his collection to Princeton when Old Clement Odell was in charge of Rare Books. He was a classmate of Philip's and a gentleman collector himself. Philip loved Princeton and it was natural for him to bring his collection here, but Old Clement Odell was certainly a factor. Buster became curator of Rare Books when Old Clement died."

"How old was Old Clement Odell?" asked McLeod.

"He was Philip's age, but he died several years ago, when he wasn't all that old. He just acted old and everybody always called him 'Old Clement.' People who knew him still refer to him that way."

"Are you saying that Philip Sheridan would not have brought his collection to Princeton if Buster Keaton had been curator?"

"Who knows? I know Old Clement was a factor in Philip's choice at the time, but that's not the only reason he did what he did. Buster is a reputable rare books person. He is widely respected. On the other hand, anybody might lose patience with him occasionally. He blusters, and Philip Sheridan didn't like bluster."

"I see," said McLeod. She was silent. While George and Natty chatted about some university matter that she'd never heard of, she knitted industriously on George's sweater and thought about all that everyone had told her about Rare Books and Special Collections.

Without thinking, she interrupted the ongoing discussion between Natty and George. "Natty, I understand there are always rivalries and tensions in any office —

although I would have thought a place like Rare Books might possibly be an exception — it's so quiet and isolated from the crass world. But I can understand it's like any other place where people work together. Feelings can run high. You said you didn't believe Philip was 'involved in serious altercations with anybody'— but can you really rule out the possibility that anybody could have hated Philip Sheridan enough to kill him? There's been a murder, and we have to be so careful."

"I realize that," said Natty. "And if I knew of anybody who felt that way about Philip — in or out of my department — I would certainly say so — and say it to the police." He sounded quite cross.

"Of course you would," said McLeod. "I didn't mean to accuse you of hiding something. I guess I'm just trying to think out loud." She knitted furiously, speaking again after a minute. "I can't think myself why anybody would want to kill him. He was kind of the goose that laid golden eggs, wasn't he?"

"I can't bear to hear Philip Sheridan referred to as a goose," said Natty.

"Oh, Natty, you know what I mean," cried McLeod. "Of course he wasn't a goose. I've said over and over again that he was one of the nicest men I ever met — remember he ordered me that first edition of the *The Vicar of Bullhampton* —"

"And a pretty penny he paid for that, dear lady," interrupted Natty, glowering.

"— I'm sure he did. And I meant that he was the source of many good things. Dodo wanted money for the Friends. I guess Buster wanted more rare books and Fanny more manuscripts . . ."

"You two had better talk about something else," said George. "How about something calming like politics or religion? Or better yet, the weather?"

"The weather's cold," said McLeod, frowning at her knitting.

"Indeed it is," said Natty agreeably. "Don't worry, George. McLeod and I won't come to blows. I guess I'm more worried than I realized about this murder. I do hope the police get it cleaned up before long."

"Have another brandy," said George, pouring.

As she placidly knitted, McLeod marveled at their capacity for alcohol. "Are they through going over your space?" she asked. "Will you be able to open up to the public Monday?"

"I think so," said Natty. "I'm pretty sure we will. They've been over the premises with a fine-tooth comb, with three or four fine-tooth combs, I guess you could say. They will continue to shut everybody, even the staff, out of Philip's space and the Belcher display, of course. They've been closed to everybody but the police the whole time. We were allowed to be in and out of our own offices in a limited way on Thursday and Friday, vacating while they used those fine-tooth combs, but I think they've done all the searching they can do. As I understand it, we can open up Monday. I must call a couple of researchers first thing Monday — maybe I should call Barry Porter tomorrow. He wants to get back to the O'Neill stuff immediately."

"The police were looking for the murder weapon, weren't they?" asked McLeod.

"I guess so," said Natty. "They never said."

"Chester said he was sure it was Philip Sheridan's paper knife," said McLeod.

"Really? I didn't know that," said Natty.

McLeod wondered why there wasn't more communication among the people in Rare Books and Special Collections, but decided not to say this out loud.

Natty was relaxing, definitely relaxing. Waving his brandy glass, he said, "You know, McLeod, speaking of people getting mad enough to kill dear Philip, we have to consider Miss Dodo."

"Dodo? Dorothy Westcott?" said McLeod.

"Yes, the would-be social queen," said Natty. "You know she has a consuming ambition to be the doyenne of Princeton society. That lust for social prominence is a great gift to me. That's why she has labored so hard as a volunteer for the Friends of the Library and why the Friends have brought in so much money for Rare Books and Special Collections. We've been able to make some really splendid acquisitions with that money. Dodo, from whatever base motives, has worked really hard and it's paid off handsomely. I, for one, appreciate it."

McLeod did not quite see what Natty meant. "But why did that make her mad at Philip Sheridan?" she asked.

"Am I not making myself clear? Oh, dear, it's late and I've had *gallons* of alcohol. My ex-student has plied me so generously . . . But back to Dodo. Yes, she has social ambitions, which, alas, are not shared by her husband. That provides no obstacle to dear Dodo, though. She saw Philip, the *ne plus ultra* of Princeton eligibility, as the means to achieve her ends. Oh, how she went after him. She invited him to little dinners at her house, to big dinners, to cocktail parties, and he wouldn't come. Sure, he would turn up for Friends' events. He was a good soldier about all that, although I believe darling Dodo was sometimes too zealous in milking him for financial support for Friends' events. But he would not turn up for a strictly social occasion at the Westcott MacMansion. He just wouldn't."

"And that made Dodo mad enough to kill him?"

"Dearest McLeod, I jest. Forgive an old man's feeble attempts at humor. But when you ask about people angry enough to kill dear Philip, I couldn't help but think about our capable, but climbing, Dodo." He paused. "That does sound like the name of a great vine, doesn't it? Climbing Dodo, or maybe Creeping Dodo."

"But Dodo couldn't have done the murder. She told me she left the library while Philip was still alive."

"Of course she would tell you that. Who knows when Dodo left? She was often hanging around after we closed. I didn't see her leave, so I can't say, of course. But remember her vinelike characteristics."

McLeod, chilled, could think of nothing to say for a minute, then forced herself to come up with something ordinary to get the conversation back on track. "I've been meaning to ask you about the Friends' annual dinner. Dodo says I ought to go. Should I?"

"Indeed you should," said Natty. "And you're coming, aren't you, dear boy?"

"I guess I'd better. I'm not a member, though. I should be."

"Well, neither am I," said McLeod. "Do I have to be a member to come to the annual dinner? I guess so. How much are the dues and how much is the dinner?"

When Natty told them, she gasped. "It must be awfully good food," she said.

"It's a fund-raiser, dear lady," said Natty. "You're a user of the collection, and George, you're an official of the university. You both must join immediately and come to the dinner."

"Oh, all right, Natty. I'll send you a check Monday," said George.

"Me, too," said McLeod.

"It's getting late," said Natty. "I'd better get home to bed. Dear boy, thank you so much for having me to dinner. And McLeod, thank you for asking me, and for cooking," he added hastily. "I certainly enjoyed talking to you and I hope I didn't snap at you too fiercely."

"Of course you didn't," said McLeod, laying her knitting aside and rising. "I've been snapped at by much fiercer dragons than you, Natty."

"You mean my august presence doesn't terrify you?"

"Natty, I'm in awe of you, but not terrified."

Natty looked pleased, and unexpectedly kissed her cheek. "Good night, dear girl," he said.

McLeod headed for the kitchen with their brandy glasses and left George to see him out. When George joined her to help clear the dishes and load the dishwasher, she apologized. "I hope Natty's not mad at me. I didn't mean to annoy him."

"Of course you didn't," said George. "He's not annoyed with you. He's afraid you're annoyed with him. He said he hoped you wouldn't give up on van Dyke because you were mad at him."

"Oh, van Dyke," said McLeod. "Phooey. Actually, I like Natty. Has he ever been married or is he gay?"

"He's not gay. He's married right now."

"What?"

"He's married. His wife has Alzheimer's. She's in an institution. Natty doesn't talk about her, but he goes to see her nearly every day."

"That's awful, but I love it that he's loyal. You know, we forgot about the break-in

Thursday. Do you suppose the police found out anything about it?"

"Not that I know of," said George. "I don't think that little break-in has a high priority with them right now."

"I guess not, but it is unnerving when you think about somebody rummaging around in your things."

"I'm sure it is," said George, appearing not at all unnerved. "Actually, I shouldn't think it would be as unnerving as finding a body."

"That was unnerving," McLeod conceded. "But so was finding the house had been burgled. This has been a high crime week. And then we're living in what they call the murder house."

"Be brave, McLeod. This, too, will pass. By the way, don't expect to ever get a look at Natty's books and pictures. He never asks people to his house."

"He goes out a lot. Doesn't he have to pay people back?"

"He takes people to restaurants from time to time. But he's such an amusing old goat that I think he gets all the invitations he can handle without doing anything in return."

"What a life!" said McLeod.

"I know. Are we all through in here? Good."

FIFTEEN

When she was in Princeton, McLeod occasionally went to services at Nassau Presbyterian Church, but on this Sunday morning, she decided that she would go to the university chapel. The chapel was Gothic and huge, not as cozy as the classic white Presbyterian Church, but she liked the service, which was interdenominational, although leaning in an Episcopal direction. She liked the prayer for Princeton University that the congregation always recited in unison, and she liked the choir, filled with fresh-faced students in black robes with the Princeton orange stoles.

After all that had happened in the past week, she found it very soothing to sit in that lofty nave and let the music wash over her. The chapel was not nearly full, but the empty spaces made it more peaceful. During the sermon, her mind wandered — McLeod always found church a great place to mull over problems — and tried to make sense of the kaleidoscopic events of the past week. There was the horrible murder in the library, of course, and then there was the burglary of George's house and the pillaging of her own belongings, not to mention the long-ago murder of Jill Murray in that very same house. Good heavens — it was all too much for one small, beautiful college town. It couldn't be true. But it was.

The sermon was over — it had seemed mercifully short — and she stood for the final hymn, piping away with the others, "Let there be light, Lord God of Hosts, let there be wisdom on the earth . . ." Let there be light and wisdom, indeed, she prayed silently.

As she moved out of the pew into the aisle, she was surprised to run into Buster Keaton, looking somewhat better groomed than he did at the library, but just as dark and gloomy.

"Hello," he said. "I'm astonished to see you here."

"Why?"

"I don't see how anybody can take the Church seriously in this day and age."

"But you're here," she pointed out.

"Oh, yes, I'm here, but I never take it seriously."

"I see," McLeod said.

"Actually, I'm here because my wife is the world's biggest religious maniac. She insists on it."

"Oh, where is she? I'd like to meet her," said McLeod politely.

"She's helping with the coffee hour — you know, where everybody is supposed to mingle in Christian fellowship after the service. All six of us."

"Oh, there were more than six people here this morning."

"Not many more. No matter." By now they were in the narthex, and McLeod noticed the volunteer ladies fluttering around the table with the big coffee urn and cookies on it.

"Which is your wife?" she said.

"That's her," said Buster inelegantly as he waved toward the urn. "Come on, I'll introduce you." He led her to a fiftyish woman with curly brown hair beginning to go gray. "Amelia, this is McLeod Dulaney. She's working on Henry van Dyke."

Amelia looked up from the coffee urn she was manning and smiled at McLeod. "So nice to meet you. Will you have some coffee? Cookies? They're homemade."

"I thought I'd take McLeod off to some place where we can sit down. I'll be back by the time you're through. Okay?" Buster said to Amelia.

"Sure," said Amelia. "Have a good time." She looked past McLeod to the man behind her. "Coffee?" she asked him.

"Come on to Small World," Buster said to McLeod. "The coffee's much better there than here. I can't go home until Amelia gets through anyway."

And he might as well kill time with me, thought McLeod; he really knows how to make a girl feel good. But why not? At least he had the sense to know Small World was better than Starbucks. "Sounds good," she said and walked with him across the courtyard and along Nassau Street to Witherspoon and the Small World coffee shop.

She ordered latte and he a cappuccino and they took their cups to a small table by the window where they could watch the passersby.

"Well, what do you think about our murder?" Buster asked her. "Or have you forgotten it?"

"How could I forget it?" McLeod asked, thinking what an oaf Buster could be, even when he was dressed up for church.

"That's right — you're the one who found the body," he said. "Too bad you had to notice it — look at all the trouble you've caused. I haven't been able to get any work done since you did it."

Was he serious? McLeod wondered. Just in case he was serious, she replied that surely it wasn't her fault that he hadn't been able to get any work done. "Somebody would have eventually looked in the window at the Belcher stuff," she said.

"I know that," he said. "I'm not a fool, although I know I look like one sometimes. But I've got enough sense to know that. I was trying to be cheerful about all this and tease you a bit. But I guess you can't joke about murder, can you?"

"It's hard," said McLeod. "Although I appreciate the effort." McLeod stirred her latte and Buster sipped his cappuccino. "It's really a particularly horrible murder because Philip Sheridan was such a nice man." She looked at Buster to see his reaction to this.

"Oh, he could be very, very nice," he said. "But he had a darker side. I guess we all do, don't we?"

"Really? What was his darker side like?"

"Oh, he was like a lot of very rich people," said Buster. "He wanted to control everything. And he used his money as a tool. Oh, don't misunderstand me — I got along famously with him. I certainly should have, since I always kowtowed like a crazy man, and it was 'Yes, Philip,' 'No, Philip,' 'Whatever you say, Philip.' That collection of his — any rare book curator in the world would kill for it. I wasn't about to let it get away from me."

McLeod thought briefly of Clement Odell, Buster's predecessor, who was responsible for acquiring the Sheridan collection. "But it was already yours, wasn't it? I mean, it was Princeton's — he'd made it over to the university, hadn't he?"

"Not exactly. It was to come to us as a legacy. It will be Princeton's now, but he loved those books so much he couldn't let them go while he was alive." Unaware that he had a bit of cream from the cappuccino on his chin, he beamed blissfully. "But now that he's dead, they belong to Princeton. It's wonderful."

Buster was a man who took happiness where he could find it, McLeod thought. Here was the benefactor, not cold in his grave, not yet even *in* his grave, and Buster was exulting over a legacy. "What I can't understand," she said, "is this: Who would want to kill that nice man? It happened Tuesday and I haven't heard about anybody yet with a real reason to kill Philip Sheridan."

Buster shrugged. "Everybody has enemies."

"Who was Philip Sheridan's enemy?" asked McLeod. "Name one."

"I don't know that she was Philip's enemy, but he was certainly hers. I mean Fanny Mobley, of course. The dame of the British Empire and the doyenne of manuscripts."

"Is she really a dame?"

"Don't be so literal," said Buster. "I was just alluding to her ethnic heritage — upper-class Brit, she is, and proud of it. Well, upper middle class, at least."

"But why would she kill Philip Sheridan? Wasn't he a benefactor to manuscripts as well as books?"

"Of course he was. But Fanny wasn't as diplomatic — or as deferential — as some of us. She didn't fawn over Philip — and perhaps she should have. He disapproved violently of some of the things she did with manuscripts, for instance. They had, shall we say, heated discussions about it. Actually they were dreadful shouting matches."

"What did she do with manuscripts that he disapproved of?" asked McLeod.

"Oh, I don't know," said Buster, lapsing into uncharacteristic vagueness. "I think he thought she didn't appreciate some of the things he had given the university."

"That's not a really terrific motive for murder, is it?" asked McLeod. "That Fanny would kill Philip because he thought she didn't appreciate the value of manuscripts he brought in. I mean, what can you do with manuscripts? Put them in acid-free boxes if they're books or stories or poems. If they're letters, you sort them and put them in acid-free folders in acid-free boxes. And then you wait for researchers to come and use them, and watch like a hawk to make sure they don't mark them or steal them."

"You describe our life work so beautifully," said Buster. "Still I think there was enough bad feeling there to justify a little investigation on the part of the police. I may have a talk with that nice lieutenant."

"Do," said McLeod. "The police will sort it out. But what about Chester? He and Philip Sheridan got along very well, didn't they?"

"I suppose," said Buster. "But who knows what goes on inside a relationship like that? Who depends on whom? Was Chester a masochist who put up with Sheridan's domination? Or did Chester have some sort of hold on Sheridan? Did he know something that gave him power? It's an interesting question, isn't it?"

McLeod thought it was an outlandish

question, but she had to admire Keaton's imagination. He should write fiction, she thought. She decided to ask one more question. "And Dodo? How did she and Philip Sheridan get along?"

"Like a house afire," said Buster. "That is to say that they were always hot with irritation at each other, believe me. Dodo wanted to use Philip for fund-raising purposes and he wouldn't let himself be trotted out for things like that."

That wasn't exactly the way Natty had put it, McLeod realized, but she was interested to see that Buster could find faults — and motives for murder — in everybody she mentioned. Still, enough was enough. "I really must go. Thanks for the coffee. And your wife must be waiting for you."

"Don't worry about Amelia," said Buster. "She'll be all right. She always stays at the chapel, talking to every single person who stops for coffee. Then she helps with the cleanup. I'll amble back toward the chapel, though. Are you going that way?"

"No, I walked from Edgehill, so I go in the other direction. See you soon."

Buster Keaton really could be quite awful, she thought as she plodded toward Edgehill Street, but this was the only time she had ever seen him stay off the subject of books for such a long time. She noticed that it had turned cloudy since she had left home that morning and it looked as though it might snow again. Horrors.

And poor Chester. He was sincerely mourning Philip Sheridan's death, she was sure, and yet people had picked him as the suspect.

What could she do to help Chester? As usual, her first thought was food. Should she ask him for dinner again tonight? What would George say? Was George going to be at home? She couldn't remember. She would find out and then decide what to do next about Chester. He reminded her somehow of her own children, although she thought that both of those two were perhaps sturdier and more independent than Chester. Rosie was working on a newspaper in Charlotte, North Carolina, and had signed a contract to do a brief biography of Nadine Gordimer. Harry was finishing his Ph.D. in art history at Yale. As a matter of fact, he had been finishing his Ph.D. for years. He had vowed to complete his dissertation this year, but then he had vowed to finish it last year. How was it coming, she wondered. Thoughts of Harry's dissertation and his elusive doctorate distracted her momentarily from worrying about Chester Holmes.

SIXTEEN

Once at home, though, McLeod thought of Chester again, that poor lad with his big brown eyes and his hair flopping in his face. George was at home, reading the Sunday papers.

"And how was church?" he asked. "Did you pray for me?"

"Of course," she lied. "And I prayed for light and wisdom. And then there's always Christian charity, although I forgot to pray for it today. But speaking of Christian charity, I ran into Buster Keaton at the chapel and he is certainly not full of it — Christian charity, I mean. First, he said he thought Fanny Mobley killed Philip Sheridan —"

George interrupted: "Fanny Mobley is that lady who always looks like she ought to be the figurehead of a sailing vessel, isn't she? Wrapped in billowing sails and that kind of thing?"

"Well, she does wear those floppy clothes

and lots of them have fringe on them."

"Are clothes like that the mark of a murderer?"

"Not necessarily, I'd say," said McLeod. "But Buster has other suspects — Chester Holmes and Dodo Westcott. Back to Christian charity, could you bear it if I asked Chester Holmes to dinner again?"

"Sure I could," said George, "since I won't be here."

"I think Sunday nights should be free of official events."

"They usually are, but didn't I tell you? I have to meet with the mayor of Princeton Borough. He chose the time, not me, but I have to talk to him about the pedestrian overpass we want to build over Washington Road. So go ahead and ask Chester if you like."

"I guess I will, then, and maybe I'll ask Fiona and Angus." Fiona and Angus McKay were childhood friends of McLeod's, and Angus taught at Princeton Theological Seminary.

"Ask them when I'm here," said George. "I want to meet them."

"All right. In that case, I'll just cook something and take it to Chester for his supper. I think it would be kind of a strain to have him here alone. What shall I cook? I think I'll do meat loaf — I'll make one for Chester and one to keep here. It's easy and the leftovers make good sandwiches."

"Something to look forward to — for me, I mean," said George. "You know it's supposed to snow tonight, so be careful when you go out."

"I will," she said.

A telephone call revealed that Chester would appreciate anything McLeod brought him, so she went off to the grocery store and then set to work in the kitchen.

When she took a basket containing a small meatloaf, mashed potatoes, lima beans, spinach salad, and cookies (the cookies were store bought, but good) over to Hibben Road, Chester was very grateful indeed.

"Won't you come in for a drink?" he asked.

"No, no, everything will get cold," she said.

"That's all right — I can heat it up in the microwave," said Chester, who looked a bit rumpled in blue jeans but a good cashmere sweater. "Do come in for a minute. You've been so good to me, and I appreciate it."

So McLeod followed him into the living room of Philip Sheridan's house, and sat down. Chester offered sherry, and she accepted, noting that it was Tio Pepe, her favorite. The living room seemed rather bare and cheerless, in spite of the spectacular paintings on the wall and the good, solid furniture. It was somewhat untidy.

"I take it Mrs. Hamilton is not here any longer," she said, sipping her sherry.

"That's right," said Chester, who had sat down in a big chair opposite her with a good stiff drink of Scotch in his hand. "She left yesterday. I must say I'm relieved."

"I can imagine," said McLeod.

"She had to go to New York to see about some business; she'll be back, of course." He paused, then spoke again, "And if it's not one thing it's another — the police have been here all day yesterday and all day today."

"What were they doing?"

"Searching, searching. Going through all of Mr. Sheridan's papers. And asking me questions. It never stopped. I'm exhausted and the house is a mess."

"It's a beautiful house," said McLeod. "Do you have a housekeeper?"

"Oh, yes. I hope when she gets here tomorrow she can tidy things up."

"I'm sure she will," said McLeod.

"But if the police come back tomorrow,

174

they'll mess things up again, I'm sure," he said.

"What were the police interested in? Do you know?"

"Everything," said Chester. "They went through all of Mr. Sheridan's papers and searched his closets and his dresser and his chest of drawers. They were interested in all of his 'relationships.' Relationships! I've gotten so I hate the word. They wanted to know about our 'relationship.' Were we lovers? Partners? I said, 'No, indeed, we were not,' but they didn't believe me. Nobody does, but we weren't. Mr. Sheridan had a partner for years and years, but he died, and I don't think Mr. Sheridan cared about anybody else. He just liked to have somebody in the house — that's why he asked me if I wanted to live here. We hardly ever went anywhere together. It was enough for me just to work for him and be with him at home some of the time. I learned so much from him. Not just about rare books and literature but about lifestyles and how to set a table and what dessert spoons and fish forks look like and about modern art and modern music. It was a graduate school education just to know him."

"What a testimonial," said McLeod. "It's good to hear you remember him so fondly."

She set down her sherry glass.

"Ms. Dulaney, don't go," said Chester. "I want to talk to you. You're a journalist. You know something about how the police work. Tell me, how long do you think it will take before they find out who killed Mr. Sheridan?"

"I have no idea, Chester," said McLeod. "I do know that Nick Perry, who's in charge of the investigation, is very good — slow, sometimes, but thorough. It hasn't been very long, you know, since the murder. Mr. Sheridan" — she switched to the passive voice — "was found on Wednesday, and today is only Sunday. I expect they're making real progress. There are a limited number of suspects. But the police tend to keep what they know to themselves, while they look for solid evidence. And you're the one who told me they're looking for the weapon — presumably Mr. Sheridan's paper knife."

"I'm not sure that they'll ever find it," said Chester. "But do you think they'll find the person who did it, the right person? Do you really?"

"I don't see how they can help finding the person," said McLeod. "It couldn't have been an outsider. It was somebody in the Department of Rare Books and Special Collections. It had to be."

"I just hope they find out soon."

"Everybody is helping the police all they can, aren't they?" said McLeod carefully. "Nobody's holding out information, are they?"

"I don't know," said Chester. His voice sounded wobbly. "I wouldn't think anybody would hold anything out. Except that they might hate to say anything that would get somebody else in trouble, somebody that they knew . . ."

"Chester, do you know something that you haven't told the police?" asked McLeod. "Is that what you're worried about?"

"Yes, it is," said Chester. "But it's not much."

"But it's something you think the police ought to know?"

"I don't know. I don't know."

"You do want the police to find out who killed Mr. Sheridan, don't you?"

"Of course I do." Chester turned his piteous eyes toward her. "It's not much really."

"What is it?" asked McLeod.

"It's something about Mr. Ledbetter."

"Natty Ledbetter didn't have any reason to kill Mr. Sheridan, did he? I mean, you don't know of any reason, do you?"

"Of course not. Nobody had a good reason to kill him. He was an angel who helped them all in every way he could. But Mr. Sheridan and Mr. Ledbetter got mad at each other on Tuesday."

"They did? What about?" asked McLeod.

"I don't know what it was about. I had to go down to the vault for Mr. Sheridan, and when I came back, I could hear loud voices, and when I opened the door, he and Mr. Ledbetter were standing up glaring at each other. And Mr. Sheridan was saying, 'Natty, I have nothing more to say on the subject at this time.' But he told him not to forget what he had said. Mr. Ledbetter left without saying anything."

"And you don't have any idea what they had been talking about?"

"No, I don't."

"You know, Chester, I think you ought to tell the police about it," said McLeod. "I don't think for a minute that Natty killed Philip Sheridan, but the police can use crumbs of information in ways that we don't realize. Tell them." She stood up.

"Don't go," said Chester, also rising. "Have another glass of sherry."

"Oh, Chester, I can't, thanks. I must get home. Thank you for the glass I had. It was very good. And tell the police about Natty."

"Thank you for listening and thank you for bringing me that delicious meal."

"Wait until you eat it before you call it delicious," McLeod said insincerely — she knew it was delicious, because she had tasted every bit of it.

"Don't need to," said Chester gallantly.

McLeod drove home and settled down with her own supper before the fire in the living room. She still had not read the important parts of *The New York Times,* the *Book Review,* or the *Times Magazine,* much less the *Week in Review,* and of course had not touched the Sunday crossword puzzle, but then George had probably worked the whole thing while she was at the chapel. Yes, he had, she discovered when she looked in the *Magazine.* Good, she thought, one less thing for her to worry about. Having polished off her meat loaf and the rest of the meal, she loaded the dishwasher and went upstairs to get a notebook and pencil.

Back downstairs, she enriched the fire with two juicy-looking logs and, armed with notebook and pencil, her tools for thinking, sat down on the sofa with her feet tucked under her.

"Dodo-Chester," she wrote and tried to remember as much as possible about Dodo's diatribe on Chester Holmes. The trouble was she couldn't remember one specific thing Dodo had said. She had just seemed rather ill natured in her anxiety to implicate Chester Holmes. Finally, after "Dodo-Chester," she wrote, "Says Chester 'like a spouse, prime suspect.' "

Then she wrote: "Find out more."

After much thought, she could still not remember anything else about the Dodo-Chester charges and she flipped a page in her notebook and wrote, "Fanny-Buster." Now what had Fanny said about Buster? She had said he had gotten tired of playing second fiddle to Philip Sheridan. Not second fiddle exactly, because Buster was clearly in charge of Rare Books at Princeton University, but playing second fiddle to Philip Sheridan's superior knowledge. Was that a motive for murder? Who knew? She wrote down, "Buster resented PS's superior expertise?" Was that right? Well, it was as right as she could get it.

She flipped the page. Who was next? Natty Ledbetter. She wrote down "Natty-Dodo." Now what had all that been about last night? Natty had seemed to imply that Dodo Westcott was mad enough to kill Philip Sheridan because he wouldn't aid and abet her social-climbing schemes. Was that a motive for murder? What were the classic motives for murder: love, money, revenge? Was this one? Well, if you were angry enough about a social snub — and kind of nutty — I suppose you could seek revenge, McLeod thought.

Dodo Westcott wasn't the world's biggest brain or the world's most integrated personality, whatever that was, but she was a woman who seemed too happy with her husband and children, her life in Princeton, and her unpaid career running the Friends of the Princeton Library to murder a man who wouldn't come to her parties. But you never knew. After "Natty-Dodo," McLeod wrote, "Mad about 'snubs'?"

This was taking time. And those logs were burning fast. With some difficulty, McLeod got up — I'm getting old, she thought, and I'm stiff — and put another log on.

On a new page she wrote "Buster-Fanny," and looked at the words a long time. Buster's theory was that Fanny had killed Philip Sheridan because Philip Sheridan had disapproved of the way she handled manuscripts and they had had shouting matches. She jotted down notes to this effect, shaking her head all the while, then quickly flipped the page.

"Chester-Natty," she wrote. This was another vague accusation, she thought. There had been cross words. Had Philip

Sheridan exchanged cross words with all of them lately, or did he always snap at people? Was it possible that Natty had become enraged at his principal donor and stolen his paper knife and stabbed him with it later? It seemed so uncharacteristic that McLeod flipped the notebook shut. Good heavens! she thought. It made no sense.

She looked outside, and was relieved to see that it had not snowed after all.

SEVENTEEN

When McLeod looked out of her window on Monday morning, she was relieved once more to see it still wasn't snowing. She walked to her office and checked her e-mail. Among the messages was one from Clark Powell, thanking her profusely for the dresses. They were awesome, he said.

What good manners he had, McLeod thought. Then the mention of the dresses reminded her of the things she had found packed in the carton with them. How could she have forgotten them? Well, a murder did tend to distract one from everything else. "It concentrates the mind wonderfully," someone, possibly Samuel Johnson, had said. He seemed to have said everything familiar.

She unlocked the bottom drawer of the file cabinet and looked at the book, the crucifix, and the box again. They still looked old and rare and beautiful. They also reeked of monetary value. How could she have forgotten them? At least she could take the book over to Rare Books; Natty Ledbetter or Buster Keaton would be able to tell her something about it.

She called to make sure Rare Books had reopened. Molly said yes, they were open and Mr. Ledbetter and Mr. Keaton were both in. McLeod took the book downstairs to the Humanities Council Office to see if she could find something to wrap it in, and was delighted when Frieda offered her a huge padded envelope.

"Just the thing," she said. "Frieda, you never fail us."

" 'Failure's no success at all,' " said Frieda. "That's from a Bob Dylan song."

"Very good," said McLeod, who found the quotation puzzling. Of course failure was no success. Oh, well.

Carrying her padded envelope as well as her check for the Friends' dues and the dinner, she walked across the court to the library. Pausing in the exhibition gallery, she looked at the window of the Belcher display and saw that a shade had been discreetly pulled across it.

In Rare Books, Molly greeted her. "Mr. Ledbetter is expecting you," she said.

McLeod went straight to Natty's office.

Natty, courtly as usual, rose from behind his desk and invited her to sit down. She laid the check and the padded envelope before him on his desk and sat down.

He looked at the check and thanked her.

"Open the big envelope," she said.

Natty sat down and reached inside the envelope and pulled out the manuscript. He laid it before him on his desk, and opened it, turning the pages gently. As McLeod watched him, he seemed to be gasping for air. When he turned to her, he looked almost frantic.

"Where did you get this?" he asked.

"I found it in a box of old clothes that had been in the garage at George's house for twenty years."

"Then it was Jill Murray's, I guess. Now it's George's — he bought the house and contents, I presume."

"I have no idea," said McLeod. "He doesn't even know I found it." She told him about the box of dresses, bringing them to Clark Powell, finding the book and forgetting about it until this morning.

"I guess the murder investigation drove the book and the other things right out of my mind," she said.

"What other things?" asked Natty.

She told him about the crucifix and the

185

heavy ivory box.

"Where are the other things?"

"Locked in a file drawer in my cubicle in Joseph Henry House," she said.

"Anybody can jimmy a file drawer," said Natty. "Bring them over here and we'll keep them in the safe in the vault."

"Oh, good. But tell me about the book."

"I can't tell you much at first glance. It's medieval. It's valuable. I don't know its provenance. You have no idea where it came from, do you?"

"Of course not," said McLeod.

"Let me get Buster in here. He knows more about this kind of thing than I do." He dialed, waited, and asked Buster to come to his office. "I have something spectacular to show you," he said.

Buster was there almost instantly. He pulled up a chair to Natty's desk and took the book that Natty handed him. He looked at it a long time, examining the cover, and carefully turning pages. He was whistling, not whistling a tune, but saying, "Whew, whew, whew," ever so softly. His dark eyes glittered when he looked up, and his dark hair seemed to quiver.

"Where did this come from?" he asked. "Is it ours?"

Natty, with occasional help from McLeod,

told him all they knew about the manuscript.

"It's early and it's of exceptional quality — I can tell that," said Buster. "It's the four Gospels. It's written in gold and it's illuminated with unusual skill. It's immensely valuable — worth millions, I'd say. Is there any way we can claim it for Princeton?"

"I don't see how we can claim it," said Natty.

Buster turned to McLeod. "Is it yours?" he asked.

"Heavens, no," she said. "Natty said he thought it would be George's since he bought the house and contents."

"George is a loyal alumnus and employee — he'll give it to us," said Buster.

"Do you have any idea where it came from?" Natty asked.

"No, not offhand. It's medieval —" Buster began.

"That's what I said," interjected Natty.

"Tenth century, maybe ninth century. Where was it done? Since it's in Latin, it's hard to say immediately what its origin is. But books do tell secrets. Let me think. Let me look at it." He was studying the book closely.

"You can leave it with us, McLeod," said Natty. "And bring the other things over here, too. I would say that box is a reli-quary."

McLeod promised that she would.

Buster looked up. "I'll find out about it," he said. "Let me do a little research. I wonder how it got to Princeton."

"All paths lead to Princeton," said Natty. "Take the book and find out about it. I'll walk McLeod back to her office and get the other two things."

"Let me get something from conservation to keep this glorious thing in," said Buster as he left.

Natty found a shopping bag from Barnes & Noble in a cabinet and took it with him as they left. McLeod had intended to spend more time in Rare Books, but decided it was a good idea to get all the treasure into the safe hands of Natty Ledbetter.

"Any news on the murder?" she asked as they walked across the court to Joseph Henry House.

"Not that I know of," said Natty. "At least the police are no longer all over the place."

When she handed over the ivory box to Natty, he took it reverently and said, "I'm sure it is a reliquary, and it probably has a shard of some saint's bones in it." He put it and the crucifix in his shopping bag and departed.

McLeod sat down to check her e-mail and phone messages. When she found nothing crucial, she decided to trail back over to Rare Books and see if she could pick up anything new about the murder. And she might even do a little work on van Dyke, who somehow didn't seem as interesting as he had once. Still, at least she could finish reading that box of papers she had planned to finish last Wednesday. She would dearly love to talk to Nick Perry and find out what the police had learned about the times when people left Rare Books on Tuesday. Could she ask people herself? Possibly. She put on her coat and set out once more for the library.

"Back again?" asked Molly when McLeod came into Rare Books.

"I'm back again but this time I'll hang up my coat and sign in formally. I shall try to do a little work on van Dyke. How's it going, Molly? Everything back to normal?"

"Hardly," said Molly. "How can things be normal where there's been a murder. Who did it? Are we safe? Is it a maniac? A serial killer?"

"Oh, it can't be a serial killer," said

McLeod. "It can't be an outsider. It was somebody that works here. So relax."

Molly digested this. "But that's even worse," she said after a minute. "I should relax because somebody in this office where I work every day is a murderer?"

"I see what you mean," said McLeod. What could she say to reassure a very young woman in the circumstances? "I'm sure we're all safe. Isn't that a proctor over there?" She nodded her head and smiled at a man in a black blazer with the Princeton crest on the pocket who sat in the shadows of the reception area. Princeton's Public Safety Office called its plain clothes officers by the old academic name of proctor.

"Oh, yes, that's Derek. Derek, this is McLeod Dulaney, one of our patrons, so to speak."

"How do you do?" said Derek.

"So you're guarding the staff, aren't you?" asked McLeod. "They're safe?"

"That's right," said Derek. "There are two of us here. We're helping out the Borough. Nothing else is going to happen here — staff *and* patrons, they're safe."

"See, Molly. You're safe. Well, I'll get to work. I'll stop off and speak to Chester — I've become quite fond of him. You know, Molly, he'd be a nice beau for you."

"Oh, yes," said Molly. "I'm sure. But he hasn't come in this morning."

"I hope he's not sick," said McLeod.

"I don't know," said Molly. "He hasn't called in."

"Hasn't called in? That's odd."

"I know," said Molly, "but everything's out of whack."

Eighteen

McLeod carried her pencil and sheets of paper to the Reading Room, where Diane greeted her warmly. "Nobody else here?" McLeod asked.

"Nope, you're the only one." Diane was a young black woman with a smile as welcoming as sunshine. McLeod always felt cheered when she entered the Reading Room.

"And it's late. I thought Barry Porter was so anxious to get on with the O'Neill stuff," said McLeod. "Didn't Natty call him? And where's Miss Swallow?"

"I don't know about either one of them," said Diane, "but they're not here."

McLeod filled out a call slip for the box with all the letters about the writing of "The Other Wise Man" and gave it to Diane, who summoned a page and passed it on to him.

Since there was no one else in the Reading Room, McLeod decided it was all right to talk to Diane. "How's your little boy?"

she asked. "Have you heard anything from that school?"

"No, I'm still waiting — and hoping."

"Good luck, Diane. How did you get along with the police last week?"

"Good. I guess," said Diane. "At least they didn't try to blame me for the murder. Everybody knew I left way before it happened. I think I was the first one to leave."

"That's great," said McLeod. Things had come to a pretty pass, she thought, when you felt like congratulating somebody because they weren't under suspicion of murder. She rolled her pencil between her fingers and asked Diane a question she had long wanted to ask: "Do you ever catch anybody actually trying to steal anything?"

"Yes, indeed," said Diane. "It was a couple of weeks ago. There was this Greek Orthodox priest that was coming in here working with some old English books that had some woodcuts in them. Later, one of the curators made a routine check of the books when he finished and discovered some plates were missing. She looked at the call slips and the register and saw that this Greek Orthodox priest had used the books last. So she told Mr. Keaton and Mr. Ledbetter and they went to see this priest — he lives real near here — and he had the prints!

He admitted it right away. Apologized. Said he just wanted to look at them at home. He had taken them out under all those black robes."

"And they got them all back?" asked McLeod.

"Every single one."

"That's amazing. But how did the priest get the prints out of the books?"

"With a razor blade," said Diane.

"How did he do all that with you sitting here?"

"That's what they all kept asking me," said Diane. "And I said I had never, never left him in here alone. He always gave me the heebie-jeebies, so I watched him. Finally, we figured out he could have slipped a book under that robe while I had my back turned for a second. Then he would go to the men's room and cut out the pictures."

"Good heavens! That's an amazing story."

"It is, isn't it?" said Diane with a satisfied air. "But that's how he did it — he admitted it."

"Is the university going to press charges?"

"I don't think so. He said he was sorry. But they told him he never could come back here. But I bet if Molly leaves and I leave, he'll just come straight back and come right in and get himself some more pictures."

"Don't ever leave, Diane," said McLeod.

"If I get a better job, I'll have to."

"That Greek Orthodox priest. I'd love to see him in here in his patriarchal robes and a hat — didn't he wear a tall black hat?"

Diane laughed heartily. "I never saw him in a tall hat."

"So people do steal things if they can?" said McLeod. "That's why you take all these precautions and keep these records."

"That's it. They sure do steal things if you don't watch them like hawks. I saw a student take a Scott Fitzgerald letter and put it in his pocket one time. I asked him if he had meant to do that and he was flabbergasted. But he was like the priest — sorry — and he said he was just absentminded, so I didn't do anything about it. I did ask one of the curators to check the box he had been using and see if anything else was missing. That's harder to do with letters — every single letter is not listed in the index. But I think that's all that student took. It's a good thing he wasn't wearing long black robes, isn't it?"

"I'm amazed," said McLeod. "Who was the curator who discovered the woodcuts were missing?"

"It was Mary Woodward."

"Mary Woodward? I don't know her. I'm

realizing there are lots of people here I don't know. How many curators are there?"

"Five or six, and then there's all the conservators."

"These are people who could have stayed late last Tuesday?"

"That's right," said Diane. "The professionals usually stay after we close. The clerical help — me and Molly and the others — we leave as quick as we can."

Jeff, the page who wrote novels, brought McLeod's box up from downstairs just then, and she turned her attention to the folders inside.

She took a few notes on the letters about "The Other Wise Man," but her heart wasn't in it. It was clear, she thought, that she was more interested in the murder than she was in van Dyke. But van Dyke was her best excuse to be in Rare Books.

She put the letters back in the folder, started to put the folder back in the box, and to her annoyance, dropped her mechanical pencil into the box. She groped around in the box looking for the pencil and couldn't locate it. She started taking folders out.

"Just take one folder out at a time," warned Diane, in a much more official voice than the one that she had used to tell about the thieving priest and student.

"I dropped my pencil down in there," said McLeod.

Diane got up. "I'll get it out," she said and came over to the table where McLeod was working, and peered down into the box. Then she began taking folders out. "What's this?" she said. "This isn't your pencil." She held up a slim ivory knife.

"That's the murder weapon!" said McLeod. "That's Philip Sheridan's paper knife. Put it down. Don't touch it again. Get that proctor out there."

"You get the proctor. I'll wait here. I can't leave you alone with the papers . . ." McLeod was gone before she could finish, and back in seconds with the proctor.

The proctor looked long and hard at the knife. "I need a plastic bag," he said.

"The conservators must have something," said Diane. She rang for a page and, when Jeff came, asked him to get a plastic bag from the conservation room downstairs.

While they waited, the proctor called the Borough Police on his cell phone. "Lieutenant Perry will be here as soon as he can," he said.

The page returned with a conservator, whom Diane greeted as Oscar. Oscar carried a large plastic envelope. The proctor told him to put it down on the table. "We'll just wait for the lieutenant," he said. Nobody left.

"How did it get in that box I was working on?" asked McLeod. "That's what I want to know."

Nobody answered. They had to wait for perhaps twenty minutes before Nick Perry came rushing in. He nodded at everyone, thanked the proctor, listened to what he had to say, and finally focused on the knife lying on the table.

"Did you touch it?" he asked McLeod.

"I did not," she said.

"I touched it," said Diane. "I didn't know what it was."

Perry took a card from his pocket, carefully nudged the knife into the plastic envelope, and left it lying on the table. Then he sighed and looked at the people again. "What happened here?"

"This is supposed to be a quiet room," said an angry voice. "What's going on in here, Diane?" It was Fanny Mobley at her most unpleasant. Today she wore a heavy gray sweater over a navy blue sweater and long black skirt with a fringe around the bottom.

"We found the murder weapon," said Diane.

"You found what? Are all these people signed in properly?"

"This is the policeman and this is a proctor," said Diane. "And you know Oscar from conservation and Jeff the page. And Ms. Dulaney is signed in."

"Oh," said Fanny.

"Nick Perry, lieutenant, chief of detectives with the Borough," said Nick.

"Oh, yes," said Fanny. "I see. I see. And that's the weapon that the murderer used?"

"It may well be," said Nick Perry. "I need to ask these people a few questions. Will it be all right if we sit in here?" He waved his hand to indicate the Reading Room.

"No, this is supposed to be a quiet room. Please use the work area," said Fanny.

"Too much coming and going," said Perry patiently. "If it's all right, I'd like to get this done. It shouldn't take long."

Fanny frowned at Diane, nodded at Perry, and said, "As you please, Lieutenant," and swept from the Reading Room.

"Let's sit down. We can see each other if we sit at the front desks. Tell me what happened here," said Perry.

"Nick, I dropped my pencil in this box of van Dyke papers, and then I couldn't get it out," said McLeod.

"She was taking all the folders out of the

box and that is not allowed," Diane interrupted. "So I came over to help, and when I had most of the folders out, I saw this knife. I pulled it out and I said, 'This is not your pencil, is it?' And she said, 'Don't touch it. Put it down. That's the murder weapon.' So I put it down right then. And she went to get the proctor and I sent for a page to go get a plastic envelope from conservation. And then you got here. That's all."

"And I brought the plastic envelope," said Oscar. "From conservation."

"I see," said Perry, and went back over it, asking more questions this time.

How does he stand it? McLeod asked herself. Listening to the same story over and over.

"All right, everybody," said Perry. "Very good. Let me get your names and addresses and let me call somebody to come get everybody's fingerprints. Nobody else touched the knife? Good. All right." He wrote down names and addresses for Diane, Oscar, and Jeff, and thanked them, asking them to make themselves available when the fingerprint man arrived. "And thank you, Miss Diane, for the use of your space. Now I need to know who had access to this box. Who could have put the knife in it?"

This was the question McLeod had asked

just before he arrived, so she waited for the answer.

Diane hesitated. "I guess you should talk to Miss Mobley. The manuscript curator. She was just in here."

"I will," said Perry. "But you tell me who you think could have done it."

"Any of the curators could have done it," said Diane. "A conservator. A page. Anybody who has access to the vault."

"You could have done it?"

"I don't go to the vault myself," said Diane. "I could have done it only when the box was up here in the Reading Room."

"How long has it been in the Reading Room?"

"It just came up a few minutes ago this morning. It hasn't been up here since Ms. Dulaney was working with it a couple of weeks ago."

"Before the murder, you mean?" asked Perry.

"That's right," said Diane.

"Is that right?" Perry asked McLeod.

"Yes," said McLeod, annoyed that Nick seemed not to take Diane's word for it.

"Who could have known that McLeod would be using this box?"

Diane shook her head. "I don't know," she said.

"Actually, everybody," said McLeod. "They keep such careful records here. They can look up and see what day any researcher came to the department and then look at call slips for that day and see what boxes he looked at. It's truly amazing how they track everything."

"Interesting," said Perry. "We'll have the medical examiner look at this knife and see if they think it was the murder weapon, and then send it to the state police laboratory so the forensics folks can look at it and tell us what they can find out, and maybe we can get somewhere. Thank you. Now, Ms. Dulaney, can I talk to you? Maybe in that conference room we used before? Let me make sure that's all right with Mr. Ledbetter. I need to ask him a few questions, too." He left, returning very shortly with Natty Ledbetter chugging along beside him like a gray tugboat.

"Go right ahead, Lieutenant, and use the conference room," Natty said. "I'm anxious to get to the bottom of this nastiness."

"Will you be around?" Perry asked the proctor. "Will you tell the fingerprint man where I am? And Mr. Ledbetter, I guess I'd better tell you a fingerprint man is coming to get fingerprints from several people. Maybe we should just go ahead and do the whole staff while he's here, if no one has any objections."

"I don't think anyone will object — everyone wants to get this solved and behind us," said Natty. "But, Lieutenant, we would like to keep the Reading Room open for use. People are here from out of town and we were closed most of last week."

"I understand. I don't see any reason why it can't be used. We went over it before. I think, though, I'll ask the university if another proctor can sit in there."

"All right," said Natty.

Perry thanked him and led McLeod to the conference room.

Nineteen

"How are you, McLeod?" Nick Perry said after they sat down at the table in the conference room. "And how about this murder? You're becoming a key player. You found the body and then you found the weapon."

"Actually, Diane found it. But it's not definite that it *is* the weapon, is it?"

"No, of course not. So what made you so sure it was the murder weapon?"

"Chester had told me about Philip Sheridan's paper knife, and he thought somebody had taken it to kill Sheridan with," said McLeod. "Didn't he tell you that?"

"Yes, he did tell us," said Perry. "And we looked high and low for that knife or for anything that could have been used for a weapon. We did not, however, go so far as to search every box in every collection of papers in the vault. Perhaps we should have."

"Why would the killer, or anybody for that matter, put it in a box that I was using? Is it just coincidence?"

"I don't think it's coincidence," said Perry. "He or she could have done it for any number of reasons. He might have wanted to incriminate you. On the other hand, maybe the murderer thought you were through with that box and would not be looking at it again, that the knife would never be found. Or perhaps he or she simply wanted it found but didn't want to give it to us himself, or herself. And then there's always the possibility that it's not the murder weapon at all and somebody is trying to confuse the issue."

"Why don't you ask Chester if this knife is indeed Philip Sheridan's?"

"I certainly intend to do that," said Nick. "I just saw Chester at home, as a matter of fact." (So that's why it took him twenty minutes to get here, thought McLeod.) "I'll talk to him again," Nick was saying. "But tell me first how you've become so involved in this case."

"I'm not so involved in this case," said McLeod. "I just happened to be acquainted with some of the people that work in Rare Books and Special Collections, and I got interested in them, especially Chester. And you know how people talk to me — I always say it's my white hair — but people have told me a whole lot of things."

"Like what?" asked Perry. "What have they told you?"

"Nothing sensational," said McLeod. "Lots of it is nonsense. If anybody had told me anything remotely important, I would have told you. I haven't talked to everybody in the department anyway."

"Who have you talked to?"

"I've talked to Chester, as I told you. I felt so sorry for him that George and I had him to dinner. And of course, Natty Ledbetter is an old friend of George's. When George was an undergraduate, he had Natty for a famous English course he taught, and Natty became his mentor, advised his senior thesis and all that. Let's see — I talked to Buster Keaton and to Fanny Mobley and to Dodo Westcott. They're just a fraction of the staff, you know."

"They may be just a fraction of the staff," said Perry, "but they're a very important fraction as far as this case is concerned."

"Why so?"

"They're the ones who stayed the longest after Rare Books was closed to the public," said Perry. "All the other people who did not leave at five have solid evidence that they were somewhere else, while every single one of the people you've named was still here."

"Are you sure?" asked McLeod. Then she realized what a stupid question that was, that Nick Perry would never have said it if he had not been sure. She was at risk of sounding like a silly old lady.

"I'm sure for the moment, unless some explosive information comes to hand," he said. He waited a few seconds. "So what did they tell you?"

"You mean the prime suspects?"

"That's right," he said.

"Well, every one of them told me he or she left early, while other people were still here," she said.

"They tell us the same thing. We're working on that as hard as we can," he said. "But of course, anybody could have killed Sheridan and left the body there while other people were still around. They tell me that hardly anybody except Chester ever went into Sheridan's room anyway. Just Miss Mobley, Buster Keaton, and Mr. Ledbetter. So clearly somebody else could have killed Sheridan, even one of the others who left much earlier, and nobody would have found the body. But what did they tell you?"

"Nick, I hate to tell you in a way. It is all

quite inconsequential. Each person seemed to want to implicate another person, but nobody had any real evidence of wrongdoing and not a semblance of a strong motive. For instance, Buster Keaton said Fanny Mobley and Philip Sheridan used to have shouting arguments — but nobody else confirms this. Dodo Westcott insisted it was Chester Holmes who had the motive for killing Sheridan, a man Chester says was his best friend. Stuff like that."

"What else?" said Perry.

"Natty Ledbetter tried to implicate Dodo. And Chester said Natty Ledbetter had been angry with Sheridan. So you see it's meaningless."

"It seems that way," said Nick, "but you never know with these ivory tower types. You've talked to all these people, so who do you think had it in for Philip Sheridan?"

"Nick, that's the hard part. I don't think anybody had it in for Philip Sheridan. He was the big benefactor who could help all of them with their pet projects — rare books, manuscripts, events for the Friends of the Library. I told Natty Ledbetter I didn't see how anybody would want to kill the goose that laid the golden eggs, and he got angry with me for calling Philip Sheridan a goose."

"Geese that lay golden eggs sometimes try to call the tunes," said Nick. "I mean the people that control the purse strings like to control other things, don't they?"

"I guess so," said McLeod.

"Well, keep listening, McLeod. People do tell you the most amazing things."

"Let me know about that knife," said McLeod.

"I will. Stay in touch. I'll ask Ledbetter about the knife right now. Then I'll ask Holmes."

"He hasn't come in. At least he hadn't a little while ago," said McLeod. "But he could identify it for sure."

"As I said, I talked to him at home. He should be here soon. Don't leave until we get your fingerprints," said Nick. "Okay?"

"Okay," said McLeod. "I'm going in the Reading Room and go through that box, if that's all right. Actually, I never got my pencil out."

"We should get any fingerprints off that box," said Nick. "And anything else we can. Do you mind waiting?"

"Okay," said McLeod again. "I can call up another box, but now I think I'll just wait for the fingerprint man. I don't feel like working on van Dyke right now."

"I'll go get that box," said Nick.

"If Diane will let you take it out of her protective custody," said McLeod.

"I'll ask nicely," said Nick. "Stay in touch."

"Sure," said McLeod. She was sitting in the work area outside the Reading Room when Barry Porter arrived.

"Still here?" said Porter.

"Oh, yes," said McLeod. "And you're back. Did it throw you off schedule when they had to close down last week and keep out researchers?"

"Not really," said Porter. "I just have a few details to clean up anyway. Much excitement, eh?"

"I'll say. And a great deal of real grief, Barry. Philip Sheridan was a benefactor and a nice man."

"Yes, I'm sure," said Barry Porter. They chatted for a few minutes until Porter said he'd better get to work and went in the Reading Room.

The fingerprint man arrived, spoke to the proctor, and sat down to take McLeod's prints. When he had finished with her, McLeod got up and went out to the reception area to get her coat and the things she had put in the locker.

On her way out, she met Chester Holmes. "The police are here," said McLeod. "And we found a knife in a box of van Dyke

210

papers. I think it must have been Philip Sheridan's."

Surprisingly, Chester seemed to brush this information aside. "Have you got a minute?" he asked her, and led her over to an alcove formed by display cases.

"Sure," said McLeod.

"I'm a suspect," said Chester. "A real suspect. The police came back to the house early this morning. Mr. Sheridan's lawyer told them that Mr. Sheridan left me some money, and the police say that gives me a real motive."

"Oh, Chester. He must have left money to a lot of people. What about his sister, isn't she an heir, or heiress?"

"I don't know," said Chester. "All I know is the police have another reason to keep hounding me."

"Chester, I trust Nick Perry. Don't give up. Right will triumph in the end. Go on in there and talk to Nick." She remembered what Chester had told her last night. "And tell him about Natty and Philip Sheridan. You might as well."

Chester stared at her and nodded. "Okay," he said. "Thanks."

It was after noon. McLeod wondered if Philip Sheridan's lawyer had told the university about the will. Had he, as promised, left his collection to Princeton? Surely he had, she thought. She picked up a sandwich and went to her office, checked for messages, and decided to forget the murder and everything else and go to a lecture on Sylvia Beach. Beach was the woman from Princeton who had run the Shakespeare and Company bookstore in Paris in the 1920s and published James Joyce's *Ulysses* when nobody else would dare. The first copy to enter the United States was the one Sylvia mailed to her father, the Reverend Sylvester Beach, pastor of the Presbyterian Church in Princeton. Lectures like that, McLeod reflected as she came out, were one of the glories of the Princeton life.

When she came out, it had finally started to snow. What a winter this was turning out to be.

As she walked home in the snow, McLeod thought about Chester. He seemed to be such a sweet boy. He had aroused her maternal instinct the day of the murder, and she had continued to fuss over him ever since. But everybody else seemed ready to suspect him of the murder. And now, he did indeed have a motive. Could that sweet, brown-eyed lad be a murderer? Things were never what they seemed, she thought, and maybe he did kill his "best friend" and "only relative." And there was Dodo's theory — the spouse or spousal figure is always the likeliest candidate to do a murder — even if Chester was telling the truth when he said he and Philip Sheridan had not been "partners."

By the time McLeod reached the little house on Edgehill, she had almost convinced herself that Chester Holmes was the murderer. On the front porch, she paused to make sure the were no signs of another break-in. Then she remembered the alarm system and opened the front door, she listened carefully for intruders before she went in.

Once inside, reality took over, and she dismissed thoughts of Chester's guilt. He really was too nice, she thought, and genuinely grateful to Philip Sheridan. It had to be somebody else, but who?

TWENTY

After George came home, they were in the kitchen, preparing to eat cold meat loaf and the baked potatoes McLeod had put in the oven when she got home. "I remember we're going to dinner at Mrs. Westcott's Wednesday night, but I won't be home tomorrow night," George said as he made the salad.

"What else is new?" asked McLeod.

"Well, the circumstances are new," said George. "I have a date."

They sat down to eat.

"You mean a girl date, not a university date?" said McLeod.

"That's right," said George. "A girl date." He poured wine in their glasses.

McLeod was astonished, surprised at the news and surprised at her own reaction to it. It was amazing how upset she felt, but determined not to show it, she said, "That's wonderful." To her shame, she heard her voice quaver. What was wrong with her? They weren't married. They weren't sleeping together. They weren't even seeing much of each other. "Who is she?"

"Her name is Polly Griffin," said George.

"Does she work at the university?"

"At the art museum," said George.

"Oh," said McLeod. It was all she could think of to say. She poured her second glass of wine and decided she should pull herself together.

And pull herself together she did. While pulling valiantly, she remembered something — the treasure. "I have never told you, George —"

"You have a date, too," he interrupted.

"Not at all," she said. "I never told you I found something that I think is pretty valuable when Dante and I cleaned out the garage."

"What?"

"A rare book," she said. "Natty and Buster Keaton think it's worth a lot of money. And I found a crucifix and a reliquary box made out of carved ivory."

"Yes?" said George, frowning at her.

"Let me tell you how it happened," she said. "I kept forgetting about it on account of the murder and finding the murder weapon."

George looked puzzled.

"I think I found the murder weapon this morning," she explained. "I mean, I found something that I think — and Nick thinks so, too — something that might be the murder weapon."

"And that is?"

"Philip Sheridan's paper knife."

"Yes?" said George again.

"Didn't you know about the paper knife? Chester said all along that the murderer must have used Philip Sheridan's paper knife to kill him. And this morning I think I found it." McLeod told him about her discovery in the Reading Room.

"I do admire the way you stay in the thick of things," said George. "But back to the treasure."

"There were all these boxes in the garage," McLeod began, telling him about the old shoes and the recipes and the dresses. "I kept the box of dresses because I thought one of my students could use them in a production at Theatre Intime. And I didn't even take the dresses out of the box until I had hauled the thing up to my office. So I looked at them just before Clark Powell — that's the student — picked them up. And that's how I found the book and the crucifix and the reliquary. I locked them in a file drawer in my cubicle. And then this morning I remembered them and I took the book over to Natty, and he and Buster were very excited about it — they say it's a medieval copy of the four Gospels. And Natty came over to Joseph Henry House and got the reliquary and the crucifix so he could keep everything safely in the vault."

"And you finally decided you'd better tell me about it," said George.

He was really angry, McLeod realized. "I'm sorry, George. I really am. I hope I did the right thing. As I said, I forgot about it. I found the stuff in the box of dresses last Wednesday, the afternoon after I found the body that morning. Remember? Then I had class on Thursday and we had the burglary on Thursday and Friday Dante came and Saturday we had Natty to dinner and Sunday I went to chapel and took supper to Chester and this morning I remembered it when I got to my office and I took it over to Natty. Then I found the murder weapon, and if you ask me, I think it's a miracle that I remembered to tell you tonight." Especially after you just told me you have a date with a girl named Polly tomorrow night, she thought.

"I see," said George.

"Do you think those things belong to you

or Little Big? Dante was sure those boxes on the rafters of the garage had been there since Jill Murray lived here."

"I think they belong to me and I'd like to see them," said George.

"They're safe in Natty's vault. Go over to the library and look at them tomorrow," said McLeod. "Get them back if you want to."

"I'll certainly go look at them."

"Don't be cross with me," said McLeod. "If I hadn't kept the box of dresses, Dante would have taken it to the dump with the other cartons."

"You are correct," George said. "You did the right thing. Thank you."

He was clearly still miffed, thought McLeod as she poured herself a third glass of wine. She would regret it later, she thought, when she woke up at three o'clock in the morning and couldn't go back to sleep. But she needed it now.

TWENTY-ONE

The next morning, Tuesday, McLeod was happy to see that it had not snowed heavily — not even an inch. Life in Princeton could go on. She would get dressed and go to Rare Books and finish that box of van Dyke papers. Surely the police were through with it.

First her office, though, to check the mail and messages. She hung up her coat on the rack downstairs and went in the Humanities Council Office. Frieda had a quotation ready: " 'God sends the snow in winter, the warmth to swell the grain, the breezes and the sunshine, and soft refreshing rain.' "

"He doesn't send snow in winter *everywhere*," said McLeod. "It never snows in Tallahassee. I can't get used to it up here."

It sounded like I was complaining, she thought as she climbed the stairs. In her alcove, she laid her mail on the desk and looked around. Something was out of whack, she thought. What was it? She looked around and saw that someone had forced open the drawers on her file cabinet. She pulled open a desk drawer and immediately felt that the intruder had also riffled through her desk. What was going on? First the house was burgled, and now her office. "I'm glad I took that book and those other things over to Rare Books," she said to herself. "Thank heavens."

She went back downstairs and reported the damage to Frieda. Frieda's eyes widened and her mouth opened. " 'O, it's broken the lock and splintered the door . . . Their boots are heavy on the floor.' Remember the Auden lines I quoted to you last week? Now it's happened."

"Hadn't we better report it to Public Safety?" asked McLeod.

"Of course, I'll do that now," said Frieda. "Was anything stolen?"

"I don't think so," said McLeod. "I don't keep anything valuable up there." At least, not anymore, she thought.

"No, it's not a good place for safekeeping," said Frieda. She punched a number on her phone.

McLeod waited around to talk to the two proctors from Public Safety. She took them up to her cubicle. "Vandalism," said one of them when she told them nothing had been taken. They went through the whole building looking for other signs of breaking and entering and found none.

McLeod went downstairs with them and they stopped in the Humanities Council Office. Everyone agreed that Joseph Henry House was pretty easy to break into.

"And those cubicles upstairs are open to the world," said one of the proctors.

"Frieda complains that the last person out doesn't always lock the doors," said McLeod.

"Isn't Public Safety supposed to check the doors at night?" asked Frieda.

"We do, but a burglar could come in after everyone left, go through those cubicles upstairs, and leave before we checked the doors," said the proctor. "We'll do what we can," he said, and the two men left.

Frieda promised she would call somebody about repairing the locks on McLeod's file drawers.

McLeod finally got to Rare Books. As she was signing in, Nick Perry was leaving. He stopped to greet her and asked her if he could come by Edgehill Street later and talk to her. "About seven?" he asked.

"Sure," she said.

Nick made sure he had the right address and left. McLeod was delighted he was coming. Maybe she could tell George that she, too, had a date.

On her way into the Reading Room, she stopped in Natty's office.

"Good morning, dear girl," he said, getting up.

"Good morning," she replied. "Sit back down, Natty. I'm not going to stay."

Natty shook his head and remained standing, so McLeod slid into a chair. Natty was so old-fashioned — he wouldn't sit down while she was standing. It was kind of nice, really. "Did you find out anything yet about the treasure?"

"Buster's working on it like a bull dog," said Natty. He paused portentously. "You know, George came by this morning to have a look at it."

"Did he take it away?"

"No, no, it's all still here."

"Oh, Natty, I forgot to tell him about it until last night. Isn't that awful? He was furious. But I just bumbled along, doing first one thing and then another and living one day, one half-day, at a time."

"Not to worry," said Natty. "George will understand eventually, if he doesn't already."

"Oh, my office was burgled," she said. "I'm very glad I got that book and the other things over here to you yesterday, or they might have been stolen."

"And so you should be," said Natty. "Buster and I are very glad you did. Buster has high hopes that dear George will give them to Princeton."

"I hope that nothing I did will keep that from happening," said McLeod.

"No, no, dear lady. I'm sure everything you did was for the best."

When she finally got to the Reading Room, McLeod saw that Celestine Swallow, the old lady — she corrected her thought to "older woman" — who had been researching flower painters before the murder, was back. She was in the work area outside the Reading Room and she was somewhat agitated, twisting a pencil in her hand.

McLeod greeted her and asked if there was anything wrong.

"It's rather troubling," said Miss Swallow. "I put in a call slip for it yesterday. And they still can't find it."

"What is it that they can't find?" asked McLeod.

"Oh, it's the plates from the *Orchidaceae of Mexico and Guatemala* — Augusta Withers illustrated it. In fact, she painted the originals that the lithographs are based on. I really want to see them."

"They will turn up, won't they?" asked McLeod.

"I certainly hope so," said Miss Swallow.

As often happened when conversation was taking place outside her office, Fanny Mobley appeared and asked crossly what the problem was.

When Miss Swallow explained about the missing plates from *Orchidaceae*, Fanny shook her head despairingly and said, "*They* do things like that," implying, McLeod deduced, that Rare Books lost things but manuscripts never did. Then she went back in her office and slammed the door.

McLeod settled down with a new box that held clips of stories about van Dyke from various publications over the years. She learned that van Dyke was small but "splendidly erect," and carried a gold-headed cane. He wore white suits before Mark Twain made them famous and smoked tiny cigars. His house in Princeton, built in 1750, had been across the street from Grover Cleveland's. Heads of caribou and moose that van Dyke had shot adorned the walls of the entrance hall. He kept three horses and liked to drive a carriage and a sleigh.

"He would turn down a lecture that would pay $1,000 (a huge sum in his lifetime) and then speak for nothing to benefit an orphanage," said one writer.

McLeod was glad enough to leave all this behind when Miss Swallow suggested quietly that they go get some lunch. They settled down in Chancellor Green with wraps and tea while Miss Swallow mourned for Augusta Withers's illustrations in the *Orchidaceae.* "The book was published in 1837," she said. "But those botanical books often got ripped apart so people could have the flower pictures for framing. Princeton has many of these loose prints, but they don't catalog them. Now they say they don't own any pages from the *Orchidaceae,* but I know they do. They had some of them in an exhibition several years ago. That exhibition was one thing that got me interested in this project. I wrote her name down. I know they're supposed to be here. It's very frustrating."

"I can imagine," said McLeod.

"The world is falling apart," said Miss Swallow.

McLeod could only agree. She told her about her vandalized office. "And the funny thing is that the house where I live was burgled last week."

"That's very strange," said Miss Swallow. "But maybe people will call it the burglar house now, instead of the murder house."

"Maybe so," said McLeod, who now called it the Murder House in capital letters to herself. "At least nothing was taken at either place," she added.

"That's the good news," said Miss Swallow, "but I'm sure you still feel violated."

"I do," said McLeod. She liked Miss Swallow. Perhaps she could be a Miss Marple or Miss Silver, an older woman who was a whiz at solving mysteries. "Well, think about it," she urged Miss Swallow. "Maybe you can figure out what's going on."

"I don't know how I could figure out anything," said Miss Swallow. "I can't figure out what happened to those orchid plates."

"Is there anything else you can be working on?" asked McLeod.

"Oh, yes. I've filled out call slips for several things," said Miss Swallow.

"Rare Books is a nice place to do research, isn't it?" said McLeod.

"Very nice," said Miss Swallow. "The Reading Room is very attractive and everyone is extremely nice." She paused, and then added, "Miss Mobley seems to be rather odd."

"She is indeed," said McLeod. "Have you noticed how she's sweet one minute and cross the next?"

"Yes, I have, as a matter of fact."

"It seems to me that she's always mean as a witch in the morning and cheerful and helpful in the afternoon. Do you suppose that's a form of bipolar disorder?"

"Is that the pattern? Cross before noon, not cross after lunch? I don't think that's bipolar."

"What then?" asked McLeod.

Miss Swallow finished her wrap, wiped her mouth daintily with the paper napkin, and said, "Hmmmm."

McLeod looked at her, waiting.

"You know what it could be?" asked Miss Swallow.

"What?" McLeod said impatiently. Get on with it, she thought.

"I tell you what — I think it just might be alcohol."

"Alcohol!"

"She may have a drinking problem," said Miss Swallow. "She might have a hangover in the morning, and until it wears off, she's miserable."

"That fits! That fits!" said McLeod. "I bet she starts drinking at lunch — and cheers up. It's not just that the hangover wears off. I sat down at the table with her here the other day when she was eating lunch and she drank from a thermos she brought from home. She brings liquor from home in that thermos and by afternoon she's cheered up."

"That's the pattern all right."

"It certainly seems possible, but how did you think of alcohol?"

"I come from a family of alcoholics," said Miss Swallow. "They didn't *swallow* alcohol, to make a bad pun, they swilled it. My grandfather, my father, my brother. They all died of cirrhosis of the liver and my mother died of grief over it. I vowed I'd never touch a drop and I don't. In a way, I wish I did. I know I miss a lot, but I'm afraid to let a whisper of whiskey pass my lips."

"You are very strong, Miss Swallow. And very wise. I love alcohol but you're not missing all that much, believe me."

"Thank you." She seemed somewhat embarrassed by her revelations, bending down to get her purse beside her chair and then standing up. "I guess I'd better get back to see if they've made any progress on Augusta Withers," she said.

McLeod absently told her goodbye and stayed on with another cup of tea. She wanted to reflect on this theory about Fanny. It made sense, but what did it mean? Did it have anything to do with the murder? Had Philip Sheridan realized what was going on and threatened to report Fanny for drinking on the job? Would that have given Fanny a motive for murder?

TWENTY-TWO

When McLeod got home that afternoon, she bustled about preparing for Nick Perry's visit. George came home, took a shower, shaved, and departed without noticing that she had put out cheese and crackers and was building a fire in the parlor. "Have a good time," she had called out as he was leaving, but her voice had sounded insincere, she thought.

Nick was so late that McLeod had to go outside for more wood to keep the fire going. When he appeared, she offered him a drink, expecting him to say no.

"Yes, I will," he said.

"Scotch? Gin?" she asked. "I don't think we have any bourbon or vodka . . ."

"Scotch on the rocks would be fine," he said. "I'll get out the ice," he added.

"Good," she said and led the way to the kitchen.

"George not here?" he asked as he popped

ice cubes out of the tray.

"He's out. He has a date," said McLeod.

"Oh," said Nick. "I thought you and he — never mind."

McLeod handed him the bottle of scotch and poured herself a glass of red wine. They went back to the parlor, and Nick began to eat crackers and cheese at a rapid rate.

"Tell me about your burglary," he said.

"How did you know about it?"

"I'm a policeman," he said.

"Why do you want to know about it?"

"I'm a policeman."

"Oh, Nick, I know that, but you're a policeman in charge of a murder investigation — what do you care about a burglary? Or maybe it's a good thing you want to talk about the burglary, not the murder. At least you'll have a drink. I don't think I ever saw you have a drink before."

"Look, I'm still investigating the murder, but I have to cover every possibility. Sergeant Popper told me he saw a breaking and entering at this address on the record and I thought I'd better look into it. I sent him home — he's been working nonstop — and came over here to talk to you. And I'm clandestinely having a drink. Okay? Now tell me about the blooming break-in."

"You've been working nonstop, too,

haven't you?" said McLeod.

"The break-in," said Nick.

"All right, all right, I'm sorry," said McLeod. "It happened last Thursday, the day after I found Philip Sheridan's body." She described the broken pane in the door and the ransacking of her room. "But nothing was taken that we know of. That's the funny thing."

"They were looking for something," said Nick. "Did you bring anything home the day you found the body?"

"Not that I know of," said McLeod. "And the funny thing is that somebody rifled my office last night."

"Really? Did you report it?"

"Frieda, the office manager at the Humanities Council, reported it to Public Safety — you know, campus security," said McLeod. "But I don't suppose anybody reported it to the police."

"McLeod, you must have something that somebody wants."

"I can't imagine what it is," she said. "Another drink?"

"Yes, but I'll make it half as big as the first one." When they had settled down again, she asked him if Chester had identified the knife in the van Dyke box.

"He's sure it's the one that belonged to

Sheridan," Nick said.

"And was it the murder weapon?"

"Yes, it was. I just got the report from the state lab. That's why I was late."

"Does that help toward a solution?" McLeod asked.

"We knew it was somebody that works in Rare Books," said Nick. "This is just icing on the cake." He took a sip of his very mild drink. "Tell me, what do you think of Ledbetter?"

"I like Natty," McLeod said. "He's full of that 'dear boy' and 'dear lady' stuff, but he seems to care about the collections and I think he must be good at his job. He's not a suspect, is he?"

"Everybody is a suspect," said Nick.

"Is Chester still a suspect?"

"Everybody is a suspect," he said. "Let's talk about something else."

"Are you hungry?" asked McLeod. "It's after nine o'clock."

Nick looked at his watch.

Does he have to check everything I say? wondered McLeod.

"Yes, I am. I'd take you out to dinner, but to tell you the truth, I don't think I'd better. As soon as we sat down, I'd get a call."

"And you don't want to be seen having

dinner with a suspect, do you?" said McLeod.

He looked at her. "You're not really a suspect, McLeod, but people might think you were. At least you're involved; you found the body. I told you I was having a clandestine drink. The whole thing is clandestine."

"That makes it interesting," said McLeod, smiling happily.

"Good. Could we order in a pizza or Chinese or something?"

"We could," McLeod said without any enthusiasm. "Or I can make grilled cheese sandwiches or scramble some eggs or something."

"Great," said Nick. He did grilled cheese and bacon sandwiches while she made a salad and found an unopened bag of potato chips.

They ate at little tables in front of the parlor fire, and McLeod seized the chance to ask him questions she had always wanted to ask. Where did he grow up and where did he go to school?

"I grew up right here in Princeton," he said. "I went to the high school and then to Yale."

"How did you happen to become a policeman?"

"It's a long story. My father was a lawyer — he's retired and lives in Florida — and I thought I'd be a lawyer. I liked the idea of being a lawyer, but by the time I was a senior in college, I couldn't stand the idea of going to law school. I decided to be a policeman. I used to read a mystery story a day. So I got a master's in criminology at Rutgers. It wasn't nearly as bad as law school and it only lasted half as long. Anyway, here I am — a law-and-order man in my hometown."

"That's great," said McLeod.

"It's all right," said Nick.

They were drinking coffee before the fire when George came home. He looked in the parlor, and then came in.

"Well, Lieutenant, how do you do?" he said.

"Fine," said Nick, getting up and shaking hands. "And you?"

"I'm good."

"You're home early," said McLeod.

"So I am," said George.

"Would you like some coffee?" asked McLeod.

"Sure, and I'll have a brandy. Brandy, Lieutenant? McLeod?"

"I'd better not," said Nick. "I have to start work early tomorrow."

"Don't we all?" said George. "McLeod?"

"No, thanks," she said.

When George returned with his brandy and coffee, he sat down with them, and said to McLeod. "Well, I saw my treasure today."

At first she thought he meant Polly What's-her-name and then realized what he was talking about. "Natty told me," she said. "Were you impressed?"

"Very. I wish I'd known about it sooner, though."

Oh dear, he was still cross, thought McLeod.

"What treasure is this?" asked Nick.

"So tell him about it," said George.

McLeod went through the story one more time — cleaning out the garage, the box of old dresses, Clark Powell, the discovery of the book and crucifix and ivory box and turning them over to Rare Books for safe-keeping.

"Let me get this straight," said Nick. "You and Dante Immordino — I know him — cleaned out the garage, and you salvaged a box of old clothes because you thought your student might be able to use them for a play, and you took the clothes to campus and opened the box and found a valuable book and relics in them. You locked them in your file cabinet on Thursday and then yesterday you took them to the library. Is that right?"

"That's right," said McLeod.

"And the drawer of your file cabinet was jimmied last night?"

"That's right."

"Don't you see?" said Nick. "Somebody is after these things."

McLeod and George looked at each other and then at Nick, who stared back. "It's plain, isn't it?"

"Plain as day," said McLeod weakly. "Now that you point it out so clearly."

Nick smiled, and started asking questions, taking them back over every detail of the break-in and going over McLeod's activities with the carton of dresses.

"I would have given you a ride to campus so you didn't have to get that carton from the garage up to Joseph Henry House," said George.

"Oh, you had already left for work before I even remembered to take the box," she said.

Nick ignored this interchange and went on with his questions. "Don't you see you got the carton out of the house just before Mr. X came in after it?" he said. "And you must have a guardian angel. You got it out of your office just before X came in there." He paused. "You know, I think I'll have someone ask Dante Immordino a few questions."

"Dante's so nice. You don't think he was trying to steal something, do you?" said McLeod.

"I don't know," said Nick. "I just think somebody should ask him some questions."

"Do you think this has anything to do with the murder?" George asked.

"I don't know, but I'm glad I came by here tonight. It was an impulse this morning when I asked you if I could come, McLeod. I thought you could tell me more about some of the people involved — you do get a lot out of people. But this is news. I'll find out if it has anything to do with the murder. And now I'd better go." He stood up, thanked them both, and departed.

"I'm sorry I drove your beau away," said George.

"He's not my beau," said McLeod. "Why are you home so early? What happened to your girl date?"

"She had a headache," said George, and grinned. "I'm glad I came home early, though, and mentioned the treasure. Good for Perry. I feel stupid that I didn't make the connection."

"What about me?" said McLeod. "You just found out about it yesterday but I've known since —"

"You just found out about your office this morning," George reminded her.

"And I did keep forgetting about that stuff. I know it's hard to understand, but —"

"I understand," said George.

McLeod was suddenly feeling better about everything.

TWENTY-THREE

George called her from his office before she left the house on Wednesday. "I just wanted to confirm that we're going to Dodo's house for dinner tonight," he said. "What time?"

"Let me look. It's late — seven-thirty. And that probably means we won't eat until nine or nine-thirty."

"I'll be home in time to get there at seven-thirty. See you."

McLeod had several conferences scheduled with students, but she could spend some time that morning in Rare Books. She could find out if anything new had happened, and there was one question she wanted to clear up.

Molly said she didn't know of anything new, so McLeod signed in so she could go back to the Reading Room and call up another van Dyke box.

Miss Swallow looked up from the large book she was perusing, stood, and beckoned her out of the Reading Room. "I just wanted to tell you that yesterday afternoon sometime after I got back from lunch I made a point of getting close to Miss Mobley and I smelled alcohol!" she said in a low, conspiratorial voice.

"In the afternoon! Then you were right," said McLeod. "Do you think she drinks enough for it to interfere with her job?"

"I don't think so," said Miss Swallow. "She seems very competent to me, but — well, volatile."

"Yes. That's very interesting. Thanks for telling me."

"And another thing," Miss Swallow was saying, "Nathaniel Ledbetter came in this morning and told me he had heard about my distress over the missing orchid prints and he said that he personally was going to make a special effort to find them for me. He said, 'I have an idea where they might be. I'll check and get back to you.' I thought that was very nice of him."

"He's a very nice man," said McLeod.

Miss Swallow agreed, said she had to get back to work, and McLeod followed her into the Reading Room. She worked on a new box of papers and was charmed by an anecdote she read. After van Dyke resigned as ambassador to the Netherlands during

World War I, he went to see his old friend, Josephus Daniel, Secretary of the Navy, and asked, "How old do you think I am?" "You look about thirty-five to me," said Daniels. "If you say I'm thirty-five, I am." He became a Navy chaplain and traveled the country urging its entry into the "righteous" war. He contributed his salary to the United States Naval Academy, which used the money to endow a prize for the best patriotic paper by a midshipman each year.

This was fairly interesting, but McLeod couldn't keep her mind on it. She left and stuck her head in Natty's office.

"Come in, come in, dear lady," said Natty, standing up as he always did.

McLeod sat down, as she always did, so Natty would sit down. "One thing's been bothering me, Natty," she said. "I know Philip Sheridan left Chester some money. What about his bequest to the university? It's safe and sound for Princeton, isn't it?"

"Oh, yes, dear lady. Philip was a man of his word. All of his incomparable collection belongs to Princeton University — or it will as soon as the will is probated. It's a magnificent gift."

"I'm so glad," said McLeod. "Congratulations." She left Natty and headed to Joseph Henry House, wondering again if Philip

Sheridan had known about Fanny Mobley's drinking and perhaps threatened to report her. It seemed to her, now that she thought about it for the second time, that such a threat provided a very good motive for murder. At least, the best motive she'd thought of so far.

Clark Powell arrived promptly for her first student conference. He seemed very pleased when she commended his rewriting efforts and then offered her two tickets to the opening night of *The Learned Ladies.* "It's tomorrow night," he said.

"That's very soon. You just got the dresses last week," she said.

"True. We were desperate for costumes. Do come if you can."

"I certainly will," she said.

After three conferences, she was dead tired and walked home, looking forward to a nap before they went out to dinner. Nap and shower refreshed her and she dressed in her good long black wool skirt and black cashmere sweater with anticipation.

George was a little late getting home so they were a little late arriving at the Westcotts' big house on Cleveland Lane and had to park some distance from the front door.

"Dodo must be having a crowd," said McLeod as they walked slowly, watching for slippery spots on the sidewalk.

"Not on a weeknight," said George. "I bet some of these cars belong to the temporary help."

Dodo, dressed in a bright blue caftan trimmed with wide gilt braid, met them at the door with great enthusiasm. "I'm so glad to see you both. Do come in. George, it's good of you to come; I know how busy you are. Do you know my husband? Bob, dear, this is McLeod Dulaney — she teaches writing at Princeton and she's writing a book on Henry van Dyke."

"I'm not sure I'm writing a book about —" began McLeod, but Dodo didn't stop or listen.

"And this is George Bridges, the new vice president for public affairs at Princeton," she was saying to her husband. Dodo finished introductions and led them into a large living room, where two other couples were standing in front of a fireplace, in which pristine birch logs were arranged beautifully but unlit. When she began further introductions, Bob Westcott said sharply, "Dorothy, let me get drinks for these people and then you can introduce them."

McLeod and George asked for martinis and agreed with a glance that Bob Westcott had his priorities straight.

The others turned out to be Cowboy Tarleton, a Princeton lawyer McLeod had met before, and his wife, Shirley, and to McLeod's astonishment, Mary and Little Big Murray. Dodo had told her, McLeod was thinking, that Mary Murray had murdered her mother-in-law, yet Dodo had invited her to dinner.

"Mary, this is McLeod Dulaney," Dodo was saying, "and George Bridges. McLeod, this is Little Big Murray. Big, you know George, don't you? He bought your old house."

"Oh, right," said Little Big. "But he didn't buy the house from me, Dodo. He bought it from that man from Texas."

Mary Murray was a diffident-looking woman with short wavy brown hair, whom McLeod thought she might not have even noticed under other circumstances. It was hard to picture her as a murderer. Little Big, on the other hand, was big. You would notice him anywhere, McLeod thought, because of his sheer size. But his face was curiously blank, and McLeod remembered that Dodo had said he was stupid.

McLeod was dying to ask Mary Murray

who she thought had murdered her mother-in-law and ask Little Big why on earth he hadn't cleaned out his mother's garage before he sold the house to the man from Texas, but obviously both of these gambits were unacceptable as dinner conversation.

George and Little Big began to chat about, of all things, golf. McLeod asked Mary Murray if she had grown up in Princeton. "I know your husband did," she said.

"Yes, I did, too," said Mary Murray. "And where are you from?"

"I live in Tallahassee, Florida."

"And you're an old friend of George Bridges?"

"Yes. He kindly offered to let me stay with him in his new house for the semester," said McLeod. "At least it's new to him. It's an old house, isn't it? I know it used to belong to your mother-in-law. How old would you say it is?"

"I think it was built in the 1880s."

"And your husband was born there?"

"In a sense. He was born in Princeton Hospital, but his parents were living there when he was born. He hasn't lived there in thirty years, and he doesn't like to talk about the house."

"I can understand that," said McLeod. "I knew his mother was murdered there. I'm sure it's a painful subject for him."

"It is. He found the body, you know." Mary Murray took a sip of her white wine. "His mother had grown up in that house and she died there."

"I don't think I knew that," said McLeod.

"Oh, yes. It was known as the Lawrence house for years."

And then it was known as the Murder House, McLeod thought. Would it someday be known as the Bridges house? "Jill Murray's name was Lawrence before she married Bigelow Murray?" she asked.

"Oh, yes. And she was very proud of being a Lawrence. After she was married, and her parents had died and her two brothers had grown up, she insisted that she and my father-in-law move back to that house. They bought out her brothers' interest — her brothers were crazy about their sister, anyway. She was quite a charmer."

"And she charmed you, too?" asked McLeod.

"Oh, no. Little Big was her only son, and nobody was good enough for him. But she charmed everybody else."

Dodo summoned them to the dining room, where McLeod found herself seated between Bob Westcott and the lawyer Cowboy Tarleton. "You commute to New York, don't you?" she asked Westcott. "Isn't it hard to come home to a dinner party?"

"It is," he said, smiling at her, "but Dorothy's wish is my command. She likes to have people in on weeknights, and I try to get here on time."

"You're the only person who doesn't call her Dodo," said McLeod.

"I hate that nickname. It began when she was a child, and it makes her sound like an idiot. And she's not an idiot. Anyway, how do you like Princeton?"

McLeod answered that she loved it, and the conversation became general. Looking around the table, McLeod wondered how Dodo was considered such a social climber — this was not a glittering group, unless the Murrays glittered socially, which she doubted.

The food was catered, but not bad, and the wine flowed freely. At one point she had a chance to talk to Cowboy Tarleton. "You were Philip Sheridan's lawyer, weren't you?" she asked him.

"I was. He was one of my favorite clients. He was a gentleman of the old school, to use a trite phrase." Cowboy was a pleasant man, tall and thin, and he smiled a lot. McLeod liked him.

"Everybody loved him, but somebody

murdered him," she said.

"It can happen to the best of people," said Cowboy. "Or I guess it can. Though in fact, I don't think I ever knew anybody so universally admired who was murdered before."

"It wasn't an accident, or a random act of violence," said McLeod, "so he must have had an enemy."

"I don't think it was an enemy, exactly."

"What do you mean?"

"I don't mean anything. I don't know why I'm saying that. I just don't think Sheridan was killed because of his character."

A maid in uniform was removing the plates. McLeod supposed George was right about the Westcotts' temporary help, or maybe the caterers provided it. "You handled his will, didn't you?" she asked.

"Yes, I did."

"Chester Holmes told me that Philip Sheridan left him some money, but the bulk of the estate goes to the university, doesn't it?"

"I'm not breaking any confidences, since the will has been filed for probate. He left his sister a substantial sum, but of course, he left the collection — the books and manuscripts — to Princeton, plus a sizable amount of money to maintain the collection and to pay for a curator."

"That was all pretty straightforward, wasn't it?"

"Absolutely. He brought in a hot-shot New York estate lawyer to oversee me on that part, to make sure it was airtight."

"Did that annoy you?" McLeod asked.

Cowboy looked at her shrewdly. "A little," he said. "But not enough to make me kill him, if that's what you mean. That was a long time ago, anyway."

"And you don't hold a grudge?"

"Not that long, believe me."

"What did you mean about his not being killed because of his character? I don't understand."

Cowboy was quiet while the maid put dessert plates before them. "I meant that Sheridan was a good man, a truly good man, but like all truly good men, he thought he knew best," Cowboy said. "He wasn't a bad man, not at all, but he had his little quirks."

"What kind of quirks?" McLeod asked.

"Oh, you know what I mean," Cowboy said, smiling again. "You knew him."

"I didn't really know him. I met him and talked to him and he showed me a Trollope manuscript and even gave me a Trollope first edition —"

"That is so typical!" broke in Cowboy. "He gave me a pair of Daumier caricatures of lawyers, all matted and framed for my office. They were prints, but original prints from the eighteenth century. They're among my proudest possessions."

McLeod plowed on. "But I didn't really have anything but the most superficial acquaintance with him. So what kind of quirks did he have?"

"He was a stickler about people doing what they were supposed to do. He was good to Chester, but if he thought Chester neglected some task, he would be very stern. Not rude, but stern."

"Chester has only the warmest praise for him," said McLeod.

"Sure, working for Philip is all that Chester knows," said Cowboy. "But still sometimes Sheridan could be quite demanding. I think sometimes the people in Rare Books felt that he went too far."

"Did he shout at people?" McLeod asked, remembering what people had told her about loud arguments between Sheridan and Fanny, Sheridan and Natty, and who else?

"Not often, that would be the ultimate. But he had a little quirk that could be quite annoying. He was always changing his mind."

"About what?"

"About everything. 'We'll go out to lunch,' he'd say. 'We'll go to the Nassau Club.' Then he'd say, 'No, we'll go to Lahiere's.' Or maybe, 'No, let's not go out to lunch today. Can we send out for sandwiches?' It could be — well, inconvenient."

"I'm sure it could. I wonder if he did that with the people in Rare Books?"

"He must have. He sure did it with me. And I know he called his broker often to tell him to buy or sell and then called him back to tell him not to do it. He was always talking to me about changing his will. Sometimes he did change it and sometimes he didn't. It was annoying, but I couldn't tell him to stop."

"But on the whole he was a good client?"

"Oh, yes, and I shouldn't complain. I started billing him for telephone time, and he paid."

Dinner was finally over, coffee was served in the living room, and everybody left fairly early, complaining that the next day was a workday.

"Thank you so much for coming," Dodo told them when they left. "George, I hope you enjoyed meeting Little Big. I thought it would be such a coup to bring you two together."

"It was, Dodo," said McLeod. George said nothing.

TWENTY-FOUR

On Thursday morning, McLeod read in the *Times* of Trenton that Nick Perry had held a brief press conference the day before. When reporters asked him if the murder of Philip Sheridan was a "cold case," or otherwise abandoned, he replied, "Absolutely not. This case will never be closed."

"Do you think it will end up like the Jill Murray case — unsolved?" a reporter asked.

"Not at all," Nick had said.

"Does that mean you're close to a solution?"

"It means I think we'll solve it," said Nick.

Good for Nick, she thought. Meanwhile, she had to get moving — this was Thursday, class today.

When she met the class that afternoon, she talked about their new assignment: to write about a person involved in the arts.

"Henry van Dyke said the two most important things in life are art and friendship," she said.

"Does that mean we have to write about a friend next time?" asked one of the students.

"What a good idea," she said. But for this assignment, they could write about people in the visual arts, or music, or the theater, she said, and she urged them to look for people who had not been publicized before. She pointed out that Clark Powell, who was in the class, was involved with the production of *The Learned Ladies,* which would open at Theatre Intime, Princeton's student-run theater, that night.

She went by herself to see the play, enjoyed the youthful actors in the performance, and paid a great deal of attention to the women's costumes. It was fun to see the long-sleeved black velvet and the pale blue lace dresses being worn by young and beautiful "learned ladies."

With all this, it was Friday before she was able to get back to Rare Books.

When she was on her way to the Reading Room, Buster Keaton came rushing out of his office and hailed her.

"There you are!" he said. "I just tried to call you. Guess what you found!"

"What?"

"It's nothing more nor less than the Litzenburg *Gospels.*"

"The what?"

"The Litzenburg *Gospels,*" said Buster impatiently.

"The Litzenburg *Gospels?*"

"This conversation has a certain repetitive quality," Buster said. "McLeod, you found the Litzenburg treasure. Come and look at these things again."

In Buster's office, she saw arrayed on his desk the gilded book, the ivory box, and the crucifix. "These are the things you found in George's garage — right?" Buster said.

"Right."

"They are part of the Litzenburg treasure, very valuable objects missing from the Schatzkammer, the treasure chamber, of the cathedral in Litzenburg, Germany," Buster said. "They've been missing since 1945, when they were apparently looted in the closing weeks of World War II. And here they are."

"How did you find out what they were?" asked McLeod.

"I'd like for you to think it was only because of the sheer power of my brain that I figured it out," said Buster. "But it wasn't too hard. The International Foundation for Art Research in New York compiles data on stolen art, and I went through its online database. They listed several things from

Litzenburg. Litzenburg is in what used to be East Germany, so not much was known about the missing pieces for a long time, but since Germany has been reunified, the people in the little town have publicized their loss."

McLeod looked from the objects to Buster and back at the objects.

"Of course, thousands of objects lost or stolen during World War II have never been recovered — and never will be," said Buster.

"Tell me what you found out about the book?" asked McLeod.

"Like I said, it's a copy of the four Gospels. It is indeed ninth century. It's a lovely book, very high quality, and very, very valuable. The church at Litzenburg used to be part of a cloistered convent and a noblewoman was the abbess — she paid for this copy of the four Gospels to be written by a famous scribe."

"For heaven's sake," said McLeod. "What about the box? Is it from Litzenburg, too?"

"The box — and it is a reliquary — is from Litzenburg. So is the crucifix. Of course, neither one of them is as valuable as the *Gospels*," said Buster.

"I can't take it all in," said McLeod, shaking her head. "It's absolutely dumbfounding."

"It's so wonderful," said Buster. "I can't take my eyes off that book. Princeton has some valuable books and manuscripts, but this would certainly be right up there at the top — if it were ours. We can keep it for a while, can't we?"

"Buster, I have no idea. They don't belong to me. They just turned up in a box I found when the handyman and I were cleaning out the garage one Saturday."

"And where was George? Why were you having to clean out *his* garage?"

"George had to work. So Dante and I went ahead and did it. There were some boxes up on the rafters that Dante said dated from Jill Murray's time, and we took them down and most of them were real junk. But one of them had several old dresses in it, and I couldn't resist them. I took that box inside. As it happened, one of my students was very interested in the old dresses for costumes for the play he was directing for Theatre Intime — it opened last night, by the way, and it is very good. I brought them to my office and didn't really look at them until just before he picked them up. That's when I found the book and the box."

"The objects stayed in your office for some time, I believe," Buster said.

"Just a few days," said McLeod.

"Well, don't take so long next time," said Buster. "Anything might happen. We'll put them back in the vault, shall we?"

"I guess so," said McLeod. "I guess that's the best place for them right now."

"Don't you want to give the *Gospels* to Princeton?" said Buster. "Just think of the tax deduction — it's worth a million, I'd say."

"Those things don't belong to me. Surely they must be returned to Litzenburg."

"They belong to George!" said Buster. "Surely he wants to donate them to his beloved alma mater."

"I'll tell him about it," McLeod promised.

When she left Buster's office, she ran into Celestine Swallow, who greeted her with great enthusiasm. "I'm so glad you came in today," she said. "I wanted to see you — I have good news. Let's go to lunch — can you?"

"Sure," said McLeod. "Let's go to the Annex instead of Chancellor Green, if that's all right."

Celestine agreed and they got their coats and purses and left the library, crossed Nassau Street, and went downstairs to the Annex.

"This is cozy," said Celestine Swallow. "I haven't been here in years."

"It's an old Princeton institution, isn't it?" said McLeod. "I love the miscellaneous collection of things on the walls." She waved a hand at the mirror on one wall, the stuffed fish and the huge, ancient smoky painting of a tiger on another wall, the still life of oysters and the hunting scene on the third. "I love the whole ambience. Have you found everything you were looking for at the library?"

"Oh, yes. Mr. Ledbetter — or Natty as everybody seems to call him — found the orchid prints. I was delighted."

"That's great," said McLeod. "Where were they? Did he say?"

"I asked him and he just said, 'Tucked away, dear lady, tucked away,' " said Celestine.

"Anything new on the Fanny Mobley mystery?"

"Everything I see confirms that she's an alcoholic. Hung over in the morning, getting drunk — or tipsy, I should say — in the afternoon."

"Do you think anybody else knows about it?" asked McLeod.

"I don't see how they can help noticing.

You and I did, and we're not here every day."

"You know how nobody notices what's before them every day, and then somebody comes in for the first time and whatever it is slaps them in the face."

"That's true," said Miss Swallow. "But I should think someone would notice her erratic behavior. It must interfere with her job."

"Apparently not," said McLeod. "I guess if she set fire to some manuscripts or something, somebody would notice."

"The people on the staff are pretty odd, aren't they?"

"They're under a strain," said McLeod. "We have to cut them some slack. They had a murder just a little over a week ago, you know."

"Of course, you're right," said Miss Swallow. "In a way they're heroic for soldiering on the way they do."

"I think so, too."

That night she told George that the treasure was from Litzenburg, and went on to tell him all that Buster had found out. "He wants you to give it to Princeton."

"McLeod, if what Buster says is true, they don't belong to me," George said. "They're stolen goods. They belong to that church in Germany where they were stolen from."

"Of course. You're right," said McLeod. "Buster will see that, once he stops to think." She took another sip of wine. They were sitting before the fire talking about where they would go to eat — it was Friday night, a bad night to eat out in Princeton, but neither one of them felt like cooking. "Buster is such a monomaniac about rare books that he loses all perspective," McLeod continued. "And he's persuasive, as well as fanatical. He's like those curators in art museums who won't return art that was stolen by the Nazis. You read about them in the newspapers all the time."

"It does seem to me that Natty should have realized who the owner is," said George.

"I didn't even see Natty when I was there today," said McLeod. "Nobody seems to be paying much attention to their jobs — except Buster, and that's all he thinks about. But everybody else is thinking about the murder, I guess."

"What about the Annex for dinner?" said George.

"I went there for lunch," said McLeod.

"Main Street?"

"Too noisy and too crowded on Friday."

"What about going over to Lambertville?"

"Too far in this cold weather," said McLeod.

"Oh, you Southern belles," said George.

"It is cold, and the forecast is for freezing rain," said McLeod.

They finally decided they might as well eat at home. George said he had steak in the freezer and could fry potatoes — George loved steak and potatoes — and McLeod said she'd make a huge salad.

While they ate, McLeod wondered, but did not ask aloud, what had happened to Polly Griffin. Was she going to turn up again?

To take her mind off Polly Griffin, she told George about Miss Swallow and the flower prints. "She must be eighty years old," she said.

George was mildly interested when she told him about Miss Swallow's deductions about Fanny Mobley.

"Is that a firing offense?" she asked him.

"I don't do personnel," he said, "but I should think the question would be whether it interfered with her work in a major way or not."

"I don't know about that," said McLeod, but she resolved to find out if she could.

After dinner, over coffee, she said, "You

know I heard something the other night at Dodo's house that I wish I could remember."

"What was it?" asked George.

"I can't remember — that's it."

"It will come to you," said George.

"I hope so."

TWENTY-FIVE

In the middle of the night, McLeod woke up and remembered what it was that someone had told her at Dodo's house, and she wrote it down before she went back to sleep.

On Saturday morning, she reached for the piece of paper on her bedside table and groaned. She couldn't read her writing. But the memory would probably come back, she thought. She had remembered it once and surely she would remember it again.

By the time she got downstairs, she had resolved to call Chester and arrange to see him. Then she remembered what she had written down in the middle of the night: Lawrence letters. Mary Murray had said that Jill Murray had been a Lawrence, and weren't those World War II letters she and Dante had found in the garage from a man named Lawrence to a woman named Lawrence?

What had she done with them? She had

brought the box into the house, intending to see if Jill's Murray's family wanted them, and never thought of them again. Had the burglar taken them? Am I sure I brought them inside? Maybe the box is still in the garage. No, Dante had cleaned it out thoroughly. Nevertheless, she went outside to the garage and opened the door and looked around. No sign of the box.

She came back inside and peered, without much hope, around the hall and the dining room and the kitchen.

"What are you looking for?" asked George, glancing up from the newspaper he was reading as he sat in one of the easy chairs in the dining room's bay window.

"A box of letters that Dante and I found when we cleaned out the garage."

"Oh, that box of letters," he said. "I found it on the floor in the hall. I was trying to tidy up so I put it on the shelf in the coat closet."

Back in the hall, McLeod opened the closet door and saw the box, almost hidden under their collection of winter hats and scarves that were piled on top of it. She retrieved the box and took it to the dining room, where she sat in the other chair in the bay window. The letters, from Lieutenant Vincent Lawrence to Mrs. John

Lawrence on Edgehill Street in Princeton, were arranged chronologically — someone had taken care with them. The letters weren't very long, just large script on lined paper. Or later, V-mail pages. Each began, "Dear Mother," and then Lieutenant Lawrence went on to describe in workaday fashion some of what he saw and heard and felt as a young American officer making his way across Europe in the closing months of World War II.

It took McLeod a long time to read them. She wasn't sure why she persisted, but she did. At one point, she got up to stretch her legs and walk around, wondering why she was willing to spend time reading the letters from one person she had never known to another person she had never known. Because I'm curious, she thought. It took some time before she got to the good part.

Lieutenant Lawrence had been part of the field artillery unit that occupied Litzenburg, Germany, at the end of the war. He described searching the war-torn countryside for weapons and ammunition and other contraband in the spring of 1945. Then he wrote his mother about some beautiful objects that he had found abandoned in an old mine shaft.

In the next letter he said he was mailing

the beautiful things home to her and urged her to take care of them for him. In later letters, he frequently referred to the "beautiful things" he had mailed home, begging to know when they arrived safely. Soon Lieutenant Lawrence began to write that he was coming home, and then the letters stopped.

"This is dynamite!" she said to George. "Guess how the Litzenburg treasure got to Edgehill Street! Vincent Lawrence mailed it home to his mother. And his mother was Jill Murray's mother."

George read the relevant letters. They agreed it was sensational.

"All that happened in 1945 — that's a long time ago," said George.

"And it was twenty years ago that somebody — I guess it was Jill Murray — put the treasure in the box of old dresses," said McLeod.

"It must have been Jill Murray," said George. "I can't think that somebody else would hide valuables in one of those boxes. It's amazing if she did it, but even more unbelievable if somebody else did it. It's lunchtime. Would you like a sandwich?"

"Sure," said McLeod.

"What kind?"

"Anything."

"Anything?"

"I'll eat anything. I'm thinking."

So she ate her peanut butter and jelly sandwich — George's looked much more imposing, she noticed, but she didn't care. She liked peanut butter. And she was indeed thinking.

"Dante Immordino put those boxes up on the rafters and he didn't sound like it was fifty years ago, either," she said when she had finished her sandwich. "We don't know when she hid the treasure in the garage, and we don't know why she did it. It wasn't a very safe place, certainly. But somehow — thanks to Little Big's indolence in not cleaning out the garage — it survived all these years."

When George brought her an Eskimo Pie for dessert, she thanked him. "I love Eskimo Pies," she said. "I didn't know there were any in the freezer. So if the burglar was looking for the treasure, it was somebody that knew the treasure was here in the first place, right? Somebody in the family? At least, somebody who knew the family?"

"It would seem so," said George.

"After he found out about the burglaries, Nick said he wanted to talk to Dante. I wonder if he did."

"Ask him," suggested George.

"I'd like to talk to Dante myself."

"You should see him soon. There's supposed to be heavy snow tomorrow. I'm going to the grocery store for more blizzard supplies. In fact, I think I'll call Dante and book him in advance for shoveling when the snow's over."

"I'll call him for you," said McLeod. "And you can go to the grocery store."

"I know you're dying to talk to him. I'll be off as soon as we make a list."

The next few minutes were very pleasant, as they discussed what they'd eat if they were snowbound for a while.

"Remember the Friends' dinner is tonight," George said. "But what can we have tomorrow and Monday, if it really snows hard?"

When George left, McLeod called Dante. He said that sure he'd come around as soon as it stopped snowing. He had planned to do that anyway, it seemed.

"Dante," she said, "do you remember those boxes we took out of the garage, the ones from the rafters? You said Mrs. Murray had asked you to put them up there."

"Yes," said Dante.

"Do you remember when you put them up there?"

"When I put them up there?" Dante said after a pause.

"That's right. When did you put them up there?"

"Oh. It was before Mrs. Murray died."

Duh, thought McLeod. She hadn't thought Mrs. Murray had asked him to put the boxes up there after she died. "Can you remember how long before she died?" she asked.

"It wasn't long," said Dante. "It was the last thing I did for her."

"Thanks, Dante," said McLeod. "See you soon, I guess."

"I want to talk to Little Big Murray about all this and I want to talk to Chester about a couple of things," McLeod told George when he got home from the grocery store.

"Be careful with Bigelow Murray," said George. "After all, his mother was murdered. And let me make it clear, I don't want to have either one of those people to dinner — a dinner invitation seems to be a key factor in your investigations."

"That was not my intention," said McLeod coldly. "It's just that, you know, my mind is like a rat in a cage. It goes from the treasure-slash-burglary to the murder in the library and back and forth."

"Think about food," said George. "It's more practical."

"I think about food all the time. I think I'll make that stew with chicken thighs for tomorrow night. It's a sort of poor man's coq au vin. And the recipe says to make it a day ahead and let it sit in the refrigerator. You got the thighs and the mushrooms and everything, didn't you?"

"I did, but you don't have to cook. I can do it."

"No, I want to do it. I'll take some to Chester when it's done. I want to ask him some questions, and he'll have the stew if he's snowed in tomorrow," said McLeod.

"You and Chester," said George. "You two are practically an item."

"Poor Chester. I feel sorry for him. But I'd better call him and see if he can use some food."

When McLeod phoned Chester, he said he certainly could use some food, and she set to work in the kitchen. When the stew was ready, she told George she'd just walk over to Hibben Road with it.

"McLeod, it's bitter cold outside," said George.

"I need the exercise," said McLeod. "I haven't been out all day."

"I never knew anybody whose curiosity was so great they'd walk a mile in the freezing cold to ask somebody some questions

— and take them dinner besides."

"Now you do," said McLeod. "And it's not a mile, even round trip. It's not even a quarter of a mile to Hibben Road." She put on her boots, heavy coat, hat, gloves, and scarf. She settled dishes in a big basket and set out.

Chester thanked her profusely for the food and emptied the basket so she could take it back. "Won't you sit down a minute?" he said. "Rest up before you walk back."

"How are things going?" she asked him as he brushed his hair out of his eyes and looked at her hopefully.

"About the same," he said. "The police still suspect me of killing the man who was my benefactor and my boss and my friend." He was clearly morose.

"Chester, help me find the real murderer and then nobody will suspect you anymore."

Chester looked puzzled. "How can I help you? I'll do anything I can to help find out who killed Mr. Sheridan, you know that." He was more endearing than ever in his earnestness. "I really will. But how do you think you can find the murderer?"

"By talking to people. Asking questions."

"You want me to talk to somebody? I wouldn't know how to do that."

"No, I want you to talk to me. You knew

Philip Sheridan better than anyone else did. You must know some reason that someone had for killing him."

"I don't, not really," said Chester. "I've told you that before."

"Let me ask you about something then," said McLeod. "It's about Fanny Mobley."

"Yes." Chester grinned at her. "What about Miss Mobley?"

"There's something about her that I wonder if Mr. Sheridan knew. First, somebody told me that Philip Sheridan disapproved of Fanny's handling of certain manuscripts. Is that true?"

"In a way. You have to understand that Mr. Sheridan was a perfectionist, and he thought that everybody should be held to high standards. I think it may be putting it too strongly to say he disapproved of her methods for caring for manuscripts, but he did mention ways that she could improve. But he thought everybody could do better."

"But he wasn't critical of her to the extent that he was a threat to her? I mean, she wouldn't have reason to kill him?" McLeod asked.

"McLeod, I don't think anybody had a reason — a valid reason — to kill Mr. Sheridan."

"I see your point. But the question is,

would a person, a neurotic person, maybe think Philip Sheridan was a threat to him or her?"

"I guess the people in Rare Books are funny, aren't they?" said Chester. "I know that. Not funny — neurotic. And Mr. Sheridan had his little quirks, too."

"Speaking of quirks, did Philip Sheridan change his mind a lot?"

"As a matter of fact, he did."

"Did it annoy anybody in Rare Books?"

"Not really. Not enough to murder him," said Chester. "I just can't see murder in the picture."

"Chester, murder is in the picture, whether you can see it or not. You told me about some strain between Mr. Sheridan and Mr. Ledbetter. Have you thought what that was about?"

"I have, actually," said Chester. "Because of some things that happened yesterday."

"What happened yesterday?"

"I'd rather not say," said Chester.

"Oh, come on," said McLeod. "Tell me."

"Well, Mr. Ledbetter was breaking some rules. I'm afraid you'll hear about it next week."

McLeod sighed. "Okay, but about Buster Keaton. Did Mr. Sheridan disapprove of him, too?"

"I've thought about this a lot since you asked me about all these people. By and large Mr. Sheridan thought Mr. Keaton was really good at his job. He admired his single-minded devotion to rare books. I think — I don't know for sure — I couldn't swear in court — but I think he had doubts about his — I don't know — his personal life."

"What about his personal life?"

"McLeod, I'd rather not say. Once you say something, it's out there, like a solid substance."

This was tough going; Chester was being downright obstructive. "One more question," she said.

Chester waited.

"Back to Fanny Mobley. There's one thing about her. I don't know whether it's true or not. Would it have annoyed Philip Sheridan so that he would be a threat to her?"

"What?" asked Chester.

"Alcohol."

"Oh, that." Chester actually laughed out loud. "Oh, yes, Mr. Sheridan knew about the way she drank. He thought it was amusing. Once in a while he'd have a little tipple with her in the afternoon. She doesn't drink much, you know. Never in the morning and a bit for lunch and little bits along toward the end of the day."

"Well, there goes my great motive for murder," said McLeod. And she laughed along with Chester. "You see, I thought perhaps he had found her out and threatened to report her, or something. And she had killed him."

"Oh, no, he wouldn't report it. And anyway there isn't anybody he could have reported it to. Mr. Ledbetter knows about it."

"You've just eliminated Fanny as a suspect — at least in my mind," said McLeod with a sigh of regret. "But can't you think of somebody else who might have killed him?"

"No, I can't," Chester said. "I told you about the cross words between Mr. Sheridan and Mr. Ledbetter — I guess they were cross words. I can't even remember anything anymore."

"But you did tell the police about that little — little whatever it was?"

"Yes, I did. Nobody seemed to think it was important."

McLeod had to leave it at that. She was, she thought as she walked home in the snow, more mystified than ever about the murder.

TWENTY-SIX

McLeod came down the stairs as dressed up as it was possible for her to be when she was without her full wardrobe, which was 1,100 miles away. She wore her long black skirt and a new glittery pink sweater that she had bought at Talbot's, hoping Dodo would think it was from some place much more exotic.

George was waiting in the hall, resplendent in black tie and dinner jacket. "Let's get going," he said. "The Friends' dinner starts early — drinks at six o'clock, dinner at seven, and it's after six now. You look very nice," he added almost as an afterthought.

"So do you," said McLeod. "I'll hurry, but it takes me forever to put on all my wraps." She began with her heavy coat, added gloves, muffler, and woolly hat. "Is it a cash bar?"

"Oh, no, drinks come with it. The Friends

pride themselves on that."

"Oh, is this what Dodo wanted Philip Sheridan to buy champagne for? I'm ready."

"I guess this is the occasion." George had slung on his black overcoat and the big wide-brimmed black hat that had enchanted her when they first met. "We're off," he said, offering his arm.

"To see the blizzard," said McLeod.

"Hope we get home before it starts. Careful on the steps."

"I can't help but think there is a connection between the murder and the treasure," McLeod said as they drove toward the Graduate College, where the Friends' dinner was to be held. "I wish we knew why the treasure was in your garage. And who came after it?"

"Your friend the policeman pointed out the connection between the burglaries and the treasure," said George. "But I don't see a connection between the treasure, as we call it, and the murder of a big Princeton benefactor in the Rare Book Department of the library."

"Rare books in both cases?" said McLeod.

"That's true — rare books are involved in both cases. Hmmm. Well, here we are."

They arrived at the Graduate College

parking lot and hurried to Procter Hall. The dining hall was modeled on the medieval halls in the colleges at Cambridge, complete with high table, vaulted, timbered ceiling, and tall Gothic windows.

Natty, looking gray as usual, in spite of his black tuxedo, golden cummerbund, and glistening white shirt, greeted them — "dear boy" and "dear lady" — but without his usual effusion. He seemed, to McLeod, to be rather subdued. "Do have a martini," he said almost absently, waving toward the bar.

McLeod had never seen so many stout, gray-headed men in tuxedos. But then there were even more white-haired ladies in long dresses. She decided there was an undeniable overlap between the membership of the Friends of the Library and the geriatric citizens of Princeton. Dodo Westcott, who looked positively juvenile in this company, came over to greet them.

"Isn't this wonderful?" she said. "Such a good turnout. But I do miss poor Philip. Natty said this would be a kind of memorial to him. Actually, I hope he doesn't make it too gloomy. Gloom turns donors off, you know."

"I'm sure he won't be too gloomy," George said, "but surely it's appropriate to remember Philip Sheridan at the Friends' dinner."

Dodo, as usual, hadn't really listened to this. "Oh, there's our featured speaker. I must go see if he needs anything," she said, and rushed off to intercept a dapper little man who had just arrived.

"So that's August Martin," McLeod said to George. "I thought he'd be bigger."

"He's big enough. He's a world figure," said George.

McLeod wished that sometime, just once, George would not be so defensive about everything concerning Princeton University. Of course, August Martin was a world figure: A professor in the Near Eastern Studies Department, his every word on the touchiest part of the world was listened to with respect by governments, journalists, and academics; his books, scholarly to the core yet accessible to the lay reader, sold in the millions. He was a jewel in the crown of the Princeton faculty. Still, he was physically an awfully small man. McLeod wondered if it was Dodo or Natty who had secured him to speak at the Friends' dinner. Whoever did it, it was a coup, she thought.

George then startled her by introducing her to Polly Griffin. McLeod, prepared to dislike any girlfriend of George's, stared at her. She was sorry to see that Polly was very nice looking — and not white haired. In fact, her hair was glorious, long, shiny, straight, and parted in the middle and shaped into a French twist at the back of her head. "I'm so glad to know you," Polly said. "George has said wonderful things about you."

"Oh, good," said McLeod inanely, admiring Polly's straight black sheath that fell gracefully to the floor.

"Polly is at the art museum," said George.

"Yes, I just came to spy out the competition," said Polly.

"Competition?" said McLeod, feeling stupid.

"I work with the Friends of the Art Museum, and I suppose in a sense we're competitors."

"Oh," said McLeod. Was she ever going to think of anything remotely interesting to say? She didn't have to — Polly and George were in animated conversation together. She wandered off and, to her surprise, ran into Bigelow Murray, looking as huge as he had when she met him at Dodo's.

"Just the man I wanted to see," she said. George had warned her to be careful with Bigelow, but he couldn't kill her in front of all these rich, elderly Friends, and she was dying to ask him some questions.

"Oh?" he said.

She didn't want to bring up the treasure, but maybe she could work the conversation around to it. "You know Dante Immordino, don't you? Isn't he wonderful? He worked for your mother and now he works for George sometimes. He uses a snow shovel that was in the garage. Dante said it belonged to your mother and he says it's better than George's. Did you mean to leave it in the garage?"

"I don't know what I meant to do," said Bigelow. "I have to tell you that I hated that house after my mother died." He paused and then began to talk rapidly. "It was a crime scene for a long time. I'm sure you know my mother was murdered there and they never found out who did it. They even suspected me for a while. And then when I finally decided to sell the house — Mary didn't want to live there and neither did I — it was hard enough to clean out the house. I just gave up before I got to the garage. The real estate agent gave me hell about it, but I don't know — I just let it go. And the house finally sold."

"Oh, I ran across some letters," said McLeod. "Written during World War II from a Lieutenant Vincent Lawrence to his mother. Is he your uncle?"

"He was. Can I get you another drink?" He was not interested in the letters, and appeared to want to turn away from her.

"No, thanks," she said. "I wondered if you wanted the letters?"

He looked faintly puzzled. "Oh, I don't think so," he said. "Toss 'em out."

He left, a pained expression on his face.

She noticed that Dodo and Natty were urging people to find their places at the long tables. They had already swept the big shots to the head table — August Martin, the president of the Friends and his wife, the director of university libraries and his wife, the president of the university and his wife.

"Here you are," said George, who came up with Polly Griffin. "Let's find seats. Polly's going to sit with us."

"Good," said McLeod, gritting her teeth. George sat between her and Polly, and although Polly kept leaning over to try to engage McLeod in conversation, it was hard. McLeod talked to the man on her other side — an editor at the Princeton University Press — but for once did not ask him any questions. Her mind wandered during Natty's graceful remarks about Philip Sheridan, "who cannot be with us tonight," but she tried valiantly to listen to August Martin as he spoke with what she was sure was great learning and wit about the situation in the Middle East. She remembered nothing of what he said.

When she and George came out of Procter Hall after the dinner, it was snowing hard and the short drive home took a long time.

It snowed all night and all of Sunday morning. When the snow finally stopped Sunday afternoon, there was a thirteen-inch "accumulation," as the weatherman on the Philadelphia television station put it.

"No newspapers today," mourned McLeod. "I miss the Sunday papers."

"Too much snow," said George. "But I do believe it's stopped."

George had already started trying to shovel — and wasn't getting very far — when Dante appeared. The two of them worked together until the driveway and the sidewalk were cleared.

"I'm going to buy a snow blower," George announced when he and Dante came in, stomping their feet on the mat in the hall and peeling off their gloves.

"That's a good idea," said Dante.

"Have some hot chocolate," said McLeod.

Dante and George looked pleased and

took off their coats and followed her into the kitchen. They held the mugs in both hands for warmth. McLeod wondered how to begin asking Dante questions — she wished George would leave — but they were all three standing uncomfortably in the kitchen. "Let's sit down," she said, leading the way to the dining room table. "I'll get some cookies."

"I'm glad you two cleaned out that garage," George said when she came back with the cookies. "At least, we didn't have to dig out the cars. I saw the people across the street hard at it — it's awful when you have this much snow. When I lived in that apartment, I always had to dig out my car when it snowed. They plowed the parking lot, but the plow would throw up big drifts behind the cars that we had to shovel out of the way. Homeownership has a lot to offer. But then if you hadn't cleaned out the garage, we would have had to shovel out the cars here."

"Dante, I wanted to ask you something about that," McLeod said. "I mean when we cleaned out the garage."

"I'll just go upstairs and get my checkbook," said George and left.

"Dante, after we cleaned out the garage, did you happen to tell anybody about the box of dresses I brought in the house?"

A shadow flickered over Dante's face. "No, I didn't tell anybody about it. Why would I do that?"

"Did the police ask you about it?"

"No. Why would the police ask me about it?" Dante sounded panicky.

"Lieutenant Perry said he was going to get somebody to talk to you. Don't worry. There was something in the box besides dresses, and —"

"I don't know anything about what was in that box," said Dante. "You just said it was old clothes and you were going to give them to a student. I just carried the box inside for you."

"That's right. I remember that. Nobody's accusing you of anything, Dante. I just wondered if perhaps you told Mr. Murray — Little Big, as everybody calls him — about it."

"No, ma'am, I didn't tell Little Big anything."

George came back with his checkbook, wrote a check for the amount Dante named (it seemed rather large to McLeod, but what did she know about snow-shoveling prices?), gave it to him, and showed him to the door.

McLeod reflected while this was going on. Dante had looked distinctly odd when she asked him if he had told anybody about the box of dresses, but then he had forcefully and, she thought, convincingly, said that he had not told Little Big. If not Little Big, then who?

The chicken stew for dinner was a huge success.

"It was really smart of you to cook this ahead of time," George said. "Even if you did it just so you could go see Chester."

"He told me something very interesting. I forgot to tell you. Everybody knew about Fanny and her drinking. Chester says they didn't think it interfered with her work." She ate more chicken, and said, "I don't believe I've ever been so frustrated. Nobody's getting anywhere on the murder. And we don't know who was after the treasure. I don't think it was Little Big Murray. He doesn't seem interested in anything about the house. I was going to tell him about the treasure, and I did tell him about the letters, but he was totally uninterested. Totally."

"I don't believe he's interested in much of anything," said George.

"Of course, it could all be a front, but it was good enough to fool me," said McLeod.

TWENTY-SEVEN

On Monday morning, the world — at least the Princeton part of it — was bright and clear, with a blue sky arching over the snow-covered houses on Edgehill Street, the snow seeming to enhance their gingerbread trim. As she walked to work on the neatly shoveled sidewalks that lay between banks of snow, McLeod admired the two fat snowmen in front of one house on Mercer Street, and she liked the way snow lay on the trees. It made a white stripe on the black branches of the bare trees and dusted the needles of the evergreens. Since she was admiring the winter scene, she decided she must be getting used to cold and snow.

She stopped by Joseph Henry House to check her snail mail (nothing of interest), e-mail (two students wanted extensions for the assignment to write about a person in the arts, and Clark Powell protested that three students in McLeod's writing class wanted to interview him and he didn't have time for them all), and her voice mail (nothing). She e-mailed the two students her refusal to extend the deadline and told Clark Powell to suggest some other student workers in Theatre Intime to the people who wanted to interview him.

She decided to go to Rare Books and see if she could do some work on van Dyke. Surely by now she could resume her work on the box where the murder weapon had been found. If not, she could always start on another box. And she could find out what was going on, if anything, with the murder investigation.

In the exhibition gallery, she noticed the curtains were at last drawn open on the replica of Governor Belcher's office. So the crime scene was clear, she thought, as she looked through the glass at the desk and globe. It was almost two weeks since the murder.

In Rare Books she greeted Molly Freeman and signed in, hung up her wraps — winter was a lot of trouble, she thought for the thousandth time — and noticed that Derek the proctor was no longer seated in the reception area. She went to the Reading Room, where she gave Diane a call slip for the "Other Wise Man" box. She nodded at

Miss Swallow, who looked up briefly from the big book she was examining, and noticed a new researcher seated at an empty back table, apparently expecting something to be brought to him. She decided that while she was waiting for her box to come up, she would go see Natty.

He wasn't in his office, but McLeod loitered, knowing it would take a while for her box to appear in the Reading Room, and eventually Natty appeared.

"Dear lady," he said, walking with her into his office. "Forgive me. I've been downstairs, looking for something." He stood by his desk.

"Sit down, sit down," she said as she hastily sat down herself, as usual. Getting Natty to sit down was like a ballet, she thought. Someone should choreograph it. "I just wanted to congratulate you on finding those prints for Miss Swallow, the orchid prints. Where were they?"

"Round and about," said Natty. "Round and about."

"Come on, Natty, you know how curious I am."

"Dear lady," he said again but without his usual animation. He rubbed a pencil between his two hands and looked at her. "You know we have many, many storage facilities.

And I remembered one particular large cabinet with those wide shallow drawers. It isn't in the vault; it's in our storage area outside the vault, and I said, 'I just bet those prints are in one of those drawers.' And they were. I'm so glad they were there. Dear Miss Swallow. Such an interesting project that she has undertaken."

"You're wonderful, Natty, to find them." She stood up, and Natty automatically stood up, too. "I've got to get to work on van Dyke," she said.

"I'm so glad you're working on dear Henry."

Natty sounded very tired, McLeod thought as she made her way back to the Reading Room. She had just settled down at one of the tables with her paper and pencil before her when a page, the same one Diane had sent for the plastic bag when they found the letter opener, burst into the Reading Room.

"The vault! The gas is on! Chester's in there!"

Diane stared at him. Miss Swallow looked up. McLeod stood and walked over to Jeff. It was obvious that something serious was wrong, but she couldn't quite understand what it was.

"What is it?" she asked Jeff. "What is the matter?"

"Chester's lying on the floor in the vault. I think he's dead. He's blue. The gas is on."

"The gas?"

"The fire extinguisher gas. It kills you in twenty seconds!" said Jeff.

"Call 911," said McLeod to Diane.

Diane seemed paralyzed. Her hand moved slowly toward the phone, but couldn't quite make it. McLeod moved swiftly, dialed the phone, and spoke to the campus police, who said they'd be there right away.

"Take me to the vault," she said to Jeff.

"What is the matter in here? Diane, can't you keep order in the Reading Room?" It was, of course, Fanny Mobley in her morning mode.

Miss Swallow stood and said firmly, "Go ahead, McLeod. Miss Mobley, there is apparently an emergency. Do you know about the gas in the vault? Go on, McLeod."

McLeod followed Jeff, as he led her to the elevator and down to the door of the vault. He used his key, plus a combination, to open the door, and stood back to let McLeod enter. She sniffed, smelled nothing unusual, walked farther into the vault — then she saw Chester.

He was lying on the floor in one of the

bays of stacks.

"Come out now," said Jeff urgently. He was standing by the door, holding it open. "The gas can kill you in twenty seconds. Come on."

"We can't just leave Chester here, Jeff," said McLeod as she tried to lift Chester under his arms. "Help me get him out. We can try CPR."

Jeff took Chester's shoulders and McLeod his feet and together they dragged Chester out into the corridor. He was indeed quite blue. She tried to remember what she had learned in the CPR class years ago — lay the victim flat on his back, make sure he has not swallowed his tongue . . . tilt his head back while lifting his chin with the other hand . . . pinch his nose and breathe into his mouth . . .

By the time she put her mouth on his, a considerable number of staff people from Rare Books had arrived, as well as two men from public safety. She gratefully relinquished her place to a proctor who had had emergency medical training.

It was soon clear, however, that it was useless. Chester was dead.

Natty, looking even grayer than he had a short while ago, was consulting with Sean O'Malley, the director of public safety, who had just appeared. "He died in the vault?" asked O'Malley. "Who moved him?"

"I did," said McLeod. "Or we did. Jeff and I."

"The gas was on," said Jeff. "It will kill a person in twenty seconds."

"Dear God," said Natty. "Everybody get back upstairs."

Nobody moved.

"Did anyone turn off the gas? Jeff?" asked Natty.

"I don't know," said Jeff. "I don't know anything about it. All I know is they told me when I came here that it was a fire-extinguishing system and it was gas and it would kill a person in twenty seconds. It was still hissing. And now I've been in there twice . . ." He rolled his eyes and seemed about to faint.

"You'll be all right, Jeff," said McLeod. She wasn't sure, but it seemed best to encourage Jeff, who had clearly taken this lecture about the fire-extinguishing system very much to heart.

O'Malley, who had been talking on his cell phone to the police, said he would turn off the gas if someone would open the vault door. "The university uses halon gas here and in the storage areas of the art museum because it smothers a fire instantly."

"All right, everybody upstairs," said Natty again. "O'Malley will want to wait here, but everybody else must leave." The staff shuffled toward the elevator, but they moved slowly, almost unwillingly.

"Can't we move Chester someplace else?" said McLeod.

"Best not to move him," said Sean O'Malley. "Wait for the doctor and the police. You moved him once." His voice was reproving.

"I thought it was the best thing to do. It never occurred to me that what happened to him could be — well, foul play," she said.

"I have to sit down," said Natty. He went down an aisle of stacks and came back carrying a low, round library stool with a step in the side and set it firmly on the floor and sat down on it. "Everybody else please go upstairs. I'll stay, and McLeod, you can stay if you insist. Everybody else go upstairs."

O'Malley looked up as Buster Keaton escorted Dr. Winchester, Nick Perry, and another proctor from the elevator, where most of the staff was waiting to get on.

The doctor knelt beside Chester, while the others waited. McLeod thought it was all oddly like the scene in Governor Belcher's office ten days ago, when Philip Sheridan's body had been found.

Nick asked Sean O'Malley if one of the proctors could go upstairs and help Sergeant Popper make sure nobody left Rare Books.

Dr. Winchester got up and spoke to Nick Perry. "Clearly he died from lack of oxygen — you can see how blue he is — and of course, there will have to be an autopsy."

Nick Perry looked at O'Malley. "What can you tell me about this, Sean?"

"It looks like the halon fire-extinguishing system got him," said O'Malley.

"Was this where the gas reached him?"

"No, it was in the vault, Lieutenant," said O'Malley. He looked to Natty for confirmation. "Wasn't it?"

"I wasn't here. They said it was the vault," said Natty.

"It was in the vault," said McLeod, deciding it was time to speak up.

"You found him?" asked Perry, obviously surprised.

"No, I didn't. It was Jeff. Jeff's a page. He came running into the Reading Room. He was very upset. He said it was the gas and Chester was in the vault. I came back down with him and we pulled Chester out here to the corridor."

"You should not have moved him," said Perry.

"Beg your pardon, sir," said the proctor who had just arrived. "It's a good thing they moved him out here. The gas is still in the vault."

Everyone was quiet. Perry looked at McLeod. "I apologize, McLeod. Sean, tell me how the system works."

"The people at OSHA know more about it than I do — they inspect the system every six months," said O'Malley.

"OSHA?"

"Occupational Safety and Health. Here's what I know about it. Halon gas is a tetrafluoroethylene polymer. It's used in high concentration where people do not work and where a water-extinguishing system would do untold damage; it's used in museums to protect works of art and in libraries with rare books or manuscripts. Halon works by sucking the ozone out of the air. As I said, you can't use it in offices or in galleries or in reading rooms where people are working, but it's all right in the vault because people are in and out fairly quickly. Actually, the university was going to replace this system — it was outlawed under the Clean Air Act."

"And it's quite lethal?" Perry asked.

"It is quite lethal to humans."

"The system's automatic? Nobody can

turn it on?"

"It's heat responsive. If it feels heat, it starts expelling gas. But there's an alarm that goes off when it expels gas."

"Did anybody hear an alarm?" asked Perry. "Mr. Ledbetter?"

"I certainly heard nothing, and nobody said anything about an alarm," said Natty.

"Let me look at this extinguishing system," said Perry.

"Lieutenant, I have to go," said Dr. Winchester. "There's nothing more I can do here."

"Yes, Doctor, thank you. Somebody should be here from the Medical Examiner's Office. I want to look at this fire extinguisher."

"The vault is full of gas —"

"Just show me quickly," Perry interrupted. "Then I want to talk to Jeff and to McLeod."

"Mr. Ledbetter, can you let us into the vault?" O'Malley asked.

Natty rose painfully from the low stool and seemed to totter over to open the door. McLeod and the proctors stayed near Chester. She could hear O'Malley showing the tanks to Perry.

"All you'd have to do is hold a match or a cigarette lighter to the sensor," O'Malley was saying. "Look at this! The alarm is off!"

Perry said nothing. McLeod looked at Natty and the others. None of them seemed to be paying any attention. But if the alarm was turned off, that meant that Chester had almost certainly been murdered.

Twenty-eight

After they finally took Chester away, McLeod went upstairs to the Reading Room. Miss Swallow had apparently been waiting for her, and led her out to the chairs in the reception area.

"What happened?" she asked.

"You were great," said McLeod. "We were all just staring at each other and you told us to get going. And you handled Fanny beautifully."

"Thank you. She was quite undone when we heard that Chester was indeed dead. She invited me into her office and offered me a drink. She said, 'I keep a flask of brandy for emergencies,' and she poured each of us a glass. She said, 'You know, I'm British at heart, and they all keep brandy around for emergencies.' "

"Handy brandy," said McLeod. "We all need a shot. But you didn't have one, did you?"

"Oh, no. I told you my family history. Miss Mobley drank my shot after she had polished off hers."

"Well, let me tell you again: You were great," said McLeod.

"I've lived a long time, and I've seen many emergencies. Is it true that Chester was killed by the gas from the fire extinguisher system in the vault?"

"It's apparently true."

"What a terrible accident," said Miss Swallow.

"It wasn't an accident. It was murder," said McLeod, and told her all she knew.

"It's perfectly dreadful," said Miss Swallow. "So that's why they told none of us to leave." They looked at each other a moment. "Well, well, I guess I'll get back to work."

"I can't do any work. In fact, I'm surprised they haven't shut down. But even if they're open, I don't have a box up here and I'm sure they can't bring anything out of the vault right now. Anyway, I truly grieve for Chester. I liked him. He was so serious and so devoted to Philip Sheridan and he hated to say anything bad about anybody. And it upset him that he thought the police suspected him of Philip's murder."

"I'll talk to you later," said Miss Swallow, rising. "Maybe when they let us leave, we could have a bite of lunch."

"Let's do it — if we can," said McLeod.

She waited in the reception area until Sergeant Popper came to tell her that Lieutenant Perry would like to talk to her in the conference room. She followed him, and met Jeff coming out.

"Sit down, McLeod," said Nick. He intoned the date and the time and her name for the tape recorder. "Now tell me exactly what happened," he said.

McLeod told him about her call slip and Jeff's return to the Reading Room, her trip down to the vault with him, and finding Chester.

"Come show me exactly where you found him," said Nick, rising. He turned off the tape machine. "We've sealed off the vault temporarily, but we'll go down — I want you to show me exactly where the body was."

McLeod went down with him. An officer standing by the vault door, which was open but barred by yellow tape, let them in. Inside, crime-scene people were at work.

"Has the gas evaporated?" McLeod asked.

"It's on the way out. We brought in these big fans and they help."

McLeod showed him where Chester — she refused to think or speak of him as "the body" — had lain.

"Okay," said Nick. "Let's go back up." When they were back in the conference room, he turned the tape machine back on and asked her if she could give him any other information about the murder.

"No, I can't. I really can't. But Nick, let me ask you something. Are you sure Chester was murdered? Couldn't the alarm system have gone off by itself? Who would turn on the fire extinguisher gas to kill somebody? Why didn't Chester just leave, too?"

"We'll know more after the autopsy."

"You mean he might have been unconscious when the fire extinguisher went on?"

"We'll know more later."

"Tell me this, then. Is Chester's murder, if it is murder, connected to Philip Sheridan's murder?"

"It's too early to say. I'm afraid I have to ask you the questions right now."

McLeod glared at him. "Just one more question. You said the break-ins at George's house and at my office were connected to the things I found in the garage. Is all that connected to either murder, if Chester was murdered?"

"Too many iffy questions," said Nick. "We'll know more later. Back to business.

Where were you this morning from nine o'clock on?"

"I walked to my office — I left home about nine-thirty. Then I came over to Rare Books. I stopped in to see Natty Ledbetter. I was in the Reading Room when Jeff came roaring in. That was about ten-thirty, I guess. And the rest you know." She looked at her watch. It was already two o'clock. No wonder she felt hungry. "But look, I can't be a suspect," she said to Nick. "If it was a murder, the murderer had to have access to the vault and that means it would have to be somebody on the staff, doesn't it?"

"Does it?" said Nick noncommittally. "You saw a good deal of Chester Holmes after Philip Sheridan's murder, didn't you? Do you have any idea who might have wanted to kill him?"

"I can't imagine," said McLeod.

"Have you anything else to tell me about him? Anything at all?"

"Nothing, Nick. Except that he was a dear boy and I had become very fond of him. He was crazy about Philip Sheridan, and I always thought you were crazy to suspect him of killing him. If Chester was murdered, too, I guess that clears him, doesn't it?"

"We'll see," said Nick, apparently determined not to give one single thing away.

"That's all, McLeod. Thanks very much for your help."

"Can you leave now?" asked Miss Swallow when McLeod appeared in the reception area. "Can you eat lunch?"

"I can leave, but can you?"

"Oh, yes. When it was determined that I didn't know Chester and that I had no way of getting into the vault, they let me go, too. Where shall we eat? It's too late for the café at Chancellor Green. The Annex? Frist?"

They settled on Frist, the still-new student center, and made their way carefully on walks that were slushy in spite of having been shoveled. When they got to Frist, they ordered pizza because it looked so good. They sat at a table by the big south-facing windows and looked out at the snow-covered plaza between them and Guyot Hall, whose window ledges and roof-top parapets were white with snow. It was warm inside Frist. We must be a pretty sight, thought McLeod — two white-haired women gobbling up pizzas in the student center.

"I was hungry, really hungry," said McLeod when she had finished.

"Me, too."

Miss Swallow had not been as ravenous as she; she was leaving uneaten a portion of her slice of anchovy/olive/cheese pizza. Miss Swallow was much more ladylike than she was, McLeod thought; she wondered if she could possibly spear her friend's uneaten pizza.

"Can you eat my leftovers?" asked Miss Swallow, reading her mind.

"Thanks so much. I was eyeing them covetously," said McLeod.

Miss Swallow smiled and did not say she had noticed. "Did you learn anything more from that nice policeman?" she asked.

"Of course not," said McLeod. "He never divulges information." Except that time he came calling, she thought. "He just picks other people's brains relentlessly."

"You know, something else that's very interesting has happened," said Miss Swallow. "You saw that man in the Reading Room?"

"Yes. Who is he?"

"His name is Allen Weinberg, and he's here to look at some bird books and bird prints. It's quite a coincidence that we're here at the same time, isn't it? Birds and flowers. Anyway, a couple of bird prints he wanted to see are missing. Like me, he saw them here once before, but they have no record of them now. I told him about my orchid prints and how helpful Mr. Ledbetter had been and he said he would ask Natty for his help, too."

"Did Natty know where they are?"

"I don't think so. He didn't say. He just shook his head and said he and the staff would all look for them."

"Poor man," said McLeod. "I meant Allen Weinberg, but poor Natty, too. He's had two murders and two cases of missing prints. He looked awful this morning."

TWENTY-NINE

When they left Frist, McLeod said she would go back to her own office since there was nothing she could work on now at Rare Books. "Keep in touch," she said, and told Miss Swallow her telephone number, "in case anything else happens."

She settled down in her cubicle with a legal pad in front of her, seriously trying to plan Thursday's class. The phone rang. It was Buster Keaton.

"I'm sorry I didn't see you before you left here," he said. "Can I come over to your office? I'm about to leave now."

McLeod glanced at her watch — it was quite late, almost five o'clock. "Come ahead," she said. "Do you know where it is?"

"Third floor of Joseph Henry House? Right. I'll be there instantly."

Very soon he arrived, puffing from climbing the stairs, unzipping his fat down jacket.

"Those stairs!" he said. "Murder."

McLeod shivered. "Don't say the word 'murder,' " she said. "But everybody does complain about the stairs."

"And nobody does anything about them," said Buster. "I hope it's all right if I barge in like this. Can I talk to you a minute?"

"Sure. What about?"

"I'll explain if I can sit down," said Buster, looking around.

"We'd better go downstairs where there are some chairs." Buster followed her. "Would you like some tea?" she asked when they had reached the sun room.

"No, thanks, I just want to talk to you."

"Can I ask you something first?" said McLeod. "How many people knew about the fire-extinguishing system in the vault? Nobody ever mentioned it to me before today."

"I don't have any idea," said Buster. "What was there to know? It isn't a sprinkler system because water would do too much damage. It's gas. That's all there is to it."

"Did everybody know you could activate it with heat?"

"I never thought about it," said Buster. "But isn't that true of any automatic fire extinguisher system?"

"I never thought about it either. I just

310

wondered if the staff talked about it, if it was general knowledge."

"I don't know. I'm sorry."

"That's all right," said McLeod. "You said you wanted to talk to me."

"Yes, I tried to reach George Bridges, but he's so busy dealing with the press about the second murder that his secretary said he couldn't even talk to me on the telephone, much less see me in his office."

"Poor George," said McLeod. "What can I do for you? I can't speak for George."

"I know, I know. But you can tell him something for me, can't you? It's about Natty. I know he really cares about Natty." Buster paused and McLeod waited. "You see, I've had to report Natty. I hated to do it, but in all good conscience, I felt that I had to." He paused again, looking, McLeod thought, terribly sad.

"What do you mean — you had to report Natty?"

"I had to squeal," said Buster.

"To whom?"

"To the director of libraries, who took it to Tom."

"Tom?"

"Tom Blackman, the president of the university."

"Of course. What on earth did you think

Natty had done?"

"I didn't 'think'; I knew," said Buster.

"Well, what is it?"

"Natty has been stealing from the Department of Rare Books and Special Collections."

"I don't believe it," said McLeod.

"You better believe it."

McLeod stared at him.

"I know it's a shock to you, and I know it's going to be a shock to George, a terrible shock," said Buster. "And I want George to know that I hated to do what I did. But I felt that I had to put a stop to what was going on . . ."

McLeod stood up and looked out the window at Nassau Hall iced with white and sitting in the midst of blinding bright snow that covered Cannon Green behind it. She turned back to stare at Buster. "You had to do it?"

"Yes, I had to do it. Because, you see, I felt that it was never going to stop unless I did something. And I couldn't stand to see the collection being pillaged like that. You know how I care about the things that are there."

"I suppose so. Yes, I guess you had to put a stop to it." She sat down again and tried to smile at him. "But what was he — oh, taking?" She found she could not use the word "stealing."

"Prints mostly. You know we have a lot of uncatalogued prints, and he was regularly helping himself to them."

"You mean like Miss Swallow's flower prints? And that man's bird prints?"

"Those are the two cases that brought things to a head," Buster said. "Fanny and I had long suspected something was rotten in the department, but those two losses put the spotlight on him."

"But he found the orchid prints! Miss Swallow was so impressed and so pleased!"

"He found the orchid prints because he had them at his house. He hadn't sold them yet, and he brought them back to the library the next day after Miss Swallow raised such a fuss."

"You're sure?" asked McLeod.

"I'm sure," said Buster.

"You mean they weren't in that cabinet with the wide drawers?"

"They were in that cabinet because he brought them in early the next morning, before anybody else on the staff got there."

"You're sure?" McLeod asked again.

"I'm sure, I'm sure," said Buster. "And furthermore, he has admitted it."

"This is terrible," said McLeod.

"It is. And I know how he and George have always been close. I just want George to know how sorry I am for my part in it."

"Of course," said McLeod. "I understand. I'll tell him what you've said. If I ever see him again, that is. He's been very busy, and from what you say, he's going to be even busier. He will probably be very late tonight. And he usually goes to work before I get downstairs, but when I see him, I'll tell him."

"Thanks, McLeod. I am so sorry about it all. I was — still am — quite fond of Natty Ledbetter."

"I know. Who wouldn't be? Did you really have to report him? Did you ask him about it first?"

"I asked him about it," said Buster. "And he admitted it, or practically did. I felt I had no choice."

"I guess you didn't," said McLeod.

"But you know, McLeod, there's something else that worries me. What if there's something else, something really bad?"

"What do you mean?"

"I mean what if Natty knew that somebody else knew about what he had done? And what if Natty wanted to cover up what he had done? And what if he took violent action against that person who knew? What about that?"

"You mean he might take violent action against you?"

"No, McLeod. He can't cover up anymore. But what if before I presented him with the evidence, somebody else had found out what he was doing and had threatened to expose him?"

"Who do you mean — 'somebody else'?"

"Think," said Buster. "What if Philip Sheridan, and then Chester, had found out that he'd been taking pieces of the collection home?"

"Do you think that's what happened? And then you're implying that Natty took 'violent action' against them?"

"I'm just worrying about it, McLeod. I don't know what to think."

"Chester did tell me that he heard Philip shouting at Natty," said McLeod.

"There you go," said Buster. "I think he's the murderer. I'm really concerned."

"Oh, that can't be true," said McLeod. "It's impossible."

"Is it?" said Buster.

THIRTY

McLeod barely had time to get back to her office when Dodo Westcott appeared, luxuriously attired in a mink coat and hat.

"Those stairs," puffed Dodo. "They're terrible."

"Everybody says that," said McLeod. "It's part of having an office on the third floor. How are you, Dodo?"

"I want to talk to you," said Dodo. "You always help me see things more clearly."

"I don't see how I do that," said McLeod. She stood up, resigned to getting no work done at all. "Let's go downstairs where we can sit in comfortable chairs," she said. On the first floor, McLeod waved Dodo to a chair. "Take off that beautiful coat and sit down. I'll get some tea. You'll have some, won't you?"

"Love it," said Dodo.

When McLeod came back with two mugs of tea, Dodo had taken off her coat and hat and looked as fashionable as usual in a turquoise suit. She took her mug of tea and held it gratefully in both hands. McLeod sat down. "Now what did you want to talk about?"

"The murder, of course. You were so helpful to me last time, and I appreciate it."

"Oh, Dodo, I wasn't helpful at all. And I have to say you were wrong, weren't you?"

"What do you mean?"

"I mean that the last time you came over here, Philip Sheridan had just been killed and you were certain that Chester had done it."

"Well?" said Dodo. "How do you mean I was wrong?"

"Isn't it obvious? I never thought Chester would have killed Philip. And now Chester's been murdered himself, so it seems clear to me that he didn't kill Philip."

"I don't see it that way. Not at all. I think that somebody was so furious with Chester for killing Philip that this person killed Chester in revenge."

McLeod pondered this for a minute. Could Dodo be serious? "Who is this somebody?"

"It could be anybody, couldn't it? Anybody on the staff, that is. Jeff, or one of the other pages. Somebody in conservation.

One of the curators. Fanny, Natty, Randall."

"Randall?" she asked.

"Randall Keaton."

"Oh, Buster." McLeod was still at a loss. "It's an interesting idea," she finally said, although she thought it was an insane idea.

"Do you think I should tell the police?"

Dodo was crazy, McLeod thought. Demented. After the first murder she had asked McLeod if she should tell the police her suspicions of Chester. Now she was wondering whether to tell the police about her suspicions of everybody else. "If you think you should, then tell the police," she said at last, thinking that there must be something she didn't understand.

"Thank you so much. You always see everything so clearly," said Dodo, getting up and reaching for the gorgeous coat. "And how's George?"

"Fine," said McLeod. "I don't see much of him these days. He works very hard."

"You must come over to our house again soon. We enjoyed you both so much. Thanks again." And Dodo was gone.

She's so crazy that she's probably the murderer, McLeod thought as she rinsed the mugs out in the tiny kitchenette of Joseph Henry House. She could be a homicidal maniac. Except that Dodo did not have access to the vault. Then she had a thought: Chester could have let her in the vault. Dodo did go downstairs and she could easily have asked Chester to let her in on some excuse or other. She wished she had not thought of that possibility.

That night she waited up for George to come home. When he had called to say he'd be very late, she had decided to cook something that could be heated up whenever he arrived. A big pot of beef stew was the result. While it simmered, she built a fire and sat down to work on George's sweater.

When George did appear, he attacked the stew, thanked her with his mouth full, and ate ravenously.

"I'm sorry you had to stay so late. Was it because of dealing with the press? I thought you were thrilled with the new communication man — Chuck Hammersmith. You said he could handle the press so well when Philip Sheridan was murdered," she said.

"Chuck is good," George said, with another mouthful impeding his speech again. "He's really good. But the press was at its worst today. Television cameramen were demanding to see the vault, and we just couldn't open up the place to the world.

The print people were asking if the library was a safe place for people to do research, for students to use, for the staff to work. 'Two murders in less than two weeks!' they kept shrieking. Chuck sent the most troublesome ones over to me, and he dealt as best he could with the more reasonable ones." He stopped talking and ate steadily.

"But you had a hard day, too, I know," he said at one point between bites. "You found another body."

"No, Jeff found it. But then I went down and tried to do CPR on poor Chester. It was pretty awful." She tried to think of a bright spot and finally said, "I didn't have to work late like you did."

"Something else came up today that unnerved me," he said, laying his knife and fork across his plate. "I think I'll have a brandy. Want one?"

"Sure," said McLeod.

"Let's sit over here." He led the way to the two armchairs in the bay window and handed her a snifter.

"What was it that unnerved you?" asked McLeod. "Was it about Natty?"

"Oh, you knew about it?"

"Buster Keaton came over to tell me about it. He was terribly upset. He wanted to talk to you but your secretary told him you were too busy to talk to him."

"I was," said George. "I could have called him back tonight or tomorrow, I guess. Tom had already told me about it. Talk about awful days. It's been a super bad day for Tom and for the director of libraries. But Tom knows how much I like and admire old Nat. He does, too, of course."

"What's not to like?" asked McLeod.

"Exactly," said George, and then added, "except that he's a thief."

"Are you sure of that?"

"Oh, yes. He admits it."

"This is the saddest thing I ever heard of," said McLeod, and it did feel that way, in spite of the two murders.

"It is even sadder when you think about why he did it," said George.

"What do you mean? Why did he do it?"

"For his wife. I think I told you that she had Alzheimer's, and she's in a very nice home. It's incredibly expensive, and Natty just didn't have the wherewithal to pay the bills."

"What will he do now? And what will happen to him?"

"Nobody wants to prosecute him, but he can't possibly stay on at Rare Books. It's not final, but I think he'll be allowed to retire. He's past retirement age. And Philip

Sheridan left him some money. Sheridan, it seems, knew about Natty's situation and always planned to help him out. At least he can use the bequest to make restitution."

"Poor Natty," said McLeod. "We'll have to have him over for dinner."

"I knew you'd say that!" said George. "That's your remedy for anything, but I guess it's a good remedy."

McLeod got up and began to clear George's dishes from the table. When George tried to help, she told him she could do it and she would load the dishwasher and turn it on. "You must be exhausted," she said.

"I am," he said.

She lingered in the kitchen, thinking about Natty. Had he known about the inheritance from Philip Sheridan? And had Philip known about the thefts, and was that what the shouting had been about? It appeared that Natty did have a good motive for both murders. But he couldn't be a murderer. If Natty had killed Chester, he would have had to do it just before she talked to him that morning — no, Natty couldn't be a murderer. But then who would have thought he could be a thief?

THIRTY-ONE

Tuesday was cold and clear — and the snow was still there when McLeod looked out her bedroom window about seven o'clock on Tuesday morning. Gray crusts already topped the tall banks of snow along the street and on either side of the sidewalk.

McLeod sighed and thought about what she would do this day. She took a shower, dressed, and went downstairs to find George still at home, reading the paper and drinking coffee.

"Good morning, Sunshine," he said. "You're up early."

"You're here late," she said. "It's good to see you at home in the morning."

"And to see you," said George, smiling at her. "Chuck Hammersmith said he'd get in early today, so I'll let him handle the first wave of media. Then I'll stay late if I have to. What's on your plate today?"

"I've got to plan my class for Thursday.

But I thought since the streets look clear today, if it's all right with you, I'd take those World War II letters around to the Murrays. The letters are from Big's uncle to his, Big's, grandmother. I don't think Vincent Lawrence had any children, did he?"

"I have no idea."

"Anyway, those letters are on my mind."

"Didn't you tell me that Big Murray told you to throw them out?"

"He did, but I thought I'd ask his wife. Somebody must want them."

"McLeod, you took the treasure away without telling me. I don't think you should give away anything else."

"George, when I took that box of dresses over to the university, I had no idea what else was in it. One thing led to another."

"I know. I shouldn't have said that. But don't give the letters away. They show how the treasure got here. If the treasure does belong to the Litzenburg cathedral, those letters will absolve us of any blame. Not that I think anybody's going to blame you or me, but still — don't give them away, for heaven's sake."

"You're right," said McLeod.

"At any rate, I've got to start the process of returning the things to Litzenburg. If I ever get a minute, I will."

"Can I help with that?" asked McLeod.

"I'll talk to the university lawyer as soon as I get time."

"I'll be happy to talk to Cowboy Tarleton about it, if that would be a help."

"Why don't you?" said George. "It would be a tremendous help to me."

"And I'll find out how to make contact with the right people in Litzenburg, too. Buster Keaton will know — that catalog of stolen art should have that, shouldn't it?"

"Great."

If I can't take the letters to Mary Murray, thought McLeod as George went back to the newspaper, I'll have to dream up some other excuse to go see her.

After George left, as McLeod was getting ready to go out, she decided that she could tell Mary she was going to write a story about the Murder House. No, that might put her off completely. She couldn't just drop in — people didn't do that anymore. Well, she'd telephone Mary and see if she could come by, and if she could, then she'd think of something on the way.

Mary Murray said of course she could come by. "I have to go to a meeting now, though," she warned. "How about this afternoon?"

After they had settled on four o'clock,

325

McLeod decided to go to the university and see Buster before she called Cowboy Tarleton. She walked up from the parking garage, all the way up Elm Drive, past the construction for the new residential college where the tennis courts used to be, past Dillon Gym, and on to the library. Rare Books was open, and researchers were at work in the Reading Room, even though the police were still around.

McLeod looked in Buster's door.

"Come in, come in," he said. "How did George take the news about Natty? Sit down."

"He had heard it, of course — from Tom Blackman. And as you thought he would be, he was very sorry for Natty. And he doesn't blame you for reporting him."

"Good. I'm glad of that."

"But you don't really think Natty did the murders, do you?"

"He just seems to be the most likely candidate at the moment," said Buster. "Of course, I'm not going to say anything like this to the police."

"It does seem unlikely to me," said McLeod. "Character means something, doesn't it? Natty just isn't capable of murder."

"He was capable of stealing."

"But think of why he did it," said McLeod. "When you think about why Natty did it, it's very hard to condemn him, isn't it?"

"What do you mean, why he did it?" asked Buster.

"Because of his wife. She has Alzheimer's and she's in that expensive private care place and he didn't have the money to pay for it."

"I didn't know that," said Buster. "Still, stealing's stealing, isn't it?"

"I guess so," said McLeod. "And that brings me to why I'm here. George wants to know the address of the church — or cathedral — in Litzenburg. He wants to return the *Gospels* and the other things."

"I thought George was going to give the *Gospels* to Princeton," said Buster. "I was really excited about this new addition to our collection."

"He says he can't give it to you; it's not his to give. It's Litzenburg's."

"Return them to Litzenburg? That's crazy. It's been so long they probably don't even know about them," said Buster.

"They're listed in that roster of stolen art," said McLeod.

"They may have forgotten they ever listed it."

"Well, as you say, 'stealing's stealing.' "

"Maybe sometimes it isn't." Buster did not sound convinced.

"You and George can get this settled," said McLeod. "When George has time."

"Who has time? With Natty gone, I have to do two jobs."

"Are you the new director?"

"Of course not, but I have to do all the work. They'll bring in some outsider who doesn't know the first thing about rare books and we'll have to train him. But for now, I'm doing the best I can. And the police are still around — it's so disorganized. I thought we should close, but the powers-that-be vetoed that. Oh, well, we'll manage."

As soon as McLeod came into the Reading Room, Miss Swallow got up and drew her out to speak to her.

"That nice policeman, the one who seems to be in charge, was asking me about you."

"You mean Nick Perry, the lieutenant?"

"That's the one. He asked me if you would be in today. I had to say I didn't know whether you would or not."

"You mean he questioned you about the case today?"

"Yes, they are now interviewing everybody who was in Rare Books yesterday. It's wonderful that they have such good records of everybody who comes in. Anyway, they've realized that the killer didn't have to have the combination to the vault himself, that the young man, the victim, could have let the murderer into the vault if he, or she, had a plausible excuse."

"You know I was thinking that about Dodo," said McLeod. "I really think she's crazy."

"I see what you mean," laughed Miss Swallow. "But aren't we all?"

"Did Nick Perry want to see me about the case? Do you know where he is?"

"No, I don't. He may still be interviewing people in the conference room."

"Thanks, I'll find him."

She looked through the glass windows and saw that Nick was indeed in there, with Lieutenant Popper and no suspect. He must have felt her gaze upon him, because he looked up and saw her. He got up immediately and came out, drawing her to one side of the work area.

"Can I come by again tonight?" he asked.

"Come for dinner," she said.

"It couldn't be until pretty late. Why don't I just come by late?"

"You need to eat. I'll wait for you. What time can you make it? Nine?"

"I'll try to get there by nine. Go ahead and eat if I'm too late. Really."

"It will be fine, Nick. I'll cook something. It won't be elaborate. I'd love to talk to you."

"Thanks," Nick said. "I'll call if something comes up that means I absolutely cannot make it."

McLeod was feeling quite sunny as she went back into the Reading Room, where she was at last able to finish the box with the material about "The Other Wise Man." Van Dyke had done a great deal of research, he said in one letter, for an article on the legends of the Magi. Then the idea for the story of a fourth Wise Man came to him. He remembered getting out of bed in the cold, groping his way over to the table, and writing down the first few sentences. He spent a year working on the story, and then read it to his congregation at Brick Church in lieu of a sermon on the Sunday before Christmas.

Cowboy Tarleton had said he could see McLeod at two o'clock, so she left the Reading Room about noon. Instead of working, she decided to take a walk and think — perhaps figure out who had done the break-ins and who had done the murders — while she walked. The walkways on campus were all clear by this time, and she decided to go down the hill and see the new Carl Icahn Laboratory building, where she knew there was a little café. Once she was inside the building, she was very glad she had come. She had read that it was designed by Rafael Viñoly but nothing prepared her for its huge atrium and immensely tall windows — they must be forty feet tall, she thought — looking out on a wood-bordered grassy field and the sweeping curve of the new ellipse-shaped dormitories.

She got a cobb salad and sat at one of the tables scattered in the atrium. The windows and the Frank Gehry "sculpture" competed for her attention and she looked from one to the other. The sculpture was called the "Armadillo" and it looked just like a huge armadillo. It was big enough to hold in its interior a small conference room with a table and chairs and a bulletin board. It was odd to have a conference room inside a sculpture, but it was interesting.

It was too bad that she had no talent at all for integrative genomics, or whatever it was that people did in this building. She still loved the older Princeton buildings like Georgian Nassau Hall, Romanesque Murray-Dodge, and soaring Gothic Mc-

Cosh, but this was something else. What a place.

Then her mind dropped architecture and took up treasure hunting again. She tried to think it through. Of course, the burglar could have searched her room and been scared off before he got around to the rest of the house. But if the burglar had been looking for the *Gospels* and the crucifix, and had thought they were in her room, he, or she, must have known that Dante had carried a box up there. Dante denied telling anybody. But people lie, she thought, all the time. Or they just forget what they said. And then the burglar had suspected the treasure might be in her office — Dante must have told someone that she had taken it to campus.

How else could the burglar possibly have known all this?

Natty couldn't have. Could he? And how could Natty be the murderer, as Buster contended? It was insane. Buster's theory would be that he killed Philip Sheridan and then Chester so his thefts would not be revealed. When did Buster denounce Natty? Was it Monday morning, right after Natty killed Chester? Wait a minute. Chester had known something about Natty on Saturday night, so Buster must have made the accusation Friday. Either way, it was no wonder Natty had been in such bad shape when Chester's body was found.

She still clung to the hope that it wasn't true about Natty, but she could see how the chain of events seemed to hang together. And if Natty wasn't the murderer, then who was? Were the two killings even connected? And were they connected to the burglaries?

I give up, she thought as she finished her lunch and walked back toward Nassau Street and Cowboy Tarleton's office.

THIRTY-TWO

She had to wait a few minutes for Cowboy to get off the phone. She could hear him explaining to a client that it would really be better if he didn't expect Cowboy to accompany him to traffic court to protest a ticket for failing to stop at a stop sign. "I'll have to charge you more than the fine would cost you. Anyway, if you show up at all, they'll probably reduce the fine."

After he hung up, he came out, smiling as usual and looking even taller than she had remembered, and waved McLeod into his office.

"I'm really here to ask you about something for George," she began as soon as the greetings were over. "It's about this stuff from Germany . . ." and she launched into an account of the treasure. "And so they're temporarily — I hope, temporarily — at the Rare Books Department of the university library. George says that the things don't belong to him, that they belong to the cathedral at Litzenburg. But he's not sure how to proceed. So this morning I asked Randall Keaton, the curator of Rare Books at the university who identified the *Gospels* and the other things, for the address. Buster wants the *Gospels* for the Rare Books collection badly, and he insists that George can keep the things and, of course, give them to Princeton."

"He's wrong," said Cowboy. "The news that you found the *Gospels* is going to get out — I'm surprised that it hasn't already — and since you know who the rightful owner is, you must indeed return everything. It's hard to believe a curator would take that attitude. A few days ago I would have told you to appeal to Nat Ledbetter. He was Keaton's boss."

"Natty Ledbetter is no longer head of Rare Books and Special Collections," she said. "I may as well tell you. He's been stealing prints from the collection."

"I know. He's a client of mine," said Cowboy sadly. "Tell me again how Keaton discovered the provenance of these objects that you found." He pulled a yellow legal pad forward and took up a pen.

"I forget the name of the agency, but they have a database on the Internet that lists stolen art from around the world. These things were listed in it and, I think, described in detail."

"McLeod, I'd advise you and George to get busy on the Internet and find this listing, or get some cyberwhiz of a student to find it. And then notify whoever you need to notify."

"Thanks. We can do that." McLeod hesitated. "I have another question for you, if you don't mind."

"What is it?"

"It's about Philip Sheridan. You mentioned to me at Dodo Westcott's that he changed his mind a lot and sometimes wanted to change his will. Did he make any changes just before he died?"

"Why do you ask?"

"From all I've learned about his murder, I've come to wonder if he planned a change in his will that would motivate a murder." She was thinking about Natty but didn't want to say so.

"I don't believe so. In fact, the police suspected his young assistant for a while and wanted to know if his bequest was in danger. It wasn't. Philip did call me about one quixotic change he was going to make, but he was killed before we could get it written."

McLeod waited. Would he tell her what the change was? Had Sheridan been about to cancel the money for Natty?

Cowboy was hesitating. Then he seemed to shrug and went on talking. "He told me he wanted to remove one thing from the legacy to Princeton, and asked me if he could still do that. I told him he could. The university might be disappointed but there wasn't anything they could do about it. So he said he wanted to leave the *Bay Psalm Book* to Bowdoin College."

"Oh, I remember somebody said the *Bay Psalm Book* was the jewel of his collection. It's the first book printed in America, and there are practically no copies around."

"Yes, that's right," said Cowboy. "Princeton was very excited indeed at the prospect of owning it."

"But why Bowdoin?"

"Love," said Cowboy. "It was where Will Trueheart — he was Philip's companion for many years — had gone to school. And Philip told me he decided he had never provided for a proper memorial for Will and he would do this final thing. Besides, he felt that his copy of the *Bay Psalm Book* should be in New England. It was originally published in Massachusetts. I thought it was a whim of Philip's. He was a devoted Princeton alumnus. He had been quite fond of Clement Odell, who was Nat's predecessor, and of course, he liked Nat himself. The agreement with Princeton was a win for both him and the university. I must say I didn't hurry about preparing the change. But I shouldn't tell you that." He shook his head. "You're too easy to talk to."

"I'm glad you think so," said McLeod. "I do appreciate your talking to me. And I'm sure George will be grateful."

"He won't be when he gets my bill," said Cowboy. "Don't worry, I won't charge him anything for this talk. When we have to do something, it will be different."

"Thanks," said McLeod again, and left.

She walked back to the campus and down to the parking garage. It was time for her to find the Murrays' house on Wilson Drive.

THIRTY-THREE

She was astonished to find that the Murrays lived in an extremely modern house, a severe white box with sheets of glass. Bauhaus comes to Princeton, she thought. Although the other houses on Wilson weren't really old like the ones on Edgehill, they were all certainly traditional architecture. The Murrays' box was conspicuous, to say the least.

Mary greeted her without enthusiasm and asked her if she'd like some tea.

"No thanks," said McLeod, but gratefully sat down on the black leather sofa in the spartan living room–dining room when Mary ushered her in. "Such an interesting house," she said.

"We love it," said Mary. "Big and I both grew up in old houses, and we wanted something different, something with clean lines and open spaces and lots of light."

"Well, you got it," said McLeod.

"Yes," said Mary, waiting.

"Mary, I wanted to come and see you to ask you a couple of questions. You know I found all these letters that Vincent Lawrence wrote to his mother during World War II, and I wonder if you wanted them. Vincent was your husband's uncle and his mother was Big's grandmother. I asked Big about them, and he wasn't interested, but I wanted to check with you. I thought they might be of interest to you or your children."

"Oh, no, I don't think we're interested, and we don't have any children, you know," said Mary.

This was a blank wall, McLeod felt, but she'd give it one more punch. "Vincent sent some beautiful things back from Europe, I understand," she said.

"He did?" said Mary. "I wasn't even born then. I hardly knew Vincent. He never married, and he died before Jill did."

McLeod could be persistent. "Mary, I wonder if you could tell me more about your mother-in-law, Jill Murray. Everybody speaks of her with such warmth and affection. And since I'm living — even temporarily — in her old house, I'm curious about her."

"She was very popular," said Mary. "Everybody thought she was wonderful. I had my problems with her — as I guess every wife does with her husband's mother — but I have to admit she was admirable. She was active in everything in town — church, garden club, the public library board — she was a great gardener, a good cook."

"Who would want to kill a paragon like that?" asked McLeod.

"They decided it was a tramp, a random act, I suppose you'd call it," said Mary.

"Do you ever think about it? Does it worry you?"

"No, I don't. It's over and done with and there's nothing I can do about it. You have to move on, put things behind you."

The blank wall was blank. She could not dredge up another question.

Mary surprised her when she spoke again. "You know, I'll tell you who might be interested in those letters — maybe. That's Amelia."

"Amelia?"

"Amelia Keaton. She's married to Randall Keaton. Somehow I thought you knew them," said Mary.

"Oh, Buster Keaton," said McLeod. "Of course, at the library. You mean Buster might want them for the manuscript collection. I had not thought of that."

"No, it's Amelia who I thought just might

be interested. You see, she was a Lawrence, too. Her father was Arthur Lawrence. He died recently. But Amelia is mad about all that family stuff."

"I'll certainly ask her," said McLeod. "I did meet her once, at the chapel one Sunday morning."

"She's big on church," said Mary. "Church and family. Like her Aunt Jill." She stood up. "And you'll have to excuse me. We're going out tonight and I have some things I have to do."

"Thanks so much," said McLeod, "and I'll get in touch with Amelia. In fact, can I use your phone book?"

"You're going right now?"

"I think I will. While it's on my mind," said McLeod.

"Let me give you her telephone number," said Mary.

McLeod wrote it down, and Mary said, "And if I were you, I'd not ask any more questions about Jill Murray."

McLeod stared at her and started to ask why, but thought better of it, and left.

Once she was in her car, McLeod called Amelia Keaton on her cell phone and asked if she could come to see her. "I met you at the chapel one Sunday morning. Buster introduced us," she said.

"I remember. Certainly. Come on by. You know where we live?"

"Actually, I don't."

Amelia gave her the address on Linden Lane and told her how to get there. It was a small house, but nicely kept, McLeod thought as she rang the bell. Like Big and Mary Murray, the Keatons, she had gathered, had no children. It did seem that the houses of childless families always looked neater and trimmer than the others. But that was only logical — they had more money, more time, fewer people cluttering up the outside and inside with things on wheels and other miscellaneous objects.

Amelia Keaton flung the door open and smiled as though she were more delighted to see McLeod than anyone in the world. "Do come in. I was just about to have some tea. You'll have some, won't you?"

"I'd love some." She had refused tea at Mary Murray's, but Amelia seemed genuinely welcoming, so she accepted. She started to follow Amelia into the kitchen, but Amelia said, "Sit down. It's all ready. I'll bring it right in." She was as good as her word. McLeod barely had time to look around the living room — noticing the antique furniture, the glass-fronted bookcase filled with what looked like very old books, and a blue and white bowl with narcissus about to burst into bloom — before Amelia was back with a silver tray bearing a silver teapot, thin china cups and saucers, and shortbread cookies. "I'll let it steep one minute," said Amelia. "How do you like Princeton, McLeod?"

"I love Princeton. This is the fourth time I've been here for any length of time, and I know it's one of the most beautiful, interesting towns in the world."

Amelia nodded approvingly and poured the tea.

"It's good!" said McLeod approvingly when she took her first sip. Amelia looked smug, and passed the cookies. She gazed at McLeod, waiting.

McLeod, in turn, hesitated. "Amelia, you know I'm just here for a semester," she said finally. "I'm staying with an old friend, George Bridges, who bought the house on Edgehill where Jill Murray used to live. Mary Murray told me she was your aunt."

"That's right. And I knew you were staying there. I even knew you cleaned out the garage."

"You did?"

"Oh, yes. Everybody knows everything in Princeton," said Amelia.

"Amazing. It's interesting because I wanted to say I found some letters in the garage. They were written from Vincent Lawrence to his mother during World War II. I told Big and Mary Murray about them but they weren't interested. Mary said you might be."

"I would be interested. I would have guessed Little Big wouldn't give a hoot about old letters, but I do. Vincent Lawrence was my uncle, my father's brother. My father adored Vincent — Vincent was older than my father. And Vincent's mother, of course, was my grandmother. Did you bring them with you? I'd love to see them."

"No, I didn't bring them. I wanted to check with you first."

"It was nice of you to do it in person."

McLeod could tell that Amelia was clearly surprised that she had come to see her when a simple telephone call would have done, but what could she do? She had wanted to see her and ask some more questions. "I came on impulse," she said.

"Have you read them? Are they interesting?" Amelia was excited.

"They are extremely interesting," McLeod said.

"I didn't know Jill had them."

"The handyman said the things up on the

rafters in the garage belonged to Jill Murray. He said he had put some cartons up there for her. And the letters were in one of those cartons."

"Isn't Dante sweet?" asked Amelia.

"Oh, you know him?"

"Yes, he used to work for my parents, as well as Jill. He works for me now, too. He's invaluable. He's old, but he's strong and he works so hard."

"So that's how you knew I cleaned out the garage on Edgehill?" said McLeod.

"Yes, that's how." Amelia laughed. "Dante told me. And then Buster told me about your finding some marvelous things in a box of old dresses. Weren't you thrilled?"

"It was quite exciting," said McLeod.

"Do you suppose there was anything valuable in those other boxes Dante took to the dump?" Amelia asked.

"No, I don't think so. One box I remember was full of nothing but old shoes. That would be a bad place to hide valuables," said McLeod.

"One does wonder how Aunt Jill got hold of them, doesn't one?" asked Amelia. She rolled her eyes and stuck her tongue in her left cheek.

Her expression made McLeod remember how she had realized that whenever her cousin Bruce stuck his tongue in his cheek and rolled his eyes like that, he was always lying. Was Amelia, this likable, churchgoing, attractive woman lying?

"Tell me about your Aunt Jill," said McLeod. "Everybody says such wonderful things about her."

"She was very popular," said Amelia, but without the enthusiasm that everyone from Dante to Natty had expressed. "But she had her downside, too. She quarreled with my father before she died. He was quite angry with her."

"That's too bad," said McLeod. "Family quarrels can be damaging, can't they?"

"Quite damaging," said Amelia.

"Did you know Vincent Lawrence?"

"Not really well. He was something of an art collector. I have a few of his things." She waved her hand at a collection of porcelain plates that hung on one wall. "Those were his — and that picture." She pointed to a seascape over the fireplace.

"Did you ever hear of anything he brought home from Europe after the war?"

"There were whispers about some things, but I never saw them."

McLeod decided she had mined this vein as thoroughly as she could. "I must be off.

I've stayed too long. I'll bring the letters over."

"I'll come right now and get them," said Amelia.

"No, I'll bring them. I put them away and I'm not sure where I put them. I'll be able to find them when I get home." Now she would have to figure out a way to give the letters to Amelia while also saving them for George. She had certainly painted herself into a corner on this one.

"Give my love to Dante when you see him," said Amelia.

THIRTY-FOUR

It was dark by the time McLeod reached the empty house on Edgehill Street. What time would George be home? And when would Nick Perry show up? She checked the phone for messages and heard George say he'd be very late; he had finished work, but Polly had invited him over and he thought he'd go. He hoped McLeod would be all right on her own. Her mind was whirling with all the new information she had gathered that day — and that was good, because she couldn't be bothered to care about George and Polly.

Why should she care, anyway? she thought. Besides, the murders and the treasure were all she could think about.

One thing she could do right away, she decided, was to take Cowboy Tarleton's advice and search online. She went upstairs to her room and turned on her laptop. Google immediately brought up dozens of references to Litzenburg, all in German. McLeod scrolled down the screen, clicking on "Translate this page" each time.

She read, in extremely odd English translations, facts about the shopping, hotels, and climate of Litzenburg. And finally she came to a mention of the church, a Romanesque monument, and its missing treasure. The Litzenburg treasure was recorded lost as "war booty" at the end of World War II. As she read farther, McLeod learned that twenty years ago, the church suddenly felt new hope for the return of its treasure — news of it had surfaced in the United States. A New York lawyer had offered what was surely the reliquary from Litzenburg to a German foundation in return for a "finder's fee." The lawyer would not reveal whom he was representing, but sources indicated that it was a brother and sister in a New Jersey town. They said that a third brother, by then deceased, had reportedly "found it in the gutter in Germany" after World War II. The foundation had refused to pay the "finder's fee." The church had protested to the United States government, but nothing further had happened.

McLeod printed out the information and continued to search, but could not find an address for the church, nor could she locate the stolen art listings.

In a way, aside from the Polly angle, it was too bad George wasn't going to be home — she was dying to tell somebody everything she had found out. Nick Perry would be coming by, but when? And if he wasn't in his "you answer questions, don't ask them" mode, he would be the ideal listener.

She sat at her desk staring at the empty computer screen. What had happened after Vincent Lawrence mailed the treasure home? She knew that years had passed. Vincent Lawrence's mother would have died, and then Vincent died. She supposed that Jill Murray and her brother, Arthur, had inherited the treasure. They were surely the "brother and sister in New Jersey." Then the two of them must have tried to sell part of the treasure. But no luck. Did they try to find another buyer, a dealer maybe? Then Jill had apparently hidden the treasure in a box of old dresses. Why had she done that? And then Jill had been murdered.

Who had murdered her?

And what connection did all this have with the murders in Rare Books?

The solution had been dawning slowly on her. One person was connected to both mysteries. Why had it taken her so long to figure it out? It now seemed so obvious.

The doorbell rang.

Oh, good — it's Nick, she thought, getting up. But I haven't cooked a thing, she lamented to herself as she rushed down the stairs and opened the door, talking already, apologizing.

"I'm so sorry I haven't —"

But it wasn't Nick who had rung the doorbell. It was Buster Keaton.

"Buster!" she said. She heard a quaver in her voice.

"Sorry to barge in at this time of night," he said.

"George isn't here," she said. She thought this would send him away — already she was regretting that she had let him know she was alone. Why, oh, why hadn't she opened the door on the chain? Because, she answered her own question, it hadn't occurred to her, and if it had, she still would have thought it was Nick.

"Oh, really," said Buster.

"I'm sorry you missed him," she said, and started to shut the door. Buster pushed it open and came inside.

She looked at him. What could she say? How could she get rid of him?

"Could I have a glass of water?" he asked.

She couldn't refuse a man's request for a glass of water, could she? "All right," she said. She turned and started for the kitchen. Buster followed her. "Ice?" she asked automatically.

"Please," he said.

"I wish George had an ice maker," she said, feeling compelled to say something as she pulled out a tray of ice cubes and popped it over the sink. She put ice in a glass, filled it with water, and turned to hand it to him.

"I saw Amelia this afternoon," she said, trying to make conversation as she handed him the water.

"I know you did." Buster took the glass of water, staring at her as he did so. What did he want? she wondered again. Was he going to wait until George came home? Why hadn't he called first? Or had he come to see her? He couldn't know how much she knew. She shivered.

"I like your house," she said.

Buster still stared at her. If only Nick — or George — would show up. She started out of the kitchen, but Buster did not move. Then habit, a lifetime's training in Southern hospitality, took over. She turned and said, "Buster, would you like a drink — something besides water? Tea? Wine? Have you eaten supper — can I offer you anything to eat?"

"Now that sounds good," Buster said. "I'll have Scotch on the rocks."

McLeod put more ice cubes in another glass and handed it to Buster. "The Scotch is on that little chest in the dining room," she said. "Help yourself. I'll rustle up something to eat."

Buster went into the dining room and came back with his glass brimming with Scotch. McLeod took a wedge of Camembert out of the refrigerator, unwrapped it, and put it on a plate with crackers.

"Let's go in the living room," she said, taking up the plate. "I'll build a fire. I'll take the cheese and crackers in and go get some wood from the porch."

"I'll get the wood," said Buster, to her surprise. They were in the front hall by this time.

An idea came to her. When he had gone outside, she stared at the new burglar alarm beside the front door, trying to remember exactly how it worked. When it was turned on, you had to turn it off when you came home to keep the alarm from going on in the security company's office. She had turned it off when she came home. But if you were home and heard a burglar, then you could push the red button and the alarm would go off. She pushed it. What harm would it do? she asked herself. And it might do some good.

Buster was back with the wood. She put the plate down on the coffee table and fetched the morning newspaper.

"I'll build the fire," Buster said, confirming McLeod's contention that no man thinks a woman can build a fire.

"Sure," said McLeod. "There's the kindling in that little pot on the hearth.

Buster set about building a fire in an odd way, placing the sticks of wood in teepee fashion on top of the newspapers and the kindling, and it took a while. McLeod watched him, still thinking about the burglar alarm. She recalled that the security people would probably telephone to see if it was a real emergency or an accidental button pressure. She started for the kitchen to be near the phone if it rang and on her way gave the red button on the burglar alarm another shove. Maybe two signals would make them move faster.

In the kitchen, she tried to think of other edibles she could offer. Food — or was it music?— to soothe the savage beast — or was it breast? She found a jar of eggplant spread in the cabinet, and was opening it when Buster came back in the kitchen.

"Fire's going," he said. "Can I have some

more ice?" He had poured more Scotch in his glass.

"Sure," she said, getting another tray out of the refrigerator and struggling to pop out the cubes.

"Here you are," she said finally, turning to Buster with the glass of ice and could scarcely believe what she saw. "What are you doing?" she shouted.

He had turned on the burners of the stove and was systematically blowing them out, leaving the gas pouring out. Then he began on the oven.

"Do you want the house to explode?" she shouted at him. "Are you mad? Turn those off." She moved toward the stove and he reached out and stopped her. She threw the glass of Scotch and ice in his face, and he hit her so hard on the side of her face that she fell down. Trying to scramble up from the floor, she looked at him. "Why are you doing this?" It was ridiculous — even at a time like this, she asked a question.

"It won't explode," he said. "I'll leave and the gas will kill you quietly and easily. You don't have a thing to worry about."

Buster had never been exactly charming, but never, with all his bluster, had he looked the way he did right now — hateful and really frightening.

She started again to get up. I'm out of shape, she thought, and I've got to get more exercise.

He kicked her in the shoulder so that she fell back.

"When you leave, I'll just get up and turn off the gas," she said.

"No, you won't," he said. "You won't be able to." He turned away from the stove and took a necktie out of his pocket. In spite of her struggles to get away or kick him, or both, he managed to tie her wrists with it.

"You really mustn't do this," McLeod said, and thought: I sound like an ineffectual mother. "It's ridiculous."

Buster, paying no attention, grabbed her flailing feet and used another tie to fasten them together. She began to bang her tied-up feet on the floor. "Stop it!" she said. "You know, the police will be here soon."

"Yeah, and so will the Easter Bunny and the Great Pumpkin." He pulled a third tie out of his pocket and said, "This will shut you up."

The doorbell rang.

"We'll just ignore that, won't we?" said Buster.

This is my last chance before he gags me, McLeod thought, and I better make it good. She screamed. She screamed as loud as she could in the few seconds before Buster clapped his hand over her mouth and then gagged her with the third necktie. Even with the gag, she could still smell the gas.

The doorbell rang again. And rang a third time, as Buster held her down. Then she heard glass splinter and the front door open. Nick Perry appeared in the kitchen door.

Buster relaxed his hold on her and stood up. Then before Nick could stop him, he vanished through the back door. Nick hurried to the stove and turned off the oven and the burners and opened a window. McLeod, on the floor, felt the cold air rush in. She had never dreamed that such cold air could feel so good. She kicked both feet against the floor to celebrate, and Nick knelt to remove her gag. Still kneeling, he pulled out his cell phone and spoke into it — a mixture of numbers and letters, ending with the address on Edgehill. Then he untied her hands and feet.

"Thank you, Nick, thank you," McLeod said as Nick helped her to her feet. "I was never so glad to see anybody in my life."

"What happened?"

"Buster knocked on the door, and I let him in. I tried to distract him from whatever he had in mind with fire and food, but he followed me to the kitchen and started turning on the gas jets. When I tried to stop him, he hit me. He knocked me down and kicked me and then he tied me up."

She was interrupted by the doorbell and loud knocking on the front door. She followed Perry as he rushed to answer it. It was Sergeant Popper.

"Everybody okay?" Popper asked. "How did you get here so fast, Lieutenant?"

"Sheer luck," said Perry. "How about you?"

"Patrolman Adams and I came to answer a burglar alarm, and just as we drove up, that guy Keaton ran out the back door. We tackled him and he's handcuffed to Adams in the patrol car."

"Good work," said Nick. "You and Adams drive him to the station and book him for assault and battery — for now."

"Nick, Buster did the murders," McLeod said, but nobody paid any attention to her.

Popper left and Nick closed the front door. "Are you all right, McLeod? He knocked you around quite a bit. You should go to the emergency room."

"No, no, I'll be all right," she said. "I really will. Nothing is broken, but it was scary — I guess Buster's crazy. I'm glad you came."

"Where's George?"

"He's at Polly Griffin's house."

"What's her number? I'll call him and tell him what's happened. He can come home and look after you. I've got to go back to the station to deal with Keaton."

"Nick, I know Buster is the murderer," McLeod said as she looked up Polly Griffin's number. She gave it to Nick, who punched it into his phone. McLeod heard him identify himself, ask to speak to George Bridges, and then give George a brief account of what had happened in his house.

"He'll be right here," said Nick. "You need to sit down. Is there a fire in the living room?"

"There was." They went in the living room to discover that Buster's fire had gone out. "I knew it wasn't any good," she said.

While Nick rebuilt it, McLeod sat on the sofa and talked. "Nick, let me tell you what I found out today. Just before he died, Philip Sheridan told his lawyer he wanted to change his will and leave the *Bay Psalm Book* to another college instead of Princeton. Buster killed him because he couldn't stand the thought of the *Bay Psalm Book* not coming to Princeton, to what he regarded as *his* collection. I know it sounds nonsensical, but this man really cares about old books. I think it's the only thing he does care about."

"I'm not surprised. It backs up what we had figured out. We knew he was our guy." Nick stood up, dusted his hands, and stood with his back to the fire.

"How did you know?"

"Forensic evidence. His fingerprints were on the cutoff valve for the fire extinguisher system."

"Fingerprints! Good old-fashioned fingerprints?"

"That's right. He wasn't your perfect murderer by any means. I went by his house this evening as soon as I got the report from the lab. He wasn't there. I decided to come and tell you I couldn't have dinner here, that I'd have to work forever."

"I'm so glad you came instead of calling," said McLeod. "And I'm really glad you broke the glass on the door and came in."

"You didn't answer the door, and I noticed the car outside. I checked the license number with the office and it was Keaton's. That was bad enough. When I heard a scream, I broke the glass," said Nick. "I'm sorry I broke the glass."

"Don't worry about that — I'll tape a piece of cardboard over it," said McLeod. "I know how to do that. Nick, I'm sorry I haven't cooked anything for us to eat. I got sidetracked."

"I can't stay and eat anyway," Nick said.

"Of course not, but I have a lot to tell you about the burglaries and the treasure . . ." Before she could begin her story, George came home and rushed into the living room.

"Are you all right?" he asked McLeod.

"I'm fine," said McLeod. "Tired. But okay. I'm glad to see you."

"Likewise," said George. To Nick, he said, "Thanks for calling me."

And Nick left, as quickly as George had come home.

THIRTY-FIVE

"Can I get you anything?" George asked. "Have you had anything to eat?"

"No, I haven't," said McLeod. "Have you?"

"No, not yet."

"I hope Polly didn't mind that you left."

"She understood," said George.

"It's a good thing you bought that burglar alarm, George," she said.

He looked at her oddly. "Here, eat some crackers and cheese," he said. "I'll bring us drinks and then I'll find something else for us to eat."

George came back with glasses of brandy and the news that he was heating up some soup and would make some sandwiches. "Now tell me. What's been going on?"

"A lot," said McLeod. "Buster Keaton came here and I wasn't sure whether he was looking for you or me. And he murdered Philip Sheridan and Chester Holmes. And he ran away."

"You're not making a lot of sense," said George. "Or maybe I'm thick. Tell me again slowly."

McLeod tried to be more coherent. "Buster Keaton came here and rang the doorbell. He hit me and tied me up and turned on the gas. He was trying to murder me. Nick Perry got here in the nick of time — I love it, Nick in the nick — and Buster ran away. But I had pressed the button on the burglar alarm and two policemen came to check out the alarm and they caught him when he ran out the back door."

It took a few more questions from George before he really understood what had happened.

Then he asked her if the crackers and cheese had been for Nick or Buster.

"For Buster. I thought I could distract him with food," McLeod said.

"McLeod, you use food to accomplish everything."

"Food is holy," said McLeod. "Maybe they haven't arrested Buster for the murder, but he killed Philip Sheridan and Chester Holmes."

"How do you know?" George asked.

"Nick Perry told me he had killed Chester. He left his fingerprints on the fire extinguisher. I'm not sure why he killed Chester. But I had figured out he killed Philip Sheridan. Just before he rang the doorbell."

She told him about her visit to Cowboy Tarleton the day before and her talks with Mary Murray and Amelia Keaton. It took some time for her to tell all the details. She had, in fact, finished a bowl of soup and a sandwich before she was through.

George immediately began to worry about the public relations problems for the university. "My God," he said, "the Rare Books curator kills a big donor and another employee. It's going to be a disaster."

"At least you know about it before the press starts calling you," said McLeod.

"What a day tomorrow's going to be."

"You can cope, George. You always do."

"Yeah. Sure."

"But Buster may have killed somebody else, too." McLeod thought that George might as well know it all.

"Who else did he kill?"

"Jill Murray, I think," she said. "But I'm trying to figure that one out."

"Why would he kill Jill Murray?"

"Jill was his wife's aunt," said McLeod.

"That's not much of a motive," said George. "You have to admit."

"Ha, ha," said McLeod. "As a matter of fact, my favorite in-law is my husband Holland's Aunt Aggie. She's hilarious. Anyway I have lots to tell you about the treasure."

"About getting it back to Litzenburg?"

"I'm working on that, but listen to the rest, although this part is a little hazy. Vincent Lawrence sent the treasure home, his mother died, he died, and then I gather Jill Murray and Arthur Lawrence inherited the *Gospels.* I found something on the Internet about the Litzenburg treasure and it said a brother and sister in New Jersey had once tried to sell the *Gospels.*"

George was staring at her. "This all happened since I saw you last?"

"That's right. And you know just before Jill Murray died — I asked Dante when it was — she put that carton of old dresses in the garage. I think she was trying to hide the *Gospels* where Arthur couldn't find it. But isn't it logical that Buster Keaton, who's a nut about old books if there ever was one, knew about the *Gospels* and killed her in the process of trying to find it? He wanted it — either for himself or for the library."

"You don't know that for sure, though," said George.

"No, but I'll find out," said McLeod, with more confidence than she felt.

They sat up quite late, discussing all the developments. Finally, when McLeod was falling asleep on the sofa, George said she really ought to be in bed.

"I know it." She tried to get up and complained that she was very stiff. George helped her climb the stairs, and said if she wasn't better in the morning, she'd have to go to the emergency room. "I'll be all right," she said.

The next morning George knocked on her door before he left for the office. "How are you?" he asked.

"Much better," she said.

"You've got an awful bruise on your face."

She got up and looked in the mirror. "It looks much worse than it feels," she said.

"If you're all right, I'm leaving," George said. "Call me if you need anything."

"Thanks."

While she was eating breakfast, Nick Perry called to tell her that Randall "Buster" Keaton had been formally charged with the murders of Philip Sheridan and Chester Holmes and was being held in Trenton, awaiting a bail hearing.

"Can you go out to dinner tonight?" Nick asked. "I can take a break for the first time in two weeks."

"I'd love it," said McLeod. "What time?"

"I'll pick you up about seven. Is that all right?"

"Fine," she said and hung up. She opened the front door, stuck her head out to get a feel for the weather, and couldn't help but smile. It was definitely warmer and the snow was melting. Still she had to bundle up in coat, gloves, hat, and scarf before she could set out for her office.

On the way she had what she thought was a brilliant idea for her students when they finished their pieces on people in the arts. She would assign them to write a story about someone in Rare Books; they would learn what it was like to interview people under stress. They could talk in class beforehand about how you can be sensitive to the pressures people endure and still get information for an article.

At the office she found an e-mail from her son, Harry. His dissertation had been approved by his committee and he would defend it in April. Could she come up for the party afterward?

McLeod was astonished. Harry had done it. He had really finished his dissertation and won approval. Defense was a mere formality, she knew, where softball, even flattering questions would be asked. Harry would shine. Of course she could come for the party. Nothing on earth could stop her. She e-mailed her congratulations and acceptance. Now all he had to do was get a job.

She bundled up again and walked over to Rare Books to find out who was in charge now that Natty was forced into retirement and Buster Keaton was in jail. Molly Freeman, the receptionist, told her Fanny Mobley had been named acting director. Fanny came out to the reception area just then, and McLeod could see that she was still sober, but not as cross as she usually was at this time of day.

"McLeod, can we help you in any way?" Fanny asked her.

"Congratulations," McLeod said. "I thought I'd drop by and see if Miss Swallow is here."

"Let's see," said Fanny. "Yes, she's signed in. Let me go get her, then you won't have to sign in and take off your coat and put your bag in a locker."

"Thanks very much," McLeod said.

"A lot has happened, hasn't it?" Miss Swallow said as soon as she appeared. They sat down in two of the stiff chairs. "I understand Buster Keaton has been arrested."

"That's right," said McLeod, and told her about her adventure with Buster the night before.

"So that's how you got that awful bruise."

"It is. And Nick Perry called to say Buster has been charged with both murders. You know now that it's over, I feel really sorry for Buster and for his wife. I was even thinking about going to see Amelia. Should I?"

"My dear, if the thought has occurred to you, you should go. It's these unfulfilled impulses that we regret later."

"You're right. I'll go home and make her a pound cake."

"That's right. And I'm nearly through here. I'll finish up today, I'm sure. But we must get together later."

"Indeed we must," said McLeod.

THIRTY-SIX

She whipped by the grocery store and, afraid that George's kitchen would not have a tube pan, went to the hardware store to buy one. When she got home, of course, she found a perfectly good tube pan. That was all right, she thought. Better to be safe than sorry. She made the pound cake and, as soon as it was done, wrapped it in plastic and took it to the Keaton house. Amelia, in sweatpants and an old sweater, her face ravaged, answered the door and stared blankly at McLeod.

"I'm so sorry about Buster," said McLeod. "You must be terribly upset." She handed her the pound cake. "It's a wonderful pound cake recipe," she added.

Amelia took it and stood stock-still, staring at McLeod.

"I just wanted to say I'm sorry, and if there's anything I can do, please let me know," said McLeod.

"Come in," said Amelia. "I'd like to talk to you." She led her into the living room and put the pound cake on the coffee table. McLeod noticed that the narcissus, which had looked so healthy yesterday, was drooping. Were plants affected by cataclysmic events in the household?

"Would you like a piece of cake?" Amelia said.

"No, thanks. It's for you."

"Maybe I'll feel like eating someday. Not right now, though." She sat down in a chair and faced McLeod. "It's good of you to bring cake after Buster hit you, or so I hear. Your face looks awful."

"It looks worse than it feels. Clearly, Buster was not himself last night," said McLeod, feeling that she was turning the other cheek until her neck hurt.

"He let himself get really carried away about that copy of the *Gospels*," said Amelia. "I'm sorry."

"Have you seen him since — ?" McLeod asked her.

"Yes, I went down this morning. I talked to him through a glass window. The judge will set bail this afternoon — Cowboy says it will probably be quite high, so I've set the wheels in motion to raise some money. I think it will be all right."

"Is Cowboy his lawyer?"

"Buster called him last night," said Amelia, "but I gather he's going to have to have somebody else. Cowboy went down last night but he said he has conflicts and said anyway he doesn't think he could defend somebody charged with murder. He said Buster would have to get a criminal lawyer. I was surprised — I thought he took on anything. But of course, Buster must have the best defense."

McLeod had to admire Amelia: She had just learned her husband was accused of murder and she was entertaining a visitor in her living room and talking about getting him the best defense. If you could do that, you were pretty tough.

"Are you all right? Do you have any family nearby? What about Buster's family?"

"I have cousins and lots of friends here in Princeton," Amelia said. "Buster's parents are very old and live in Michigan. To tell you the truth, I haven't told them yet. But I will. I haven't told anybody, as a matter of fact. I guess everyone will know soon enough."

"Yes, I'm afraid everyone will know," said McLeod. "It will be in the papers. I was surprised the Trenton *Times* didn't have anything about it this morning — but they will."

"I guess so."

"Can somebody stay with you, Amelia? Or can you stay with a relative or a friend?"

"I'll see," said Amelia. "Buster will be home soon, I'm sure. You're very kind to think about me. I appreciate it." She paused. "You're kind of a part of this, though, aren't you?"

"What do you mean?"

"You're the one who found those things from Germany, aren't you? In the garage?"

"Well, yes, I am."

"You see Dante told me about cleaning out Jill's garage and said that you had taken a box of old dresses up to your room. I thought right away, that's where Jill hid that stuff from Germany." She stood up. "Would you like some coffee? I've had too much already today but I'm going to have another cup."

McLeod stood up, too. "Let me help you," she said. "I'd love a cup." She would really rather have tea, but she was too interested in what Amelia might have to say to even bring it up. Coffee would be fine, she told herself.

"It's all ready," said Amelia, heading toward the kitchen. "I had just put on a

fresh pot when you came. Sit back down."
She came back with a tray holding a pot of
coffee and two cups and saucers. They sat
down and Amelia poured the coffee.

"What made you think there was something hidden in that box of clothes?" asked
McLeod. "I certainly had no idea when I
had Dante bring the box upstairs."

"You see, I knew about the things that
Vincent got in Germany. Everybody in the
family knew he'd found some valuable
things. Me, Little Big, everybody. Buster,
Mary Murray. Vincent said he'd found them
in the gutter. I didn't know he'd stolen
them. I never dreamed of that. After Vincent died, my father talked about the stuff
with me. He was, as you know, Jill's brother,
and since Vincent had no children, Jill and
Arthur, my father, inherited everything. My
father and Jill tried to sell the things, and
they weren't getting anywhere. The Ger-
mans were saying the things were stolen. So
Jill said they should hold on to the things.
But my father was desperate for money at
one point and he tried to get Jill to divide
up the stuff. But she wouldn't do it. And
she wouldn't tell my father where it was. He
told her it ought to be in the vault at the
bank, but she just smiled and told him not
to worry. It was all perfectly safe, she said."

"That must have been maddening," said McLeod.

"After Jill was killed, my father went through the house and couldn't find a trace of the things from Germany. We all helped Little Big clean out the house when he finally sold it a few years ago. There was absolutely no trace of Vincent's things. I can vouch for that. But we never thought about the garage. That seems like such a crazy place to hide anything. It wasn't even locked."

"It does seem crazy," said McLeod. "But from all I've heard, Jill was not crazy."

"No, she was smart," said Amelia. "And blind selfish. Look, I feel better talking about this. I'm going to cut the pound cake. Would you like a piece?"

"Sure," said McLeod, and waited while Amelia went to the kitchen and returned with a cake knife.

"This looks very good," said Amelia. "It was so nice of you to make it and bring it over." She put a slice of cake on McLeod's saucer and one on her own.

They munched cake for a few seconds and McLeod felt extremely relieved that the cake had turned out so well.

Amelia finished her cake and licked her fingers. "As I was saying," she said, "when

Dante told me about those boxes out there on those rafters in the garage, I knew that was where Jill had hidden the things Vincent found. I'll always wonder if some of it didn't go to the dump in those other boxes."

"Surely there wasn't more stolen from Litzenburg," said McLeod.

"I'm not sure how much Vincent brought home," said Amelia. "But anyway —"

"Wait a minute," said McLeod. "Who broke into our house looking for the treasure?"

"You don't know?"

"No, I didn't know. Until last night — that's when I began to think it was Buster. Was it you?"

"No, it wasn't I," said Amelia. "And it wasn't Buster. You see, I told Mary Murray what Dante had told me and she broke into the house."

"Mary Murray! She told me she didn't know about any treasure, as I called it," said McLeod.

"Of course she'd say that," said Amelia. "She's known about it forever."

"I'm always astonished when people lie to me," said McLeod. "But Mary did, and Dante did. He told me he hadn't told anybody about the box of dresses."

"I'm sure Dante told everybody in town,"

said Amelia. "But it was Mary who went in the house on Edgehill. She thought that she and Little Big were entitled to half of Vincent's things. And then she went to your office when Dante told her you had taken the dresses to the university. A lot of people think Mary is mousy, but she's not."

"And I thought it was you or Buster —"

"Think about it," said Amelia. "Buster had the stuff in his hands before your office was burgled. He knew where it was by that time. Mary didn't."

"But Mary seemed so ignorant all the time."

"She can seem that way."

"She certainly doesn't seem like somebody who could break into Joseph Henry House and jimmy a file drawer lock."

"Joseph Henry House was unlocked," said Amelia.

"How did you know all this?"

"Mary told me what she did. We're friends, as well as cousins-in-law."

"Could you stay with them for a while?" McLeod was worried about this woman, who seemed so alone.

"Sure I could. But I'm all right, I really am." She cut herself another small sliver of cake and ate it. "Buster told me about it as soon as you brought the *Gospels* to Rare

Books. We knew immediately it must be one of the things Vincent had found in Germany. Buster was surprised, I must say, to find out they were stolen. As I said, Vincent always said he found them in the gutter."

"Was Jill Murray killed because of the *Gospels* and the crucifix and the reliquary?"

"Of course she was."

"Who did it? Was it Buster?"

"Heavens, no. I'm sure it was my father."

McLeod looked at her, and pity surged. Here was a woman, an attractive woman, a woman who went to church — and her husband was accused of two murders and she calmly said her father had done another.

Amelia seemed to read her mind. "I've wondered today if it's me, something about me, that makes men murder. Not that I'm a femme fatale, far from it, but am I a really bad influence?"

"Of course not," said McLeod firmly. "Of course not. And are you sure it was your father?"

"He never said he did it," said Amelia. "The police never suspected him. He had an alibi. But he had a terrible temper, and it got worse after Jill died."

"Who was his alibi?" asked McLeod.

"I was," said Amelia.

"You were?"

"He asked me to tell the police he was with me that afternoon. We were together for a little while that day, but not for as long as I told the police. What could I do? He was my father. It wouldn't bring Jill back if he were convicted. And God forgives everything — why shouldn't I?"

THIRTY-SEVEN

George was home early that evening.

"I'm sorry you're going out," he said when he found out she and Nick were going to dinner.

"I'll be back," McLeod said. "Don't worry."

George greeted Nick warmly when he arrived and suggested they all have a drink. They had martinis and talked about the murders — naturally.

"Okay, you had evidence that Buster killed Chester," said McLeod. "What about Philip Sheridan? Were Buster's fingerprints on the paper knife?"

"His and everybody else's," said Nick. "Everybody that came in that office must have picked up that knife and fiddled with it. But we suspected him and you gave us the motive. Thanks."

"But what about Chester? Why did Buster kill him?"

"Chester knew everything. He knew about Sheridan wanting to change his will and after a while he figured out that Keaton had done the murder. He tried a little blackmail — or Keaton thought he was trying to blackmail him — and that was enough to set Keaton off again. He was half mad by that time."

"But what about the treasure?" asked George. "Does it have any connection with the murders at the university?"

"Not as far as we know," said Nick. "The murders of Sheridan and Holmes were all about the fact that the *Bay Psalm Book* might go to some place besides Princeton."

"Did the old murder in this house have anything to do with the treasure?" asked George.

"It might have. We'll reactivate the Jill Murray case," said Nick. "There's no statute of limitations on murder."

"What if the murderer is dead?" asked McLeod.

"It would be good to know who the murderer was, alive or dead," said Nick.

"This is just a theoretical question," said McLeod. "What if somebody had given the murderer a false alibi and the murderer is dead, would that witness be prosecuted now?"

"I can't say offhand," said Nick. "It would be nice to know who that murderer was."

Someday, I might tell him, thought McLeod.

When she and Nick left for dinner, George seemed rather forlorn. "I won't be long," she told him.

RECIPES

Pork Chop, Apple, and Sweet Potato Casserole

6 loin pork chops
1/4 cup vegetable oil
4 medium sweet potatoes, peeled and sliced
3 medium tart apples, peeled, cored, and sliced
1/2 cup apple juice.

Preheat oven to 350°. Grease a large casserole and set aside.

Salt and pepper the pork chops. Heat the oil in a heavy skillet; brown the pork chops in the skillet and place in the casserole.

Layer half the sweet potatoes over the chops, then layer half the apples. Repeat, seasoning each layer with salt and pepper. Pour the apple juice over the top. Cover and bake until the chops are tender, about 1 1/4 hours. Uncover and bake, allowing the pork chops to brown for about 15 minutes.

Serves 6.

CHOCOLATE MOUSSE

6 ounces semi-sweet chocolate bits
4 organic or pasteurized eggs, separated
1 teaspoon sherry

Melt chocolate bits. Beat egg yolks until pale and lemon-colored. Slowly stir in the chocolate and blend well. Beat the egg whites until stiff. Add a third of the whites to the yolks and chocolate, add the sherry, mix well. Fold in the remaining whites. Spoon into a serving bowl. Cover and chill at least 8 hours before serving.

Serves 4.

SCALLOP SOUP

4 tablespoons olive oil
6 shallots, chopped
1/2 fennel bulb, chopped
1/2 pound mushrooms, chopped
1 pound scallops
1/4 pound spinach
1 can boiled potatoes
1 cup clam juice
1 cup white wine

2 cups water
1/8 teaspoon Tabasco sauce
few threads saffron

Heat oil, add shallots, fennel, and mushrooms, and cook 7 minutes. Add other ingredients, bring to boil, reduce heat, and simmer 3 to 4 minutes.

Serves 3 or 4. Double for 6.